A Dirge for the Temporal

by Darren Speegle

A Dirge for the Temporal Copyright © 2004
by Darren Speegle

Published by Raw Dog Screaming Press
Hyattsville, MD

First printing 2004

Cover image: Mike Bohatch www.eyesofchaos.com
Book design: Jennifer C. Barnes

Printed in the United States of America

ISBN: 0-9745031-3-4

Library of Congress Control Number: 2004093337

www.rawdogscreaming.com

For my brothers
Josh and Joe

Acknowledgments

September first published in *Fortean Bureau*, Sep 2002

Indulgence first published in *The Dream People*, Apr 2002

The Whole Circus first published in *Here and Now*, Aug 2003

Illusions of Amber first published in *Underworlds*, Apr 2004

Merging Tableaux first published in *Horrorfind*, Mar 2004

The Crookedness of Being first published in *3AM Magazine*, Oct 2001

Triangle first published in *Plots with Guns*, Mar 2002

A Dirge for the Temporal first published in *Rogue Worlds*, Oct 2002

Eyes of Hazel, Kiss the Earth first published in *Darkness Rising 6*, Jun 2003

The Ego Game first published in *Antipodean SF*, Mar 2003

The Day It Rained Apricots first published in *EOTU*, Oct 2001

Papa Bo's Big-Ass Barbecue first published in *Of Flesh and Hunger*, Jun 2003

Junkyard Fetish first published in *Bloodfetish*, May 2002

Clockwork first published in *The Dream People*, Feb 2002

On the Job first published in *Horrorfind*, Dec 2002

Along the Footpath to Oblivion first published in *Underworlds*, Dec 2002

Hush Hush Little Kitty first published in *Redsine*, Jul 2002

A Fixture on River Street first published in *Aoife's Kiss*, Sep 2002

Mousse first published in *Horrorfind*, Jul 2002

Humpty Dumpty Had a Great Fall first published in *The Dream People*, Aug 2002

The Curse of Lianderin first published *Futures*, Aug 2001

Dandelion Girl first published in *Chiaroscuro*, Apr 2001

rhyme or reason, Dear God first published in *5_Trope*, Aug 2001

Table of Contents

The Lunatic Mystique

It was fitting that her eyes were the feature he came into contact with first. Physically, those forever changing pools were the most disconcerting thing about her. Even in that pre-introductory glimpse, as her face slipped between the vertical windows that teased him with the reality of the world, he saw twin fans of color unfold within them. She had been looking in at him, in advance of drumming her fingers on the pane, her eyes magnified in the secret glass. Then he was opening the door, and those opalescent vessels became a faintest watery blue, the pupil a pinpoint tunnel that sucked his soul like thread through a button hole.

"Yes?" It was the most clever thing he could come up with, in the face of her magnificence.

Her beauty, savage as it happened to be, was secondary to her eyes, falling from them like radiance from diamonds; yet not unnoticed as its elegant curves flooded his senses. The face alone was worthy of wow, darkly exotic setting for her prize jewels. Still, the jewels themselves...

"Good morning, Mr. Avian. My name is Cocoa. I am originally from South America. Because I love your daily column so ferociously, I've come to collect you from yourself. It is time you recognized Danny Avian as the sole player in a boxed-in game."

For all his newspaper eloquence, he could produce nothing better than: "Huh?"

"I've been reading your column for years, Mr. Avian. Your insights and observations demonstrate a keen understanding of our universe, but beneath your bright truths fester loneliness and isolation. I have a sense for such things. And having fallen under the spell of your *poetry*, I feel it is my obligation to help you."

"I'm sorry but is this one of those celebrity worship things? Because I simply don't have any room for that kind of nonsense…"

"No, I sense there is very little free space in your box," she said. "Look at me. Do I look like a celebrity worshiper?"

It was an opportunity to more fully gather in her whole delicious form, but he continued to drink only from the wells of her eyes, which now had grown silvery with the quality of a ghostly mirror.

"You look like a test," he said. "Did Vanguard send you? He knows better than to distract me. It may seem like I simply ramble off my poetry, as you've referred to it, but a lot of time and concentration goes into it."

"You are an exciting man, Danny Avian. May I come in while you pack?"

"Pack?"

"A few days' worth will do."

"Well, that answers whether or not Vanguard sent you. There's no way the paper would *offer* me a vacation, even though I haven't had one in three years."

"It's time you did…Danny. May I…?"

He wasn't sure whether she meant come in or call him Danny, so he merely nodded a hopeless head. He wasn't feeling well right now…about any of this. People just didn't come by. And when they intended to, they warned him well in advance. So maybe Danny did live in a box, but it was his box.

"Can I offer you something?" he said, closing the door behind her.

"May I see your hand?"

She hovered inside the door, by the mahogany rack on which hung a single coat and a single hat. She didn't wear a coat herself, though it was March, and her hair was in a high, luxuriant knot, exposing her elegant neck. Maybe these were symptoms, in the way her name was a symptom, of that tropical mystique of hers. He noticed the caramel delicacy of her hands as she took his.

It was the first touch. His nerves wailed as he managed to say, "Don't tell me you read palms."

She caressed his thumb, as though for imperfections. "No. I am not as obvious as my name."

"I didn't mean to imply."

She released his hand. "Better, I think, that you cease with the apologies and the self-consciousness and all that other stuff that comes out of being stuck in your boxed-in game. Be the poet, not the person who is the poet. Simplify things. It's not as though you invented the poet. Talk to me as you would talk to the blank word processor screen. Let me discover on my own what's beneath."

He looked at her. Cocoa's eyes, as they returned the stare, were clear—like truth. Beside him, his discarded hand was naked, impotent.

"I find you...intriguing company," he said, discovering her advice in his words, though he hadn't consciously applied it.

"Then pack."

"For what type of climate? Will there be a computer? May I submit my column from there?"

"Whatever you wish on all counts. Just leave the box behind."

"You make conditions?"

"It doesn't matter. Your willingness to come means you're abandoning the box."

This made him wonder as to her layers. Nonetheless, he did his wondering as he packed. Manipulator, madwoman or messiah, she moved him. And that was enough for a graying columnist with fading intellectual dreams.

She had followed him back, and stood in the doorway to his bedroom as he threw casual articles into a casual bag. "In your column you said something once, something that deserved a Pulitzer, as far as I'm concerned. 'Life grows without mystery into worms.' It stinks of cynicism but delights the senses with its accuracy."

"Are you really here?"

She was. He wondered whether to toss his passport into the bag. Did, just because.

If Avian was surprised to find that their transportation matched the standard for the semi-rural setting where he made his abode, he was even more surprised to find a man behind the wheel of the old rusty pick-up. A four-fingered hand came off the vinyl to wave as he walked down the footpath to the drive. Avian couldn't help but notice that the hand still holding the wheel also lacked a thumb.

"Abe is the Gatherer," Cocoa introduced him. "Abe, this is Danny."

"Gatherer?" Danny said as he accepted the other's hand through the open window. The experience of the nubble was surreal.

"It is my calling," the man said. And didn't expound.

Cocoa tossed Danny's bag in the bed, then hopped in the cab, scooting over to the middle. As Danny got in Abe started up the truck, the four fingers of his right hand dropping the shifter into gear.

"So do we know where we're going?" Danny asked.

"'There is a road,'" she said, looking at him through steely gray orbs. As nonchalant a statement as it was, he recognized immediately that she was quoting him. "'One that winds all the way to the end of the universe. That is the road I decided to take, in my search for nothing and everything: tomorrow, the moon, a Jazz musician on the street corner, cigarette protruding from one of the valves of his sax. It has no number, this road, nor does it have a specific destination. If it possessed a name, that name would be Mystery.'"

It touched him in varying ways that she knew it to the word. He looked across her at the driver, with his leathery skin and whiskers, eyes at once intense and lost as they searched for the road at the foot of the drive. Perhaps these two had been lured into his life by that specific column—the same one in fact that had produced the quote about life growing without mystery into worms. But that had been at least two years ago.

"Do you remember the party Vanguard threw for you," Cocoa said, "when your column went to syndication? You wouldn't remember I was there. I doubt you remember reading to us a short story you had written some time before. You said you had intended to market the piece, only to watch it *devolve*—as you put it—into material for your column. You were terribly stoned."

They were on the road now and heading away from newspaper routes.

"I don't attend parties," he said quietly. "And if I did, I wouldn't read."

"Sure you did. The story was in the first person, about you and a girl named Jan. I've been intensely jealous of her ever since." She laughed, but he didn't like it.

He didn't like being sabotaged out of his burial grounds.

She persisted, reciting: "'Which is why we quit our jobs, sold our furniture, packed our bags, and went. For most of us, life grows without mystery into worms, and that is our legacy. Jan and I sought more.'"

If it had been, it had been destroyed. Posterity had his columns. The four winds had the ashes of everything else.

Nodding Fog was the first place of interest. We rolled in about nine o'clock in the evening, having outlasted an annoying clog in the fuel line of the old Ford truck, which we were committed to dumping when it finally gave up. Nodding Fog was a small village, maybe thirty roofs and a circular fountain in the middle. There was parking by the fountain, which we used, and a bunch of rowdies pitching down beers and celebrating Friday. "Where's the store," Jan wanted to know of one of them. "We don't have no stores, we don't have no motels, go home strangers." Apparently the town was on the way to somewhere, and we weren't the first to have dropped in.

The wind on the highway had whipped Jan's hair into a frenzy, she had on no makeup and looked like Medusa at sunup. Otherwise, from my experience, the boys and the beer would have been asking her to please please stay. Ah well, there were no mysteries here anyway, it was plain to see, and—but wait, what did they have there in the fountain?

The wind blew now against the passage of the truck. He could hear it in the failing seals of the window. March whined, and Cocoa's neck was close enough to kiss.

"Mystery," she said softly, letting her eyelids fall sleepily over silver novae. "I was brought up in a place where epiphanies and strange sightings were routine. The villagers devoured the prospect of sharing the world with the unknown. I was one such epiphany. My natural parents, who lived in a village on the other side of the mountain, had thrown me away. They threw me away because I ate a poisonous plant and did not die. They threw me away because I went into forbidden places in the forest, walked among the fantastic, the others, angels and shadow people. They threw me away because of my eyes. Even then, before I was given real sight." She opened them to him, newspapers bleeding smoky ink into water. "They threw me away, Danny, because of my thumbs."

Jan had already seen, and had stepped up to the brink to have a look in.

"Thumbs?" He looked down at his own, turning them, touching the pad of one, the knuckle of the other.

Thumbs, mister. That's what we have in the fountain. Thumbs little, thumbs big, thumbs whole, thumbs rotting.

"Had to kill all the dogs, all the cats, 'cause they kept dragging them off."

"You know what I mean, Danny," smiled Cocoa. "Only you know what I mean." She put her head on his shoulder and closed her eyes again. Her hair smelled of...

Despite himself, with the hammers of Abe's disembodied thumbs pounding alarm bells in his head, his chest, his groin, he followed her into that sleepy place, drawn on whiffs of...of...chlorine?

Jan had taken the one speaking by the arm, and sure enough, he was a nubbin. Same with the boy to his left, same with all of them. She peered for some moments into the pool, Jan did. At last she asked.

"Do you want one of mine?"

"Residents of Nodding Fog only. Foreign thumbs are tainted. Sorry."

She nodded. But I don't think either of us really understood.

I watched for a moment. Some of the thumbs floated, some had settled to the bottom, some had begun to dissolve. Then a thought occurred to me. If the road that Nodding Fog was on really led somewhere, then that somewhere probably had a lot of stores.

When I asked one of the boys, I was told Banshee Creek had twenty thousand people by last count. He knew, his aunt lived there when she wasn't in Manitoba. "Which way?" "Same as you were going when you stopped."

Jan and I hopped in the Ford and headed for Banshee Creek. I didn't have to tell her I had an idea. She knew me. We don't go on the mystery tour with those we don't know. Banshee proved just big enough to have the sort of place I was looking for. The question now was: Did they have anything exotic? He showed us gold ones, imperial ones, ones that had whiskers, translucent ones, and yes, exotic ones. We chose one of each.

By the time we got back—it was now midnight or so—the boys had wandered home.

We dumped all twenty-one of our little friends into the fountain, went to find a spot in the woods, spread the blanket in the back of the truck, went to sleep. We were up with the birds. Since we were only a mile out, we left the truck there and walked back to town.

We sat on the church steps across the street from the fountain and had to wait a while for the first of the nubbins to emerge. She was a woman, and we could clearly see her nubs against the red shaft of the broom when she paused from her gutter sweeping to nod at us.

Right by the fountain she went, without a peek. Jan, more anxious than myself, took a quarter from her pocket, tossed it across the road into the fountain. The woman swept on. Jan found a piece of concrete at the corner of the step, tossed it just as accurately. Now the woman turned, a look of apprehension coming to her face. As she approached the fountain, that look became one of peering fascination. Carefully, as if retrieving a bubbly-hot pancake with a spatula, she put the flat end of her broom into the pool—the pool was ankle deep at best—then brought it up again with a sudden, quick motion. Two fishes and part of a thumb landed on the cement. The fishes flopped once or twice, and then rested their engorged bodies from the strain of it.

The scream that came out of that woman woke the whole village. People came running from every house to look into the fountain. The reaction was the same, one and all, a yelp of horror followed by flight. We passed them still running three miles out of Nodding Fog.

And that was the first of our adventures on the Road of Mystery.

Danny Avian woke to find that he was no longer being transported to mysterious places in an old pickup truck. He had arrived.

"What is this place? Who are you people?" he demanded.

"Hello to you, sir. Our home is your home."

Avian shook his head violently. His nostrils felt burn-cleaned, as if he'd been inhaling fire; he wiped at his ears, imagined dry chemicals seeping from orifices. His 'under-attended' was swollen between his legs. Everything was hot and chlorinated.

He was on a reclining lawn chair by a pool. Tile and cement and men of all shapes and sizes surrounded him. The pool, to his eyes, his fire-hollowed nose, stank of myriad nightmares, bubbling and drifting in patches of filth. Around the whole affair, pool and deck and brothers and all, were tall hedges, open at one end to a staircase and house of wood and glass. Cocoa was nowhere to be seen; nor her driver, Abe.

The man who had spoken, naked like all of them, held out his hand. Avian started.

For it was decidedly thumbless.

The man lifted his other hand, also disfigured. "But if I still had another, I would offer it to you," he told Avian.

"What *happened?*" Avian whispered.

"Don't you know? As the original Gatherer, surely *you* must know..."

Gatherer? Gatherer of what?!

He was afraid to ask aloud.

"Cocoa says that through your dreams they were gathered. That—" He sliced the thought cleanly as flesh beneath a razor, and with a certain religious grace, fell to his knees.

Around the deck, all of them dropped to the position of obeisance. Or worship.

Avian turned and there she was, their exotic goddess, bound in gold cloth, eyes opening up passages before her. In her wake, the glass of the house beneath which the terrace sprawled seemed to settle back into shape. As her eyes fell on Avian, his knees began to bend.

"No!" she said. "Not you. Not ever you."

"What is this place?" his voice quivered.

"Your palace. These pitiful creatures surrounding the well still do not comprehend that it is to you, the honor, the harvest is given. Hear me! you worms. Place your hands before you! Place your hands before *him!*"

They did...out in front of them like a prayer...and not one among them possessed a thumb.

"I don't want it." Lord God, no.

"Was that your sentiment when you commanded one side of the mountain to invade the other, stealing the thumbs of every captive taken?"

He didn't intend for it to come blurting out. "You are a lunatic, woman!"

"I remember their faces, my mother and father, when they discovered that I, alone in the whole village, had somehow been spared. I remember their faces when they dropped me down the well. They threw me away, Danny, but because they did, I came to know the fishes that are gods and the fishes gave me these eyes. With these eyes I swam through the mountain. With these eyes I appeared, in a spring, to the village I would come to know as home. With these *thumbs*, I escaped my origins. Since

14

all of my birth village had been harvested, I could only have come from other realms."

He gaped at her. Not because she was a lunatic, not because he was in the claws of some cult, and God knew where on the map, but because he had dreamed it. The recurring nightmare had inspired him, hadn't it? He had indeed attended a party, and at his own house. She had been there, eyes turning him to dripping butter. "Cocoa from South America," Vanguard had introduced her.

Let me see your hand, she'd said. She had led him by his hand into his bedroom.

No, he mustn't think of it.

In his bedroom, she had been a woman to him, a woman who became something more as he caressed her, kissed her delicate, shiny, scaly skin. Her eyes poured into his as his horrified hands, and thumbs pressing into her windpipe, choked her, turned her face to rich colors by the shadows of the strange room out of time and place and reality.

No, Vanguard, she tried to...she wasn't human, *Vanguard.*

Sober up. We'll take her to the river, Vanguard said. *No one will ever know what has happened.*

Sober up. Two words that had followed him out of his burial grounds. Lamenting the past abuse of alcohol and drugs made it easier to forget what really lay beneath the shoveled earth.

Or surface of the river. Her spectral jewels transfixing him, burning their image into his tissue, as her dead body drifted away.

"River? Did you mention the river, Danny?"

Cocoa's eyes transfixed him now.

He found himself falling, falling down the shaft of a well, to his knees.

"Forgive me, Cocoa."

"*Not ever you,* I said. Rise. Rise, poet."

He rose.

She turned to the glass, secret glass, her gaze warping its properties as she summoned the whiskered man, Abe.

"Abe has gathered and Abe has fed the hungry mouths. Now Abe will step aside for the original Gatherer, for whom all of this exists. You know what to do, Danny, yes?"

He stared.

15

"Lay him gently beneath the surface. It is poetry that way."

"No."

"If I do it, Danny, I fear it won't be the same."

"I won't do it."

"Let me show you how easy…"

She walked Abe to the edge of the murky stew. "He has given the thumbs of his hands. Now we will give the rest. Job well done, Abe." And he did not resist as she pushed him over the bank.

The entire surface of the pool came to life as the mouths converged on him, and in seconds his body and its pieces had disappeared beneath.

"There is but one thing left then," she said, turning back to Avian.

"To wake up?"

Shaking her head, she held out her thumbs.

She held out her thumbs.

September

As he drove by the sign marking the limit of the village, Galen compulsively shifted his gaze to the mirror. This side of the sign provided the same information as the other, except the word had a slash through it, to indicate one was leaving town. *Sept*, the metal plate bluntly maintained. Out in the middle of nowhere, a village bearing his own surname. What were the odds?

The road had followed a rushing Alpine stream for the past twenty kilometers or so, venturing deeper into the mountains than his ambling path had previously carried him. The village lay in a wider area of the canyon, its thirty-odd structures located along both sides of the stream. Two parallel streets joined by a bridge appeared to be the extent of Sept's road plan.

Sept. The village was pristinely beautiful, contrary to the way those four letters had served Galen in his youth. *Septic Tank* they had called him in middle school; in high school it had been a more concise *Septic*. The handle had been used by all save one, a girl who wrote poetry and told him how insecure he was behind his handsome face. To Ginger he was *September*. Funny that he should think of her now, funny that he should think of school, for these belonged to that taboo place, the past. When his wife, Laura, walked out after four years of marriage, he had decreed the past a place not to be visited. Laura had told him she needed to go home to be with her family, but he knew it was forever. He knew what being abroad had done to each of them. The sense of setting had nearly consumed him, to her alienation. The sense of distance had gotten her, to his alienation.

That sense of setting was at its peak now as he pulled into a space that might have been reserved for him. A lovely, gnarled chestnut tree stood between his car and a painted footbridge over the stream. Beyond the bridge, chimneys poured smoke into the nippy afternoon air. Beyond the roofs of the houses, golden unharvested fields lapped at the base of a steep fir-covered slope. To his right stood a small church, stained glass windows narrow and arched in its rough yellow wall. Galen looked at his watch, wondering if he need go any further than this village today. Four o'clock resounded no—as if the time of day might really be a factor when the gods had brought him here to a village by his own name.

Stepping out of the car, he looked around for the inevitable Gasthaus, staple of central European villages. He spotted the friendly structure on the other side of the street, near the motorist bridge. He left the car where it was and walked the short distance, admiring the building as he approached. A scene from farm life had been painted on the side of it: the proverbial plump, aproned Austrian woman bending to scoop up a handful of hay. On the half-timbered façade hung some of the implements of that life, painted black to stand out against the ivory stucco. Windows were plenty, their ledges covered in red flowers, their curtains drawn back to let in the sunshine. The house itself was the solid body of construction they all were, tall and deep in its dimensions. If Galen had stayed in one of these, he had stayed in a half dozen, more often than not to Laura's protests because she had once found a pair of pubic hairs on the seat of the community bathroom. She had always regretted the shortage of big American hotels.

The small lobby was lit by electric lamps made to look like wick and oil jobs. A massive disgruntled boar's head dominated one wall, while against the adjacent one rested a cigarette machine and a feeble supply of travel brochures. A set of stairs stood straight ahead, and to the left was the reception counter, with a bell. Galen rang it and waited. Emerging from a door in the wall behind the counter, a young woman interrupted his stare-down with the boar.

"*Gross Gott,*" she said, smiling. She wasn't plump, she didn't wear an apron, she smelled nothing like the farm.

"*Gross Gott,*" he said. "*Sprechen Sie Englisch?*"

"A little, yes."

"I would like a room for the night."

"How many in your party, sir?"

"One, if you count me."

She didn't seem to get it—and there was nothing to get anyway. She produced a registration card, and as he accepted it, their hands brushed. The brief sensation reminded him how far along the road of loneliness he was. Yes, he had shared an office with females during this past year of his separation from his wife, but co-workers didn't count. Did Austrians? he wondered. Did Europeans? Did the whole blessed gender?

"I'm curious," he said as he tapped the card with the pen, brows furled with the effort of remembering his new address in Brussels. "How did Sept come by its name?"

When she didn't answer immediately, he glanced up. She was looking at his name on the card.

Their eyes met. Hers were a rich brown touched by a certain joylessness, like his own. Her cascading hair was brown as well, more than complementing her eyes—lending to their momentary intensity.

"You are Austrian?" she asked.

"I'm of German ancestry...maybe Austrian, I don't know. Is it an Austrian name?"

"I..." She hesitated, frowning. "I do not really know, sir. If so, it is uncommon."

He nodded.

"Where are you coming from, Mr. Sept?"

"I've lived in Vienna for the past three years, working for the Atomic Energy Agency." He gestured behind him with his thumb. "Today I'm coming from Salzburg."

"What brought you...here?"

He shrugged. "I'm being transferred to Brussels. I'm not due there for a few weeks, so I thought I would wander some of the less traveled roads. I'm at the whim of my path, if you like."

"No map?"

He mirrored her look, which was markedly strange. "No map."

Slowly, with an elegance that moved him, she extended her hand. "Verena," she said.

He shook it without his usual flare because he was disturbed.

"Shall I get the key?" she said, glancing down. He realized he still held her hand.

"Yes of course. I'm sorry."

"Please," she said, smiling.

He assumed she was coming right back, that the key would be hanging on a rack behind the door, or somewhere equally convenient. When she didn't, he wandered over to the brochures. One showed a skier, radiant against a clear blue sky as her streamlined superimposed image jumped Olympic distances. Another depicted the very house in which he stood. Yet another was for the village itself, the word *Sept* appearing above a silvery picture of the mountain stream. A fourth leaflet was apparently a map of the region. He picked up one of these.

There was nothing inside.

He picked up another of the maps. Nothing. Shrugging, he picked up one of the skiing brochures. This time the absence of printed matter startled him. He picked up the Gasthaus brochure. Nothing. The last one...again nothing.

"Mr. Sept?"

"Yes," he said, turning. "Yeah...these brochures, they're..."

"You aren't supposed to look at them," she smiled, wrinkling her nose. "They are...the word—it is *ornaments?*"

"Like a Christmas tree?" he said with irony. And realized as he said it that it wasn't fair. She was the one making the effort to use his language.

As he stepped up to the counter, she gestured at his hand. "You wear a wedding band. May I ask...where is she?"

He thought about this for several seconds. At last he gave her the answer he felt spoke to the greater truth:

"Not here."

She nodded, led him up the stairs, skeleton key dangling on a ring.

At the door to Room 11 she stopped, inserted the key, stood back to let him enter. Again he brushed her. Again he was reminded.

She waited as he glanced around the room. "It is OK?"

"Yes, very much. Before you go, can you recommend a place for dinner?"

She smiled. "Our own restaurant perhaps? A table has been waiting, I think, for a long time."

"What do you mean?"

"We don't get many visitors here, Mr. Sept. We are honored to have you."

Leaving the key, she closed the door, and he was alone.

Room 11 was on the back side of the building, with a balcony and a view that swallowed him into its oblivions upon the moment of first contact. The slope behind the Gasthaus was rocky and steep, one section boasting a waterfall draping in quivering iridescence from the lip of a high cliff. A scent not especially pleasant, but raw, real, came off the pool formed by the falls. On the brink of the sheer face stood trees whose twisted roots dug into the stone, forming the knitted, contemplative brow of a sage old man. Down by the pool stood another chestnut tree, and another, and grass as green as May.

> *But May is September, September is May,*
> *The fields that we play in, we always will play*

He could not recall where the verse came from, and chose not to go searching among the relics. The past was not to be visited; so it had been decreed. Then why could he not avoid his images as he gazed out across the rich grass? Delete the waterfall and wasn't this the park where he had lain with his poet Ginger and understood the secrets of the universe? Hadn't he made love to her only there, beneath the tree, while she spoke to him in whispers of September, that whispering time of year? Ah, the verse was hers, of course. Where did she go, with stars in her brown eyes, poet of his?

She had been his inspiration for dabbling in the arts himself. He had taken up painting, then photography, then, in college, writing. After a year of submitting his fiction to the same responses—mainly that he spent too much time on exposition and not enough on narration—he gave it up. The psychiatrist his mother was seeing at the time—a probing, discerning man—had expounded on the theory for him. Galen's approach to literature was Galen's approach to life. If he spent as much time actually living his life as he did setting it up, he would live as living was meant to be. The aside was that almost all people took the approach Galen did. This gratis observation no doubt encouraged Galen's falling

21

into the European setting with such love. With only one year separating his degree from its application, he had leapt into the world offered to him, perhaps at Laura's expense. While she screamed permanence, he belted about the rare opportunity they had. They'd best seize it while it was in their grasp because one day it would be back to Iowa and they would have missed their chance to live.

The fields that we play in, we always will play.

"Excuse me, Mr. Sept..."

Her voice came from below. He leaned over the balcony rail to find her smiling up at him. Something belonging to the moment, something about the unassuming expression on her oval face, or the last of the afternoon sun dancing in her hair, made her look especially youthful. He wondered how old she was, but there was no answer to be found in gazing upon her rather wistful, though lovely, features. Her eyes belied her visage, and vice versa.

"Please call me Galen...Verena."

"Of course. If you would like, I will have dinner ready for you, Galen."

"You prepare it yourself?" he asked.

"There is no one else. Not for a very long time."

He confessed, "I'm confused. Earlier you referred to it as *our* restaurant. You said, '*We* don't get many visitors.'"

"It is...how do you say...a figure of speech?"

He looked at her a moment before asking, "Did you come back here expecting to find me on the balcony?"

"I was going to the waterfall to wash my hands." She held up the right one, palm to him. "I must know if it will wash away."

"Wash away..." Seeing nothing there, he shook his head to suggest that he did not understand her. But she was already walking in the direction of the waterfall.

"There's a nip on the air," he called after her.

"It is always so," she called back. "In Sept it only pretends to grow cold. As it only pretends to grow warm."

As with other things about her, which occurred to him seemingly at random, only now did he notice what she wore. Both sweater and pants were a nondescript beige, in harmony with her elegance. Her feet, he was alarmed to see, were bare. He thought to call again, but opted instead to treat his eyes, without further interruption, to her grace. She moved with a fluidity that enchanted; she was the first zephyr of September, a specter, a muse. When she reached the pool, she pulled up the legs of her pants, patted out into the water. She extended one naked foot, teasing the falling water, teasing the senses of the man standing on the balcony watching her. More tentatively, she reached out her hand, middle finger stretching as if to test the shimmering column of fire cascading from the mountain. When it was not burned, she plunged her hand into the flame; when her hand remained whole, she lay back her head and laughed happily.

Stepping back out of the water, she found his gaze across the reaches, holding her palm to him, triumphant. He waved back...as he had waved at Laura, her own palm white and segmented against the misty window of the cab. She hadn't even let him see her to the airport, though he went anyway, without her knowledge, saluting again as the plane flew away.

Verena wasn't flying away. Verena was coming back. Verena was here, now, alive to him, accessible...though he had watched her bathe in the sacred falls. The moroseness he had glimpsed had been replaced by something incalculably more difficult to define.

"Will you come soon?" she said.

"To...oh yes, of course. Dinner. Would you care to...I mean, may I invite you...?"

"Loneliness dwells with me too, Galen. I know."

Yes. She knew. Somehow he knew that she knew.

"Look," she said, holding up her palm. "It didn't wash away."

"What didn't wash away?"

"My hand...the hand that you touched."

Now an emotion that he did not like visited him. An emotion with tentacles that wrapped themselves around his nerve bundles, caused his breath to come sudden. Its name was old, old, and it chilled in any season, though the mercury never drop and the wind never blow.

He reached for her suddenly, as if he could compel his arm to stretch that far, far enough to take her hand in his own. "What has happened here?" he queried. "Where is everyone?"

"I've told you," she answered, a curtain falling over her features. "There is no one."

A Dirge for the Temporal

"I'm afraid," he said quietly.

"Shhh. Be still," she said.

He was, not realizing what he was opening his senses to. Almost immediately the perception of place warped out of all familiarity. A sound that was both deeper and more vast than silence held him suspended. It was as if the Void were coming in like a great sighing maw to devour them.

"What is it?" he whispered, eyes darting around him, up at the purpling sky.

"The gears of September," she said. "Your return has brought them to life again."

His skin felt as if it were being pulled from his bones. He clutched his head between his fists and prayed it go away. When he opened his eyes, a tear emerged, slipping down his cheek. In its magnificence she was reflected. He knew; he saw her at the same time in the waterfall.

"Your table will be ready within the half hour," she said.

He fled into his room, sliding the glass door shut. As the compartment pressed in on him, with its strange, mysterious objects and props—TV, pictures, safe, bed, mirror, *mirror*—he knew he could not remain here. Not now.

He left the Gasthaus for a ship that might right itself again without him aboard. The lobby was empty as he passed.

Outside, the afternoon grew a deeper purple, the sun long gone behind a ridge. The stream flowed inevitably. Smoke pumped inevitably. Yet there were no cars except for the wagon he had brought in. There were no people save him. He felt as if he existed in the lull of nightmarish sleep. He foresaw the key turning in the ignition, the engine coming to life, the tires snatching at the asphalt in their haste to obey him. He saw the sign as it would appear in his rearview mirror. Would Verena run after him, pleading about the gears of September?

September is May and May is September,
Nor free to forsake, when bound to remember.

He would laugh as he drove away, he swore. Laugh for the being done to. For the goddamn being done to, Laura. The keys in his fist were like tangible her, biting into his skin, cold, inflexible. He shook from the others the one key that mattered. The noise of the stream lifted as he neared the wagon.

"Galen!" came the voice of Verena over the rushing water.

He wasn't going to look back. He stepped around to the driver's side of the car, key in front of him like the stolen screwdriver or ice pick in the hand of the prison escapee. As he grasped the handle of the door, he caught sight of something on the stream.

His eyes locked on the object, instantly recognizing it as a body, a limp, naked human body riding the flow from the direction of the high Alps, now passing under the footbridge, a rag doll at the will of the current. A half second elapsed between its clearing the shadow of the bridge and passing the line of Galen's vehicle, but it was enough time to reveal the change that visited the body, a shift which shook Galen the witness down to the bone and marrow.

The body had turned on the current and opened its eyes to mark him.

No sooner had he beheld this terror than another body passed under the bridge, emerging in a similar surprise of flesh and awakened eyes, rolling against the force of the current, pulling and dragging as if to impede its momentum. In its wake came a third—the other two now having swept out of sight—and behind the third came a fourth. In all Galen counted seven before their abrupt cessation reminded him that he was supposed to be inside his wagon and on his way out of this haunted pass in the foothills of the Alps.

Slamming the door behind him, he turned the key to the beautiful greeting of a trusty engine waking from a doze. He pulled the shifter into reverse and backed out somewhat slower than he would have liked, in case Verena had decided to come running up behind with her plea. He caught her in his mirror as he shifted again, preparing to speed off in the direction from which he'd come. Out in the street in front of the Gasthaus, she stood akimbo, striking him—rather perversely—as stirringly sexy in the pose. Nonetheless, he put the pedal to the floor and was almost out of there when they appeared in the road in front of him—four, five, six, seven of them, all sexless, of a sickly yellow hue, flesh leeching to their bones.

He slammed on the brakes—too late as one went flying over the top of the car and another buckled underneath. As the others stared through the windshield at him, mouths stretched in every rictus and scowl, he saw that their expressions were the only thing of life they possessed, making them, as he saw it, fair game. As he yanked it in reverse, however, bringing the RPM to critical mass, the creatures divided, rushing by the car, more interested in what was behind it than what was inside.

Verena! He let reverse carry the car all the way around, one hundred and eighty degrees, paused only long enough to convince himself that he wasn't about to invite real-life blood into a hallucinatory reality, then he rode them down like pylons in a road course, too tempting to leave be. Having punched through the last of them, he found himself and his wagon, in a haze of hot rubber and clutch and brakes, facing Verena. Verena and the akimbo. Would he or would he not come to dinner?

She did not protest, in spite of her impatient stance, as he dragged his victims one by one back to the stream, where the water accepted them eagerly, instantly sweeping them away. He never looked at them as he did the work. He did not know their nature and did not want to know. To his hands they were cool, moist; it was enough. He glanced once they were in the clutch of the stream, then just for a second, to make sure they obeyed.

He left the wagon in the middle of the road. It was an admission.

To be denied no longer, Verena held out her hand to him.

Inside, at their neatly laid table, the candles provided a scent as well as light, but the light was exclusive and the shapes of their faces drifted radiantly. She made him eat the petals of flowers, drink water from the falls, kiss her face when there wasn't enough. She was Laura, she said. And Ginger.

"Once, a long, long time ago," she recalled, "a stranger ambled in off the *Wanderweg*. His arrival caused the gears of September to freeze. His presence caused the stream to flow backwards into the wilderness of ice and snow, carrying with it the vitality of our little village at the end of civilization. Now you have returned."

"Sept is a delightful name for a village."

"Your village," she said. She raised a glass. "Unforsaken."

Indulgence

My mother was a manic-depressive, my father was a circus clown, and I have never suffered for it more than now, nearly twenty years since their departure.

The hunger-lust, in one form or another, has been around since my adolescence, but the ritual is developed. Things dark or red, sweetly decadent, satisfy my cravings. Things reminiscent of my deeper moods, things that can be savored by candlelight. You might say I am a sort of vampire for cherry pies and chocolate cakes, Bloody Mary mixes and richly red wines. My mother's binges, on the other hand, went somewhat beyond the sweet tooth. But I become one with her through abandon not mimicry. Abandon is bliss.

Abandon is when the curtains are drawn, the candle lit and the feast spread out before me. Only then may I cease to suppress my magnificent appetite. Only then may I fully give over to the voraciousness and savagery that define my nightly indulgences. But the banquet goes not without its pauses, moments to close the eyes and to relish our finding each other over the chasm, my mother and I, dripping fingers interlocking, feet gingerly balancing on the red polka dots scattered across the whispery white fabric that serves as the bridge.

I often use my father's only surviving costume as a tablecloth. The reds have long since bled into one another—thanks to my utter lack of etiquette—but there is some comfort in having the clown suit there, some...sanity. One day I will burn it. One day, when its simple motif is no longer recognizable, I will set the candle flame to its flowery cuffs and listen to the clown scream. As for tonight, I will let it serve the practical purpose. I am hungry, after all, and the shadows are already dancing around me.

Ah, the rich, the delectable, the sinful and luscious! How I do anticipate these feasts. From the early office hours to the bakery's last call, it is all I can do to contain myself. You see, my deeper moods have become my shallower moods, abiding, as familiar to me as my own face. And the darks and reds blur my vision with such incessancy that the lenses of my glasses might as well be tainted. The ritual becomes as much a leash as a release, and the world is spared the monster even as the monster suffers.

Though the only suffering I know now is the oblivious suffering of gluttony.

But—a syrupy cherry has fallen from my maw. And—I look at it against a brief, very brief patch of white, watching it saturate like ink, like blood, the ridiculously virginal bit of fabric. Now the flicker of the candle...the flicker, flicker, moth wings...

You bitch, you bitch, you BITCH! I have watched you deteriorate to this state, throwing your black shadow over our home, devouring every-thing in sight, for the last time!

Ah, Daddy, home from work at last, still in his clown costume...

I've had damn well enough. Do you understand me, you bitch? ENOUGH!

...wielding his bottle of bourbon like a club.

There! How'd that feel? Still hungry, you?

Now like a knife.

I'm going to take you apart like a chicken!

Daddy, home and screaming. Must be in that sort of black mood Mommy gets.

The tablecloth's motif is scarcely discernible, I notice. The polka dots are no longer distinguishable from the rest of it, the entire garment now saturated by the ritual syrup. I should do the baptism tonight. Baptize. Uncle Trace used that word after they took Daddy, naked and screaming, away. *The costume—my god, we'll have to baptize it with gasoline and a match.* Uncle Trace is my mother's side.

Like a chicken! Know why? Cause I can't help it, that's why! I'm fam-ished! Ravenous as a wild dog!

28

Now like a fork. A dinner fork.

The candle flame to the tablecloth's flowery cuffs and listen to the clown scream. This time in pain. And not the sort that a painted tear and a bottle of cheap bourbon describe.

The Shades of New Geneva

Funny, they had built the great triangular Prism in the center of New Geneva as a symbol of what they called "unity in diversity." Now the dispersed bands of light melted into the miasma enveloping the city, creating a spectral stew. Like the population itself. Like the streets of the dreadful place.

As he stood looking down into the valley of the city, Lane didn't want to go back in there. He would never speak those words to Leah, who stood tautly beside him, her temporarily concrete-colored eyes refusing to reflect the weird lights below. She had lost something to New Geneva, something intrinsic, and she had finally summoned the courage to go searching for it. He would not compromise that. The strange silence surrounding their merged roads, an infection of which she was the source, must end. The possibility of leaving her had long since evaporated. She had infected him too thoroughly.

He glanced at her, finding that she had fixed on a point beyond the valley, in the direction of the sea. He followed her gaze to a motley object sewn into the deceptively clear fabric of the morning sky. It was a hot air balloon, and moving towards the basin, as if to enhance its navigator's high with the toxic vapors of the city. The French Alps to the north and the Mediterranean to the south, New Geneva had once been a favorite destination for adventurers and their colorful toys. Not anymore. If pleasure was the function of this vehicle, then it was piloted by either a fool or a madman.

"Come," he said, motioning her ahead of him. She led the way down the path with a sureness to her light step, the familiarity its own brand of homecoming. They wouldn't be giving her a parade in New Geneva. They might toss her a dwarf or a senseless riddle, ogle her with swollen tongues and drunken serenades. They might even allow her to pop off a few shots at the rats, or pose for the *spiegel*, or partake of the *âme*, but they wouldn't be giving her a parade. New Geneva took more than New Geneva gave. Lane knew because he had been here multiple times on business. Lane knew because Leah knew; she had been a citizen.

As they descended, the city's structures sank into its miasmal aura, leaving only the Prism itself, filtering the rising sun into the chaos over which it stood sentinel. The hot air balloon grew, letters beginning to take shape out of its stripes. As the city welcomed them, so did the obsolete advertisement: *unity in diversity.*

The city got its name from the melting pot of cultures and languages and peoples that Swiss Geneva was. Only the namesake was to be an even more civilized, more organized, more modern-day Babel. *unity in diversity.* Lane looked around him and he saw exactly one half of that equation, to the extent that he suddenly felt physically distanced from Leah, who was right beside him, her hand grasped tightly in his. The eyes she turned on him told tales of their own. The concrete color had dissolved to make way for the iridescence which he had seen on occasion, a quivering rainbow stolen from the armor of a beached fish in the sun's glare. Or from the swamp lights drifting within New Geneva's poisonous nimbus.

Before them, along a narrow street cut in half by shadow, the corruption unfolded. Bloated men on stick legs pecked about like chickens, looking for anything into which they might stab their beaks. Sleek favor girls—fingers glistening with the adhesive they used to secure their deposits—stuck their bottom lips out in a contest of who could pout the loudest. From neomodernrococo upper windows in the flanking walls, buxom citywives yelled down at their husbands and sons not to bring anything raunchy home, or they'd put them out with the garbage. The word garbage was instantly absorbed into the refuse spilling out from the crevices between business concerns. The entrances of these establishments were vague outlines behind exhaled vapors. A street in New Geneva was like the canal through which a fart traveled, without the expulsion of air.

Leah must have had one of these joints in mind all along; otherwise they would have already been in the city center, with its fake antique European walls and cobblestone avenues. Someone knew something about something. Lane trusted her judgment implicitly, even though he was the infiltrator by trade. The sunken inner door didn't fit well in its frame; dried up posters clung to flaking paint; the withins were dark and full of Miles Davis riffs and ripoffs.

Over the sounds of the trumpet, a slurred voice made itself audible, addressing the player. "You *are* my man Miles, ain't ya? Goddamn, how did you find your way here to the Jazzy Sloth?"

The Jazzy Sloth. Indeed, where else would one be?

Leah went straight to the bar, something of the mood of the place appearing in her eyes as she leaned up on her toes and elbows to address the bartender, whose back was turned to them. "Joy, it's me. Leah."

"Leee-uh!" exclaimed a sandpaper voice as the woman twirled. "Hello, you beautiful bitch!"

"I'm back to reclaim what belongs to me," Leah said plainly. "Joy, let me introduce you to Lane. Lane is my...he is my Lane."

Lane felt a patter of delicate little feet race through him, hearing this confession from her.

"Wait a minute," said Joy in her abrasive voice. "You're the one Leah hired to find her sister Gena."

"Yeah," said Lane. Hearing the name reminded him that their mother had spelled it with an *e* so that it read like an abbreviation of Geneva, in honor of the splendid modern city where the sisters had been born.

"Did you?"

"She was a *spiegel*." He looked over at Leah, whose eyes were the lightest suggestion of blue as they gazed at the trumpeteer on stage. He continued, "I forced her to come, nearly had to drag her, but we didn't make it."

"She do herself?"

"*Fuck!*" Leah let out unexpectedly. For the scattered patrons, she might have been hurling her frustrations at the musician. Joy passed Lane a protracted glance.

It had been the last gig for Lane. For years he had been entering the city, finding them and bringing them out—or *not* bringing them out. The whole operation had come to an end when Gena, a not so random number, threw herself under a passing vehicle's tires. He didn't realize his level of investment until he delivered the news to Leah, who absorbed it without movement, her eyes the color of silence. In that moment in time he became lost with her. Through Leah and through his own sorties into New Geneva's jungles, the city had sunk its claws into him, a non-citizen.

Rarely did such outbursts come from Leah. Perhaps it was the being back. He felt the intensity, and the desolation, too.

intensity in desolation. Our new motto in New Geneva.

He put his hand on her shoulder, and she was stoical again. For a moment her eyes assumed the quality her sister's had, which bespoke the absence of anything to offer this city which had developed its own desires and motives.

"I need to know where the *âme* is brightest lately," Leah said to her friend.

"I can't say really, as more and more are offering themselves. Don't drink! The more of us who've joined, the greater its allure."

"Don't say 'us,' Joy. Never say 'us.'"

Lane watched Joy's expression, saw the shift in the hue of *her* eyes, to that of a glassy office-building exterior. God, if that ever happened to him...no, he mustn't think of it. As long as he was rescuing *them*, he was sane.

Joy said, "It's just that waves of the city's population go blindly—"

"Go *where*, Joy? Where is the most active area? That's what we need to know."

Joy considered. "I suppose there is a lot of activity in Germantown these days. But really every part of the city center is game."

"Thank you," Leah said. "I'll see you again. Stay here and don't let anything change your mind."

"Leah," Joy's voice reached coarsely. "If you come across what was taken from me, will you retrieve it, too?"

Leah's hand went to her throat, realm of the larynx and its vocal cords. Joy nodded.

"If I do, Joy."

In her silence, Leah focused through the congestion on the image of the item stolen from her. It was a simple thing, but an intrinsic one, with enormous personal value. Its color was that of the richest purple Holland tulip. Its material was that of wings, the birds of the air and aether. It had belonged to her mother and been a gift from her father. Both were dead. Leah's thoughts were never silent.

As she led Lane like an umbilical cord from a sister dead in blood on a concrete field, she thought of her father, who had locked himself in a room with four bottles of absinthe, three packs of non-filter cigarettes, and his wife's corpse. When the authorities came, with the hint of New Geneva in their eyes even then, they found a burnt-out cigarette resting between Leah's mother's dead lips, dry as her body and memory. Dad, meanwhile, was not so easily approached, all the hallucinations standing like ranks of soldiers in defense of him. His tongue hung out and his eyes bulged towards the treasure at the flat end of an empty green goddess bottle. Granted. Let nothingness process you while your children face the city alone.

Baby sister in her arms, Leah had fought her way through the officers—whom she had phoned when she could not get into the room—to look at him a last time. His soundless voice cut through the images on which his eyes still fixed to remind her that the biblical Leah had lovely eyes too, and to encourage her to wrap herself in her feathery prize and run until her feet turned to wings. He had known what he would do when he had given the article to her that morning, before brushing away her tears and singing her to sleep again. Looking at her mother, whose eyes did not stare, she had demanded the officials tell her what they had done with the gift. They didn't know what she was talking about but allowed her to look around while they did what they could to shield the madness that had been her parents. For a moment it was there, hanging from the mirror like Hollywood and tropical islands, but no, that was one of the lingering hallucinations.

Soon enough she found it in her own room, coiled around the pillow, some of its feathers distorted from her tears. She put it around her neck, and remembered that her mom hadn't been able to recall where it came from. Some dime store. Some souvenir shop. Somewhere unimportant.

Leah felt its whispery comfort around her neck now, but refused to reach up and caress a phantom. Before her, before the silence of her, cherubs winked from beneath their brimmed hats as the neomodernrococo gates of the alley gave way to sleek perpendicular scapes of reflective gray. She looked to her right and saw herself, her naked shoulders in the surface. The lucid illusion, like a lucid dream, died. She squeezed Lane's hand, but it was as cold as the condensation that formed to obscure even the nakedness. She looked up at the polished walls hemming them in and felt her diminutiveness and powerlessness.

Ahead, at yet another architectural change, an archway of stone-substitute displayed the message: *Ein Bißchen Deutschland*

The inner city thrived on their ghosts before them. The *âme*, on vagabond tongues, pushed out to meet them. Ragged preachermen cried contradictions: God would tear New Geneva down; God greatly favored New Geneva, hence the *âme*; God *was* New Geneva. Behind these came the voices of unity. Of merging. Of urban nirvana. Then came the *âme* itself, in faint, luminous faces and figures, those who had given themselves willingly. Occasionally the eyes of a *spiegel* appeared, mirroring the decorative corners, the strangers and citizens that were Leah and Lane, but not the specters that comprised the *âme*. For the *spiegel* were the antithesis of the *âme*, in that the latter gave everything while the former had nothing to give, or take from.

Leah, at last, touched her shoulder, but the boa was not there.

There was a fountain in the middle of Germantown, and that's where it was happening.

Half-timbered houses with flowers and maidens in Bavarian outfits huddled around the square, while propaganda posters were flown on flagpoles. Shaven NeoNazi heads rolled angrily by, only to be thumped, when accessible, by hater haters. Brät and Schnitzel stank the place, and beer fountained like the gods.

Lane cautioned Leah not to act on emotion, but advice like that was snatched right out of the air like electricity. She moved with the flow to the rim of the pool and, against the pull of his arm, splashed her face, licking her lips, her eyes becoming like the water, like the *âme*. He knew she sought to get into the "active thought" of the city, but as she turned her head towards the sky, he wondered if she would begin to speak in tongues. Looking around at the other pilgrims wishing to unite with the *âme*, he discovered similar textures.

He surrendered to the reverse gravity, eyes drawn upward. Amazingly, something had punctured the miasmal shelf, a small dark something which he deduced immediately to be made of wicker. Luxurious, temperamental flames gushed occasionally, as from a dragon's mouth. Nylon broke the miasma, stripes of color seeming to pour from aloft. The balloon blossomed over Germantown's square. Cheers rose, calling not for *unity in diversity* but for the owner of a strange, unconnected name.

"Who...?" Leah said to Lane.

"Citygirl!" a voice chided them. "Only the biggest pop star in the *world!*"

"Aha," Lane said, looking at Leah. But she was engrossed again, eyes only for the heavens.

A crackling sounded as speakers came to life and music spat upon the square.

"Citygirl!" they shouted in a shatter of unison.

As the basket descended, its passengers came into view. One face made itself visible, one voice singing down:

"I walk the streets, the streets walk me..."

Lane was about to tell Leah that he believed he had heard the song before, but her expression froze him.

In her silence, Leah did not lose sight. Faces from balloons were faces from balloons, even when they circled into the face of her mother.

Her mother had been terrified of whirlpools. Something about them had imbedded in her subconscious and many a morning had been spent untangling herself from the tornado of the covers. She had stilled her lips and eyes and illogic when Leah's dad had purchased just such a toy to enhance their New Geneva-style home. Leah had heard her say, "You use it, Edward. I will rely on my boa."

"One night I'll convince you to join me," he said. "You'd have the time of your life."

One drunken night she had dived in on her own. The intoxication, like its wellspring, had great power. Gena existed in a toddler whirlpool of her own, Leah in nightmares that hadn't fully formed. But so did many in this new enlightened age, in this its model city, with the alcohol pouring from every fountain and every faucet and the philosophers dancing in the streets. Yes, one night their mother had dived in on her own—but not until after she had tucked her two girls in, confessing that fears must be confronted, doors musn't be left ajar letting light spill in from the hall. The little girls hadn't argued because they could see Mom's own light shining in her eyes. As it turned out, she had missed securing the door in its frame and her voice sang thickly and cheerily as she faded along the hall. "Swimming," she sang. "I'm going swimming."

Leah had never known how it happened. Whether the city had sucked her through its pipes, pinning her against the drain, breathing water into her lungs. Or whether Leah's dad, who had been out on the sofa, had woken into a moment of clarity and performed the deed himself. Still another possibility was that their mother had set the example for Gena to follow, maddened beyond repair by the snap-together city she called her home, committing the act against herself. Leah knew only that she woke to her dad's howls sometime in the night. She found him standing over the whirlpool, holding the boa in his fists, perhaps the only article Leah's mom had worn to her date with death. The reflections on the walls were the color of skin.

As Leah looked up at the face in the wicker basket, it sang that special song from childhood. *I'm going swimming.*

The square cheered the singer on and the singer raised a hand to wave at them. Clutched in it was a feathery scarf of Holland tulip purple.

Leah opened her mouth, but her silence would not let it out.

Her eyes had become the hue of the scarf that Citygirl waved. Lane grew alarmed as several *spiegel*, perhaps sensing the local temperature change, began to gather around Leah. The silky tulip purple reflected in the mirrors that were their eyes. Lane pulled her against his chest, feeling enveloped as he always did when she was this close, spinning her silence around him. Eager hands caught the balloon's basket at it landed in the square. The speakers posted about the place continued to pump the music of the pop diva. The mirrors abandoned Leah for her, the petal flames whispering out in their eyes. With the release a single word spilled out of Leah's mouth:

"*Mine!*"

Lane watched her raise an accusatory finger, but for a moment could make no sense of it. Then realization, on its own parachute, arrived.

"Is that it?" he said. "The thing in her hand?"

"That's it," she said.

"Then by God, let's grab it now." He tried to lead her through the pressing throng, but was squeezed out. Looking around, he located a patch of *âme* converging on the same icon that attracted everyone else. Using Leah's envelope of silence as a sail, he steered them into the ghostly caravan. The physics of it were such that the pocket of liquid and light swept them along as part of its own. Citygirl grew into a face with features, a voice with nuances. And suddenly the sail narrowed to the pitch of a knife's honed edge.

"That voice..." Leah said. "I know that voice."

Lane looked at her narrowly. "Don't say it's Joy's voice. Don't you say it's Joy's voice appearing with your scarf. There are a million people in this city."

"Yes, but Joy's voice is *in* that voice. Maybe this Citygirl is a product of all the most unique voices, a thousand of them, combined."

He looked from her face to that of the pop star. Muttered, "...in diversity."

The caravan bore them to the very rim of the basket, the transparent arms of the *âme* reaching out to caress Citygirl lovingly. As Citygirl's eyes turned on Leah, Lane saw the bands of the spectrum exhibited there, mimicking the panels of the parachute above her. And he understood that the creature he looked upon was the city of New Geneva personified.

In her poised, tense, fragile silence, so did Leah. She raised her open hand to the girl whose eyes were ribbons of color, and the girl accepted the invitation, bringing the boa with her as her hand landed in Leah's grasp. At that instant, as if in obedience to a separate instinct, burners exploded with air-heating flames, and the balloon began to lift. Leah would not let the boa go and felt her body rise on its toes, then off the ground, then suddenly lurching upward, arm nearly dislocating from the socket. Her lungs took in the air of the event as she turned to look down at Lane. His arm, its hand extended futilely, grew smaller, more desperate with every clenching of the fist.

The people and their own empty hands and their recorded music diminished. The miasma embraced. The glass monolith that was the Prism appeared, rising through color-wrenched strata, and Citygirl, in a swirl of purple feathers, entered Leah's sphere. Hostess breathed of her guest and when her guest didn't object, tossed the scarf around Leah's neck and put her mouth over hers, pulling at the silence within her. Losing all sense of who and what and where she was, Leah broke the contact, and in the interim the bands of the spectrum warped and spiraled. She felt herself falling.

The rush of air was noise again, great mysterious noise again. A hand reached down towards her, but it had no rope to reach so far, no feathers on which to hitch a ride.

The city did not have a name now. Leah had been a name and more to Lane. Gena had been a name. Even Joy, whom he did not know, was a name. But now…

He moved through the center on feet of lead. Although their numbers only increased as he went, the *âme* relinquished him gladly, for he was a bruise to them. The inner city burned like a beacon, hot across windowsills and stoops, singeing the hair of rats, searing the tongues of the prophets. When he entered the park and the walls of the Prism became visible, Lane wished only to take shelter there, like some lighthouse keeper, out of the storm of nothingness.

There was such an individual, though he'd no optic with which to work, nor ships to guide. A look at his aging face as he rose from the base of the Prism, where he'd been immersed in a sandwich, revealed as much. Lane told him he was looking for a girl. She'd last been seen in a balloon over Germantown. Without realizing he was doing so, his hands pirouetted before his face, describing Leah's eyes. The man's amusement drew attention to the fact that the man himself bore no signs, not in his vessels of sight nor anywhere else.

"But how?" Lane said.

"I do my duty," said the man. "I see that the Prism remains functional and unmolested. The city needs me for no other purpose."

"Have you seen or heard anything of her?" Lane said.

The man shook his head.

"If you were to take me up into the Prism…"

"That would not be neutral," said the man.

"Can you be neutral? Knowing what New Geneva has become?"

The man took a bite of his sandwich, chewed with an enunciative care and deliberateness. When he swallowed finally, he opened his eyes wide, that there be no mistake as to their naturalness.

Lane said, "Those may be the eyes you were born with, but what do they *see*?"

The Prism keeper sucked his teeth. "I'll tell you what they see. They see a fella who'd best be on his way. I have lost my patience."

Lane was swift in his assault, driving the keeper against the glass wall, where he jolted the man's head to erase the present. The old man was stout and stood there on powerful legs, dazed, while Lane searched his pockets for the key. Lane found it in short order, clutching the means in his fist as he scanned his surroundings. Some ghosts and some mirrors hovered on the fringes of the park. The language of the former spoke more to amusement than concern, while the latter related in the only way they could, by reflecting. Satisfied, Lane turned to the task at hand.

The door in the Prism's base proved small and plain, the monolith having never been a place for tours. The narrowest of passages wound upward through its glass composition. It might have been sculpted out of an iceberg, but for the absence of ice. As he reached the lower miasmal strata, the colors clothed him. The vertical edges of the triangular body, otherwise undetectable, expressed themselves by splitting those colors so that the pigments seemed to flood the visitor's senses from all sides. The glass trapped heat, which spread through Lane's own material, writing out a definition of integration. The claustrophobia was less kind, pressing him within a house of mirrors, depriving him of oxygen. His mind, of its own accord, turned to the question of what he had to offer New Geneva. He wasn't a citizen, but he was a thief, as solid a fixture on the urban set.

Nevertheless, he rode the stairless spiral up through the invisible roofs of surrounding buildings, imagining melting ice and released oxygen even as the drops of sweat fell from his brow. Perception overtook this retreat, however, as the whole tower turned upside down and he was sliding along its spiral tunnel towards cool water in which to plunge. The colors began to dissolve as speed and altitude and depth became one thing. An effulgence of fire encompassed him. He looked outward and saw a fan of color dispersing from his own person. The fire dissipated into clarity, and clarity reigned. The nimbus roiled below his position as he realized he could breathe again, he could taste with his senses again. He was above the city. He was above the prophets.

Hands of clear liquid glass, clearer than the substance of the incorporeal *âme*, took his hands and led him to a terrace. Motion and color disturbed the clarity. As he stepped out into the air, he realized that the disturbance came from beneath his feet. There, in the transparent floor, lay Leah. Her arms moved wildly, her mouth formed infinitudes of expression, her eyes shone ice-clear as she stared up at him through her prison. The noise of air, hot and rushed, sounded above him. He looked up to see the bottom of the wicker basket. The boa dangled from its rim like a temptation out of the Garden of Eden, the serpent in its ultimate allure, with promises of a wonderful something just beyond the mortal grasp.

In her silence, Leah's tears fell from her eyes to become drops of glass on her cheeks. Her arms waved the gift away, she didn't want it after all, the city could have it if only she could be allowed to go where her sister had gone. The air smelled like smog. The sky looked like nuclear winter. Lane expressed like some prophet out of the dumpster. His hands were smeared with dirt and blood, his eyes had grown the color of girders. Words came out of his mouth, but she couldn't understand them through the silence. The gift lolled over his back, like a teasing tongue. It didn't mean anything, the dime store thing. Voices, things…nothing was intrinsic except the fascination. No one belonged within.

Which was why the tears did not continue to fall as she watched the tulip-purple boa wrap around Lane's neck, seizing him tightly and drawing him upwards, against his bulging eyes and his rotten tongue. He swung out there in the nothingness filled with sun, and the tears on her face began to melt. She rose up out of the silence, spreading out over the miasma, and she felt, in every molecule of her, the call of New Geneva. She looked down into the swirl, laughing for the pleasure of it, and as she surrendered herself she felt the hands of the *âme* rise up out of the storm of nothingness to catch her and bring her down gently to the urban beds that had been calling for her in shouts and screams of silence.

As Lane stepped out of the Prism into the park, he caught the flash of the old man's eyes. He stepped over to where the man slumped against the wall, gazing into mirrors that had not been there before. The thought—*the old man has betrayed his city and now he can only reflect it*—was replaced by the reflection itself. The image of his own eyes. Miasmal, spectral, exhibiting the rainbows through which he had just descended. The shock dissipated into the question, *But what....?*

He searched his clothes, his pockets. What had he given in return? What did he own that had such intrinsic value to him? Certainly no material thing, nor even a symbolic thing.

The question was answered as he emerged from the park to find a solitary *âme* approaching him, the outlines of her body and face as familiar to him as his own. Her name from his lips sounded every bit as ghostly as her appearance. She seemed to recognize him, seemed to be acting in humor when she crossed her forefingers and placed them over each of her eyes, but the silence surrounding her had crystallized, and there was no breaking it. Not now. Never.

As he walked back in the direction of the only place that seemed connected in any way to anything, he could almost hear the trumpet calling to him, its voiceless notes reaching across the strange urban surfaces to temper the harrowing stillness.

The Whole Circus

The nearer you were to Chaos, the more numerous and glaring its symptoms. It was hard to believe that only a decade ago it was still known as Orlando, entertainment capital of the world. Always State of the Art, the city had been the first to go fully automated. Too late New Orleans, Miami and Las Vegas saw Orlando's error. They were now suffering the same fate. They would likely never achieve the state of electronic and social bedlam their forerunner had, but they were nonetheless places you would not want to take your children.

To Shelley, who knew all too well about symptoms, Chaos was home. Even now, as his captor led him along the tubular passage, he experienced that strange sense of connection, that feeling of needing only a terminal to bring it all into glorious focus. He saw it mirrored in the eyes of the people he passed. The lust for life had been replaced by a shimmering brought on by the phantasmagorial splendor of electrons and currents and information bombardment.

Surrounding the flow of foot traffic in the tunnel, screens displayed nonsensical, indecipherable, illogical messages. In the ceiling, light panels dimmed and intensified, dimmed and intensified, contributing to the routine surreal quality of the scene. The lower half of a hominoid robot strode by, drawing scarcely a glance as it journeyed to someplace remembered by its legs. Pieces and parts of things, not always inorganic, cluttered the base of the walls. Homing spheres, seeking to deliver certified messages that had long since lost their relevance to anything, hummed by, occasionally colliding with a public access monitor, someone's head or

44

shoulder, another sphere. A random scream, or peal of laughter, echoed and shuddered along the passage. And all this in an auxiliary tubeway outside city limits.

As Shelley felt the mysteries deepen around him, reminding him that they were approaching the moving tube, direction Anarchy, he craved his Psycho. Ian, his captor, had promised it to him in periodic, small doses, but he'd yet to see the first drop—except as depicted in the frequent, passing flash ads, whose scare tactics were far more effective when you were on the stuff. In the heart of Chaos you would have to search hard to find such propaganda. Out here on the fringes, it was all you could do to escape the picture of the eager human face, the poised dropper, the single luminous teardrop of Self-replicating Psychedelic Chemical Organism freefalling towards a bloodshot eye. The image itself was actually quite delicious; the footer is what got you: *PSYCHO WILL FUCK UP YOUR MIND.*

Shelley knew it had fucked up his. Why else had he allowed himself to turn rat against Silver, Prince of Psycho? On one side of the scale, a life sentence; on the other, a death sentence. He had chosen the latter. Did he despise Silver for what the man represented, what the man commanded? Did he despise himself for being the dependent on Silver's candy that he was? Was he so repelled by the idea of a foreign organism taking up residence inside his body that he wanted to die? For reasons beyond the grasp of his depleted layman's gray matter, the duration of the high and the lifespan of the organism did not agree. The high on average lasted some fifteen hours per the standard dose of one cc, while the organism continued to grow indefinitely. There was an antibiotic which, when combined with an electrochemical application of some sort, was said to rid the body of the invitee. But a single treatment ran fifty thousand dollars.

Shelley had no money, which was why he had been put in this position in the first damn place. Silver, whose labs generated the purest strains of the city's supply, had dangled Psycho, and Shelley killed three men for him. The job had gone down to the north, in Ocala, where there remained some semblance of law. The three men had been Ocala's biggest pushers, but they were still three men. Shelley had been an easy arrest. Electronic eyes watched him commit, electronic eyes watched him go into a tube, human hands apprehended. Officer Ian, as the man introduced himself, had not been soft. He had manhandled Shelley, inserting a device into his neck below the base of his cranium. The device was activated by Ian's voice; when he spoke in anything other than an even tone, pain tore through Shelley's nervous system. It had been easy to give in to the officer's demands.

But the device had not been the reason Shelley had acquiesced. Coercion was as worthless on him as self analysis. And no matter how much of the latter he did, he kept returning to the single most disturbing of possibilities—that he was simply amusing himself. PSYCHO WILL FUCK UP YOUR MIND.

They arrived at the Lakeland-Orlando Tubeway. Its name was somewhat misleading, as it had actually been diverted outside of Lakeland, same as the tube in Ocala, and Daytona, and wherever the hell else they wanted to cut themselves off from Chaos. Such measures amounted to temporary fixes of course, for nothing could prevent the seeping. As Shelley and his captor stood in the press of bodies, a digit above the portal registered the minutes to window, when a maximum of ten could step aboard. The Orlando-Lakeland, which ran above the Lakeland-Orlando, was accessed via an elevator, which also accepted ten. Odd, Shelley thought as he compared the queues, that as many people seemed to be traveling *to* Chaos.

Four minutes they waited. Before the zero had appeared, Shelley was begging of his captor a drop, the merest drop. The bathroom was right there if the officer was concerned about it being a spectacle. Ian shook his head and Shelley was beginning to lose patience.

As they stepped from the auxiliary into the main tube, he recalled the last time he had lost his patience: a month ago, after an overdose. The doctor had told him that even if he quit now, the damage would go on. "What damage?" Shelley had wanted to know.

"The damage to your body."

"What damage to my body?"

The doctor's spiel had been an impressive one, a smattering of three-dollar words alongside the latest platitudes and mannerisms, but Shelley had seen the truth—perhaps the Psycho within him had seen the truth—which was that they didn't fucking know. He told the doctor just how transparent he found him, but the fact was, the doctor was just doing what he thought best. Shelley was left wondering if this Self-replicating Psychedelic Chemical Organism and its effect on the human body mightn't prove to be a microcosm of full automation on Orlando. They called the result Chaos, yet what was chaos?

The craving was chaotic, no doubt there. He envisioned sinking his teeth into Ian's jugular, his own body twisting in agony as Ian's choked scream flung to the end of every nerve in him. He'd have his hands on the dropper then, or be broken or dead, the same result that would come of delivering Ian to the Prince of Psycho. What would Ian do anyway? Put up your hands, Silver! Give it all up, Silver! Your labs, your warehouses, your army!

Yeah, same result either way.

Another thought occurred to him. Get out of the range of Ian's voice, where the device, unless the officer had other means, could not be activated. But where would he go? To fucked-up Psycho clown boys with triple homicide notches, that was the mother of existential questions. Not the profound *Where did I come from?* but the abyssal *Where do I go?*

The dropper was in his face suddenly, the officer's frowning countenance behind it.

Shelley seized the dropper, pulled back his eyelid and let two, four, five, six—was the jerk going to stop him?—seven teardrops of salvation into his eye. The blood vessels were right there, the nerve trailed the retina like a tentacle, then the brain itself, poised and hungry. Seven drops of sweet agony like homage to the psyche.

"Do you really enjoy it?" said Ian in a mercifully even tone.

Shelley considered. "I have a better understanding of what is going on around me when I'm Psycho."

"Do you know what is so abhorrent about your Silver?"

"Not *my* Silver," Shelley said.

"That he exploits chaos—the condition of chaos—itself."

"Maybe chaos exploits him."

Ian smirked. "Sure. And he systematically sends out his slaves to eliminate the inconveniences in his world."

"Who said there's no system to the circus?" As he spoke Shelley scanned his surroundings with some intensity.

47

"What are you looking for?" said Ian, put off.

"A terminal."

A woman standing nearby turned to Shelley. "You are seeking a terminal?"

She was svelte and beautiful; flawless, he observed, recognizing at once the significance of that fact. As she turned her back to him, raising her blouse to reveal the perfect contour of her back, he remembered her model's name: *Ethereal*.

"If you wish you may use mine," she said, indicating a standard outlet in her flesh, "but be conscious of time."

"I didn't mean...that is, I wasn't looking for..."

"Ah," she said, dropping her blouse. "It's the other you want."

"No...No." He looked back at Ian, embarrassed.

He had meant a wall terminal, thinking he might persuade Ian to let him borrow the unit the officer wore on his belt. Already scintillating, Shelley wanted that feeling, that *knowledge* of being hooked up to the whole crazy circus. A robot was too much though...at least at this early, extremely self-conscious stage...there were people...

As he scanned for others inspired by his recently attained lack of anonymity, the female hominoid remained tuned to him.

"Look at this," she invited. "Behind each of my eyes are two electrodes and a capsule of sodium vapor. Watch."

Shelley watched as her eyes began to glow, one yellow, one green.

"Ian—" he said, confused.

"I don't know what you want," Ian said. "Shall I be Joseph in his Technicolor Dreamcoat?" His tone veered slightly off the even and the sudden riot in Shelley's nervous system was almost an oasis from the external.

"I don't want anything," Shelley said. "I'll cool it."

He thought he saw, but couldn't be certain, a look pass between the hominoid and Ian.

Seven were too many drops. Heightened awareness and hallucination were intermingling. Twenty-seven individuals occupied the section of tube, seventeen men, three women, three certain androids (including the Ethereal model) and four possibles. He hadn't counted; he simply knew. Psycho was like that. On a really acute trip, you might be able to say

Darren Speegle

which of the lot were married, who had children, who would die first. This was becoming one of those trips and more. That he had confidently picked out three hominoid robots in a field of twenty-seven individuals was testament to the fact. As to the possibles…that's where the hallucinations came into play. He was seeing beneath the skin of these four bodies to blood vessels, wires, tubes…

He caught one of them looking back at him. The body of the male had over-developed musculature, which was unusual in androids—or anyone else, when those muscles were visible beneath the skin, shimmering along their contours. The male, blinking three distinct times, increased the width of his stance, then stretched out his arms perpendicular to his frame, becoming da Vinci's Vitruvian Man. Shelley clearly perceived the circle formed of his perfect proportions, and imagined it wheeling down the tubeway, the figure within it a spoke conceived by a cartoonist.

The other three of these possibles had become no less fantastic—a life-sized doll, a science prop, a superhero—and every eye among them looking Shelley down. He wondered if perhaps that's what made them possibles, that they probed him in return. Maybe they too were under the influence of seven drops of Psycho. Maybe he had skin the color of water and was exposed to them. He looked down at his arms, his legs, becoming immediately fascinated by the concept that he *was* covered.

"Hey!"

His flesh caught fire at this liberal exclamation from his captor's mouth.

"Hey, we're almost there, Shelley. You need to hold it together." The words evened out as they came, and the fire subsided.

"Don't worry," Shelley said. "I know precisely where he is, and that's where I will take you."

"Keep focused. I will not be pleased if you fail us."

Us? Shelley saw it again. That look passing between sets of eyes.

Even as he narrowed in on that word, the doors of his senses were swinging wider, the self-consciousness fading into the howling song-noise of limited particularity. Pleasure, meanwhile, Shelley did not relinquish. Pleasure was in the participating, in being consumed by the whole beautiful circus. He was transported momentarily to an Orlando of a dozen years ago, a city of sprawling lights and action, dinner shows, night clubs, roller coasters, machines of all sorts at your whim and desire. *Ah youth*, he thought as he echoed back to the present.

But on his tongue was the word and question: *"Us?"*

Ian said, "We have been unsuccessful at breaking down Silver's superior strains of the drug. He uses some sort of code that we cannot decipher."

"When you say *we...?*"

Ian's voice was smooth as the surface beneath their feet. "There was a maxim among the fully automated law enforcement, tourism, and other services of former Orlando."

The ever present Ethereal spoke it:

"Entertainment is primary."

Shelley peered, trying to make sense of it.

"The maxim of course was installed," Ian said.

"So?"

"So...this naturally conflicted with the taboos imposed upon artificial intelligence."

Shelley let his eyes drift around the compartment. How strangely attentive was this random car on the Lakeland-Orlando Tubeway.

Ian went on, "The Matrix was approached by a union of independent intelligences—by 'independent' I refer to those intelligences which are well armed with human brain cells and do not have to rely on programs. These intelligences extolled the virtues of experimentation. Little did we know where those experiments would lead..."

He produced the dropper that Shelley had taken a shower beneath. As he held it over his eye, everyone else within the car followed suit.

"Little did we know," Ian repeated, blinking.

Shelley looked from face to face, eye to eye, realizing that the ratio was far more fantastic than he had figured. Psycho, it seemed, would fuck up more than human minds.

It was beginning to look like those labs and warehouses were obtainable after all.

Turning to the Ethereal model, all the more beautiful for her glistening, Psycho-awakened eye, Shelley asked her if that terminal was still available.

Illusions of Amber

My first thought, as I opened the motel room door to find the stranger standing there, was that Death had wandered into the rural, nickel-sized town of Amber, Indiana, seeking to fill his quota. Why he found it necessary to look farther than the gangsters and drug pushers in the big city was a question which hadn't time to formulate before he was extending a well-manicured hand and introducing himself to me.

"I apologize for the intrusion, sir. My name is Pike. Doctor Edward Pike."

I looked from his sober bearded countenance to his dark, official-looking suit, simply adorned at the cuffs and absent of the merest wrinkle, and I had to wonder when they started bestowing the prestigious title of "Doctor" on morticians. He certainly wasn't a medical doctor. Not from this county. He wore no bow tie.

"What kind of doctor?" I asked, purposely withholding my name. I sounded to my own ears as stiff as he looked.

"A surgeon, sir. But that is neither here nor there. I call on you not in a professional capacity but as an agent of the townspeople of Amber, who wish you to participate in an affair this evening."

"You do not know me, Doctor—Pike, is it? You do not know me, and the townspeople of Amber do not know me. I am passing through."

"I know that you occupy Room One at this motel, as almost all who stay here do. I know that you are from elsewhere. I need to know no more."

I let my opinion of this insufficient explanation wear nakedly across my face (as if I actually needed to demonstrate to him just how strange I thought the whole situation). My interest, however, was piqued.

"What sort of affair?"

"You know, sort of a country affair."

"No sir, I do not know."

"A little thing in town with balloons and children and games."

Of course. Children, balloons, games and *me*. I shifted back into first gear. "Let me ask you something, Doc. What is a surgeon doing in humble Amber, Indiana?"

"Amber is my summer home. I am a prominent and, if it pleases you, well-to-do member of the medical community, and find myself with the luxury of being able to spend the warm months in this little town where I was born. But again, my capacity today—"

"What happens to the show?" I interrupted.

"The show?"

"Surgery. You just up and leave it. What happens to it?"

"I should hardly think that is any of your concern, sir."

"It wasn't I who came calling on you."

He ignored this with an unapologetic deftness which I found easy to admire. "As I was saying, my capacity today is that of town spokesman. The festivities begin in less than an hour and we would dearly like to have you as a participant."

I gave him a long once-over then. But I already knew my answer. I had been wondering how I would spend my evening in this microscopic dot on the map.

"Would you be escorting me to this...*affair*, or would I be allowed simply to show up?"

The grave doctor actually smiled as he said, "Why, the latter of course. There are too many frightening characters in today's world to entrust oneself to strangers."

Impulsively I glanced down at my left tennis shoe, where the latest stain still lingered. When I looked back up, I found him staring fixedly into my eyes. As though he would not deign to cast a downward glance.

"And when and where will this affair be taking place?"

"Seven o'clock, center of town."

"I'll think it over."

"Very good. But do not think too long, sir. We would hate for you to miss any of the fun."

"Goodbye, Doctor Pike."

"Goodbye, Mr....?"

"You mean you haven't already looked at the guest register?"

"That would seem pointless, don't you think? So often false names are given to motor inn clerks."

"Burke," I said, smiling, and closed the door.

I took a brief shower, threw on a pair of cargo pants and a cutoff tee shirt. Somewhere along the way I had lost the inclination to blow dry my hair before going out, leaving it to the whim of the wind through the car's open window. But when I ventured out into the summer air of Amber, Indiana that evening, I saw I wouldn't be driving.

I hadn't realized when I pulled into the motel that the main of town was less than a quarter mile down the road which intersected the highway. Stepping around the corner to the parking area in back of the building, I was facing downtown Amber. Colorful carnival lights were blinking to life even as my eyes fell upon my destination, and somehow a great part of the mystery, in that moment of time, was lost. The deluge of childhood memories did not prevent the tickle that spread through my body like the cold tentacles of fear. It could not. Just like that, I was bound to my own mystery now, damn them for ever knocking on Room One's door. Whatever their game, mine was the more shocking. Whatever they'd in store for me, I'd far worse in store for them.

I checked a pocket, wondered why I had brought it along when all I'd meant to do was humor them.

The summer air felt good. Hot, dry and still. Moth wings whapped beneath streetlights, generating the only breezes that blew. Houses were black, as if there were no medium: you were either at the affair or you were buried away in your sanctum hidden from its terrors. I passed a balding, withering woman.

Are you Mr. Burke? she did not say.

Who is Mr. Burke?

Along behind her, a boy, eleven or twelve, squeeching rubber shoes.

Are you from Room One? said he not.

I am here. Isn't that enough? Must we ask questions with our eyes, tell our souls with our shoes? Mine is the mystery and yours is the show.

And here it was at last, the laughter and the lights, the banners and

53

the barking, the wheels and the witless, and the costumes wear us all. Blossom and splendor and a great hole in Amber, Indiana, because the carnival was not trucked in but homemade—its secret corridors ambling through tents and the town's buildings themselves—which made not for a carnival but an exposé of the hollowness of the soul.

Out of this blossom and splendor appeared Doctor Pike, descending upon me as if we were brethren in arms. "Welcome, Mr. Burke! Welcome to the affair!"

"Wouldn't have missed it, Doc. Did you do the costumes? I mean, when you weren't performing surgery?"

Laughing: "Mr. Burke, I am always performing surgery."

"I've no doubt." And imagined how he was going to be as a patient.

He showed me first the House of Mirrors, guiding me by his own hand, forgetting suddenly his luxury and his summer cool. I thought to express my true feelings to him then and there, shards of reflective glass and the illusions of existence, but decided I might be intruding upon *his* game.

He showed me next the House of Freaks, notice the mutations and the distortions and the deformities as you drift among them. Notice the pig-man with his absurd features, the caves of his nostrils. Notice the crisscross man with his wondrously strange dermis. See the African serpentess with her scales and her black forked tongue—

"You," I said to her. "Where did you come from?"

The doctor seemed both displeased and pleased that I was engaging her in speech, ssss.

Her beady eyes, her tongue darting in and out, an apology somewhere amidst it all. "Room One at the Travelers Lodge."

I stood there some seconds in my amazement, fetched it out with the practiced simplicity of a pro, tucking it up behind the wrist, turning to him slowly.

"What does she mean, Doc?"

"A fantasy of hers. She is a deceiver and a liar, beware."

"What are you, then?"

He regarded me as if through a fragment of stained glass. "I have not stayed in Room One."

The bellow of the bull-man one cage over. The screech of the mermaid one tank back. The howl of the wolf-man...

54

"All of them?"

He slipped away through folds of canvas. The freaks ingested and digested and spat him out again before I emerged. What is that in your hand?

I *am* the House of Horrors. Between the courthouse and the library, the House of Fun and the House of Imagination, beneath the banner whose message is scrawled in crimson, beyond the stairs slippery with blood, there will you find me. I am the House of Horrors. Come unto me, Doctor.

Yet as I slipped past the doorman who asked for no ticket, into shadows requiring only that I be checked in at Room One of the Travelers Lodge, I could not separate myself of the feeling that I was coming unto him.

Around every corner, through every door, upon every stair, shadows protracted as if beneath unfolding wings, reaching out to rake me in. You know where you are going, Mr. Burke, you are going where the screams originate. Their muffled agonies seemed to come from deep within the place, the cries of the unborn in the womb, out of the womb, on the slab that is earthly existence. These eloquent sounds fell on my thirsty ears, and I knew I would have been drawn to this jubilee even if Dr. Pike had never bothered to fetch me out of the motel. I looked at the thing in my hand. It suddenly seemed such an insignificant instrument...after all the service it had given me.

Double doors admitted me, and there, over the table, was the surgeon. His patient's arms and legs were stretched out infinitely, and the lolling, wailing thing at the end of the trunk was more a distension than a head, presumably from all the fluids fed through tubes into its facial tissue. In the doctor's hand was a scalpel very much like my own, on his face an unsoiled surgical mask. The blade of the scalpel, like my own, shined pristinely.

"I try to determine," he said, waving the tool, "where to insert, where to cut, but I'm tempted to start slicing senselessly. As you see, I have been unable to come up with a theme for him. Unlike the others in our menagerie, where the finished product reflects either the nature of the subject or the nature of the subject's transgressions, this creature has left me at loss. His actions were so utterly random, his mind so chaotic in its workings, I've no motif with which to work. He wasn't even fleeing when he landed at the Travelers Lodge. All of you flee something—persons, deeds, memories. He fled nothing."

"What do I flee, Doc?" I asked as I stepped deeper into the room.

"Ah," he said, gliding in his long white coat around the table to meet me. "The illusion, I think, is what you flee."

"What illusion?"

We came to a halt simultaneously, one slashing stride between us. The agony of the monstrosity on the table wrecked every potential for scholarly debate.

"The illusion that surrounds the instrument in your hand, the blood stain on your shoe."

I would not deign to cast a downward glance. "Yeah…"

"The illusion that killing does not exalt you, that blood does not darken the mystery of you."

"But blood always darkens the mys—"

I felt the pain in a long swift angle, the warm fluid swell beneath my tee shirt, the foulness of the air as I sought to have more of it in my lungs suddenly.

"It will require some nipping and tucking," said the surgeon, "but I think you will be our magician. For here in Amber you cannot escape your illusions."

Merging Tableaux

Everyone has at least one scene that they cannot erase from memory, a fragment of the past that affected them so profoundly it now occupies a permanent place in their consciousness. I have two such scenes, one overlapping the other, textures blending without diminishing the shocking vibrancy of the details. The motion of surplus body fat, the smells of carnal appetite gathering in the air, the duet of bestial fulfillment and malignant laughter, the splatter of poppies.

If I had let the past remain where it belonged, I never would have known the second tableau. No matter the catalyst, returning after nearly two decades had the flavor of psychosis. The demons had been at rest for a considerable while when unexpected contact from across space and time reawakened them. I've no doubt that had I but ignored the call, they would have lain still again, grotesque but inanimate, like poor Dirk. Alas, I boarded a plane within the week, shying away from the stewardess during the twelve-hour flight because of her dark, reminiscent eyes.

Visually, nothing had changed, as nothing ever does over there. As I turned onto *Salmstrasse*, driving slowly in order to fully savor the impressions, I could see the *Rothaus* was still intact, though its paint had faded to a brownish red. In the fields behind the durable three-story structure poppies appeared, wild red-orange blooms peeping out of high grass, just as they had that spring of eighteen years before. The barn emerged from its hiding place, the surrounding weeds touched by a breeze, breaths and moans, the restless limbs of the chestnut tree.

The yard was in a state of low maintenance, a tractor perhaps having swept through once or twice since winter. I pulled into the drive, its ruptured paving stones flanked by *Brennessel*—burn nettles—already abuzz with insects, and this only the first week of June. I'd come straight from the airport in the rental, and had to grope around for the right controls before separating myself from the compact. The house looked vacant except for the curtains in the second-floor windows. But they might have been relics, their patterns formed by cobwebs behind the grimy glass. Outside the tableau itself, I couldn't remember such particulars.

Poppies bright as blood, foliage sharp as jagged glass recalled an artist's sudden, revelatory strokes, while the odors were no less direct in their assault upon my senses. Resin, earth, grass, rotting boards. Sweat. Metal. The ting of copper in the ears, on the tongue. I reached out and touched the side of the barn. Moist, always moist, as if it retained every sin ever committed. I heard, felt activity around my shoe, looked down to freeze the image—not of the snake wriggling out from under the weeds, but rather the bizarre American icon that was my tennis shoe, its bright white laces interweaving with the blades of vegetation. I held that frame for long seconds.

Yes, here I was, back on foreign soil, which I had so longed to leave as a teenager. And approaching the exact spot which had changed my every perception of who and what I was, and where I fit in the global career path my parents had chosen. As I stepped around the side of the barn, I suddenly didn't want to see the spot again, though I knew that in the immediate sense I would simply be looking at more of the jungle surrounding me. I cursed myself, my demons.

Somehow there was no moment of discovery, no emergency of the heart, and yet neither was it just another patch of jungle. Very little grew in the spot, perhaps because of the shade created by the chestnut and the barn, perhaps because it was otherwise tattooed. The tableau didn't rematerialize instantly, but waited for nourishment. I wanted to give it that. I had come a long way to give it that. Inexplicably, a discomfort expanded in my groin. When I reached down I realized I was erect. That was certainly *not* how I wanted to remember. But what had I expected?

A movement caused me to jerk my hand away from myself. I looked behind me, nothing. It was another occurrence of wind, necromancy, legerdemain. My errant hand wandered again, only this time it found its way to my pocket. I pulled out the letter, at once a confession, a rite, a statement of charges against me.

It was the fiftieth time I had read it, and as with the other forty-nine times, I was alarmed by its command of English and, more so, by its poetic nature. She had been a poet, reading to the class as if we were manipulable characters in her dream. It was what had first caused me to take notice of her, just preceding her eyes, her aura, all the rest of her.

That noise again, like an imp about no good. I sat against the barn and read aloud, in the quietest voice lest I wake the dead.

"What she does to me just looking at her. Such eyes, such grace, such everything. My father would laugh to see how his experiment has fared thus far. Six weeks at a German school and I'm not only chasing the language, I'm also chasing one of the girls. She has read a poem in class recently, has looked at me with those onyx eyes of hers, and now I find myself following her like an animal."

The entire letter was written that way, recounting events from my point of view, and in an unsettlingly accurate way. She must have researched everything about me and my family, strangers in her village, toys.

"The Rothaus is no destination for a girl. The villagers gossip that it is a home of half-wits and monsters. What business can you have there, Svenja? If only I could persuade you to notice me. Was that the briefest look? Should I hide?"

It was. God knows, I did.

"Whose voice is that from behind the barn? 'Svenja!' it calls. Can it be the boy named Dirk? Would she spare him a pot to piss in? But then, I'm a stranger and it's all a mystery to me. For all I know they are lovers and I am wasting my life away with the perceptions that have been imposed upon me by my world."

How could a creature like her philosophize? Philosophy from her was like excess venom dripping onto the letter, smearing the ink.

"My mother loves this field, flowers like flames she says, and here I am walking through it. How would I explain my being here to her? I pass through your vision, Mother, to validate my own. But I know it is baser than that. Even now the sounds I'm hearing give me a raw feeling. Grunts of servility, hints of subtle laughter. I know you, Svenja, I have seen you looking at me over literature and gods. I know you and I don't know you and I hate you if it is as I suspect it is."

Which was where the letter's author began to lose me, I began to lose myself, pure verse took over.

"It *is* as I suspect. There they are, behind the barn, Svenja on the whale-like massiveness of Dirk, forcing out the expulsions as she strokes his swollen penis, taking her own fashion of glee from the enterprise. I will discover the secrets of this, I will blackmail her a thousand times for a taste of what she is doing to him. But I can see there are stranger forces at work. Why would the half-wit want the wine that she pours over him, licking it off his face as she laughs like the first dawn? Why, in the midst of his awful ascent towards climax, would he laugh with her as she swings the bottle in the air, bringing it down smashing against his forehead, spilling its poppies over his face?

"And why, for the love of Christ, would he continue to moan in pleasure as the petals tear open his face, his neck, my own eyes as I witness this monstrosity?"

From this point on I could not share her vision, for the pleasure had been Svenja's and Svenja's alone as she devoured those moans, the sacrifice of him to her. At the last she must have released that part of him she clutched in her fist's bitter vise, for a bellow of agonized liberation pierced the deafness that had befallen my ears, the blindness that had overcome my eyes. I found her looking straight at me, through the splash of poppies behind which I crouched.

Those spots appeared on my retinae now, making the words impossible to read for a moment. I shifted to the last line, but as it came into focus, I could not read it aloud. No matter, for the author herself intervened.

"'And I wonder, has she lured me here?'"

Heart thundering, I turned my head slowly to the left, where she had emerged from the corner of the barn. Like her voice, her appearance had scarcely changed. And her eyes possessed the permanence of onyx as well as its polish and opaqueness. Poets speak of the pools of a lover's eyes. Hers threw you back like gates, even as they forbade you from retreating.

"Did you?" I said, hearing the feebleness of my words in my ears.

"Lure you here?" she said. "Which time?"

It mocked. Which was her language.

"You let them put Dirk's father away for what you did."

"*I?*"

That word, that single syllable contained force untold. I found it difficult to construct a sentence. "You...you threatened to make it my crime if I spoke the truth. You—"

"Shhh," she said. "It doesn't matter now, does it, David?"

David. She had spoken my name to me only once before, as she knelt before me among the poppies. The stark, fiery flowers had become a cage around me after what I had witnessed. *David, what have you done here?* she'd said in some Deutsch/English blend that had emphasized as much as conveyed her point. *As the daughter of the Burgermeister, can I let myself look the other way?*

She approached me, but now there was no cage and I rose quickly to my feet. The hand I used to keep her at a distance was also the hand that held the letter.

"Okay, David," she said. "But you might admit to yourself that if you had wanted anything other than to see me, to kiss me as we did then, in the field out there, you would have taken the letter to the authorities."

"I'm going to take it to your father," I said stupidly.

She plucked the paper from my hand, let the breeze lift it in a lazy spiral towards that first dawn of which her verse spoke. She smiled as she offered her lips to me. I closed my mouth tightly against the softness of her kisses, the warmth of her breath on my face. I had reacted the same way then and met with failure, succumbing to her beautiful, delicious mouth in spite of all. I used the past as a distraction, focusing on what might have happened on that occasion if Dirk's equally half-witted father hadn't emerged from the Rothaus, slamming the door in his wake.

"You needn't feel such guilt," she breathed as she tried to tease my mouth open with her tongue. "They sent him to a mental hospital. He was out again in eight years."

It wouldn't have shocked me to learn they had decided never to let him out, considering Svenja's performance that day. She would have been convincing no matter who she made her scapegoat, breaking our kiss to run out of the field screaming about the horror she had witnessed. By the time people had arrived on the scene, Dirk's father stood crying over Dirk's dead bulk, touching his tattered face, confessing that the boy was in a better house now—which quote had become the focal point of the trial.

"How long would they have kept *you* locked away?" I wondered to her. But the question allowed the sought opening, and her tongue was in my mouth.

Svenja's hunger met my own despised lusts in a marriage as Godforsaken as the site of murder and madness where it occurred. I tried to push her away, but my hands found her body and its exquisiteness, and oblivion threatened to set in. Through the caresses and the sighs and all the dark magic at work came remembered sounds, sounds that had interrupted us the one other time we had made physical contact. Like everything I had ever known since encountering her, it made no relative sense.

She pressed me against the side of the barn, hands finding the fastenings that held me together. When she loosed my grotesquely engorged shame, I wanted to die there, upon the ground of murder and madness, but more than dying I wanted to live, inside her, one with her, my Svenja, why had she waited so long to call?

I clutched her buttocks, pulling her against me, but her hands were in the way, one of them gripping me so tightly the scream itself choked, the other lifting a familiar something, accessory, device. Where had it come from, the mouth of jagged teeth? Would it bring me exaltation? Her onyx eyes asked me if I wanted it, and somehow, in every way, I did. But as she drew her hand back, to share the whole of herself, every petal and shard with me, a shape loomed behind her. I recognized the man's hulking clumsiness as his shadow became the backdrop, his facial contortions the accents of my new tableau.

The foreground filled my vision, her expression widening in an ecstasy my eyes had rejected eighteen years ago, but which now seemed a thing stolen from me. Poppies spilled out of her mouth as Dirk's father stepped back, carrying her body with him, the tool's handle still in his grip. I could not bear to witness it and turned my face to the barn, to the comfort of boards pungent with the retention of every sin ever committed.

The Crookedness of Being

My piss fled back into my organ. At the foot of the wall opposite, on the ground, was a body—a woman. I stepped over, knowing she was dead, turned away at the sight of the dark fluid that surrounded her. She'd been shot.

Sometimes the strangest part about being there is being there. That was damn well the case that night in *The Whaler* as I sipped my hard Scotch and wondered how many years it had been since I'd had genuine *déjà vu*. The feeling had hit me the moment I walked in from the December night, and hung with me well after I was obliged to answer the *Whuddya have?* of the embittered bartender. He obviously wanted nothing better than to have a greasy glass in front of me so he wouldn't have to think about my patch of counter again for awhile. Not that he had a booming business tonight. It was Christmas Eve, and only the most pathetic of us were out.

Christmas Eve. It was why I was here, actually. My regular haunts were closed—as any self-respecting dive should have been—so I'd come down Waterfront to see what was about. Now common sense says that a man who enjoys his meager existence does his best to stay away from the Waterfront. I wish I'd had some of that, instead of the blues, that Friday night couple years back. Wish I'd had even a snifter of that. 'Cause I was ripe for the undoing the moment I first stepped foot in that Godforsaken hole. Goddamn all of us, I say, but bring us home again when you're finished, old man.

Déjà—everloving—*vu*. Can you believe that? I think drink or age or both takes away our ability to tap into the recesses, you know, into the

63

deeper psyche...oh hell, I was never much for philosophy. Fact was, if I hadn't been here before, I'd damn sure as hell dreamed I had, and the whiskey glass and the tinkle of ice and the lazy drone of Bing Crosby through the cheap speaker boxes, dreaming his own dreams, White Christmases my ass. When you're married to your misery, and Scotch on ice, all the Christmases are the same dull shade of bleak. Take it from me, folks.

Six customers besides myself, three at the bar, three at tables, all isolated, each cupping his or her drink as if it were the last, or better yet, some mind-opening eggnog surprise, with the secrets of the cosmos spinning in its milky depths. Occasionally we looked at each other wondering what the other was thinking, what the other was doing here, if the other were drifting on that same wave of *déjà vu*. I remembered clearly remembering that before. You'd think I would have known better than to get up and saunter over to the nearest of my lonely cousins at the bar.

"May I sit?" I said, and hoped my expression elaborated, *Is it really an intrusion when it has already happened?*

"Not at all." Coldly.

I offered her a drink, which she accepted, the bartender refreshed her glass, frowning, and we were old friends now, chestnuts and snuggly blankets.

"They call me Jock," I said apologetically.

"Miriam."

"Miriam is really nice."

I would have sworn I'd said it before.

"I'm not Miriam," she said.

"What?"

"Oh, never mind. Never mind, Jock."

What was I supposed to say now? I'm not Jock? This isn't *The Whaler*? We are not on the Waterfront?

She pointed at the wall, a fishnet, wheel and anchor adorning the aged wood. "My father was a fisherman. But you know that, I guess."

I remember your telling me...

Perhaps I had been drunk at the time. "Yes, of course, Miriam...I mean..."

She smiled sort of a crooked smile, a humorless smile.

The bartender was passing. "The bathroom?" I requested.

"Out of order."

"Out of order? But this is a bar."

"Go out back." And moved on. To nowhere.

I glanced over my shoulder at a door in the back of the place, metal affair, emergency bar. It appeared to be ajar. No bells, no alarms, good.

I told the lady I'd be back and fired up a cigarette as I parted with the stool, dragging deeply as you might, worrying a lot, wishing it weren't Christmas. Wishing the feeling would go.

The door was waiting for me, heavy, plodding on its works. A wall came into view, other side, other side of what proved to be an alley, might have guessed. The seedy side of the city and its alleyways.

I stepped over by a big dumpster, unzipped, freed the thing, and as men are prone to do, looked around whistling. My piss fled back into my organ. At the foot of the wall opposite, on the ground, was a body—a woman. I stepped over, knowing she was dead, turned away at the sight of the dark fluid that surrounded her. She'd been shot. In the head, in the face, the rest was hidden to me. She lay belly-down in the alley, long fox coat spread about her like a blanket, its fur saturated.

I backed all the way to the door, which I had left ajar, slipped inside, that feeling of *déjà vu* so strong now I might have myself scripted the events of the night.

I didn't wait till I was seated. "John—Whiskey John!"

The bartender was not pleased. He'd offered his handle as a matter of routine only.

"But she's dead," I said, gesturing backwards with my thumb.

"Someone you know?"

What?

"Miriam," said the lady.

I turned towards the lady. She was so very familiar, I felt as if we were both from another planet, and everyone else, the vignette of a Christmas Eve on the Waterfront. Funny, none of them were in the least bit concerned about my proclamation of death. Perhaps they hadn't heard.

"There is a woman lying back there in the alley with her brains blown out. Does that concern any of you?"

If it did, they weren't saying.

The bartender pointed at me hard. "You are really beginning to fuck up the peace."

I was nearly dumbstruck. "Fuck...fuck up the peace?!"

"Fuck up the fucking peace, yes. Peace on Earth, man. It's Christmas, for Christsake."

"There is—"

"Yeah, yeah, a woman with her brains blown out. I'm sure we've never seen *that* before. Look, if it's what you're worrying about, I can get you another fur." He turned to the lady. "How'd you like that, Wanda?"

She looked straight at me. "I think that's up to Jock." As she twirled the hem of her synthetic with the nose of her revolver.

Rupture Zone

As I pulled up in a snarl of dust at the barrier, the idiot wandering around in the cacti yelled at me. I'd seen him as I approached, but I was coming fast and didn't have time to ponder the notion of some fool hoofin' it out in the middle of nowhere under the murderously scorching sun. I leaned out of my open jeep wanting to know what the fuck was going on. I had someplace to go, and now I had a barrier and this character all in the same stroke of karma.

I'd no idea where I was anymore—New Mexico? Arizona? All I knew was Jagged was coming hard—a goddamn right metaphor for her—armed to the brim, and salivating for my blood. What's worse, her gas tank was nearly twice the size of mine. I had two full metal cans bouncing like jugs of nitro in back, but she had *four* if I remembered right. Bitch. Always on top of it. Another right-on metaphor.

"What the hell do you want?" I said to the man as he trotted up gasping for air, bent over himself, long streaked hair hanging almost to the ground. I swear I could practically see the vapor rising out of his head. My right hand stroked the handle of the expensive Israeli handgun I had stolen from Jagged, favorite hobby of hers. Clock on the dash said ten past, and that was fucking high noon.

"Can't," he heaved. "Can't...go in there...past the barricade."

"Why?"

"It's the rupture zone," he managed to get out all in one stream.

"What the fuck is that?" My hand on the steel relaxed. He seemed a harmless customer.

He looked at me through curtains of hair so that I couldn't get a fix

67

on his expression. "You ain't from around?"

I chuckled. "Yeah. Lately, around in circles."

"You ain't got no radio?"

The fuck was bothering me with his suspense routine, though I didn't think it was intentional. I got the impression he'd lost a few cells along the way. I knew a little bit about what that lifestyle did to you. I had a mirror. Hadn't bathed or moteled maybe in a week, but I had the rearview, at least half of which was still usable after the bullet she'd put in it.

I turned on the radio, stock job out of some other fifteen-year-old car. Crackle, sssss, crackle, crackle...Lack of an antenna and an abundance of oblivion will do you a lot of hiss. "Just spill it, man," I growled at him.

"I—they're—it's a war zone now." He gestured. "Hey, if you stand up in there, you might be able to see this end of the thing."

I gazed out beyond the barrier and saw nothing but dust and scrub and cactus. Nonetheless, I stood up in the jeep and, under the visor of my hand, surveyed the flat landscape.

"Follow the road with your eye," he said, pointing. "See the crack in the earth, runs right across it?"

I did now. It looked like a mutant version of the fractures that covered the whole slab of desert.

"Earthquake?" I asked him.

He shook his head, very slowly, very deliberately, as though it were nothing so pansy as a something-point-something.

I fell into my seat, shifted into gear and rode the accelerator against the brake, signaling to the dude you comin'?

He shook his head, hair all in his face, eyes wide like I was the freak. Maybe I was.

Spinning desert all over the guy's peyote-stained clothes, I went round the barrier and off in search of hope in the fangs of the spider. War zone? Didn't know what the fuck it meant, but it sounded like a good place to lead Jagged. There hadn't been another road for more than fifty miles, and that last junction no doubt had my tracks all over it. I'd seen her once yesterday—her truck, that is—cresting a vapor-warped hill in the bullet-blasted rearview. She'd be along shortly, and Mescal back there would tell her all about it.

"Come on, Jag, come on, Jag," I sang as I sped across the flat. I'd no idea the hell I was committing myself to. But I knew hell. Jagged was fucking hell incarnate.

The crack became a black grin in the earth, growing meaner and meaner as I drew closer. The ragged, heat-soaked blur of its lip became an undulating flutter of motion. I soon saw that the culprits were vultures teemed along the rupture's rim, jabbing at the ground, like getting their grit for digestive purposes.

I braked late in the approach, scattering the bastards from my side of the ravine over to the other. Jesus, it was wide, at least thirty feet across. To my left, maybe a hundred feet from the road, the end of it could be seen, dry wrinkled corner of the mouth it was. To the right, it stretched on and on, widening to at least twice the gap in the road.

Stepping to the brink, I saw what the scavengers had been tearing at. Pieces of dried, collapsed matter that might once have been tubular and bright like the coils of intestines lay draped around and over the brink of the ravine. Whatever moisture the stuff had contained was all but gone, leaving what resembled snakeskins without scales. I reached down and picked one up, losing my equilibrium for a second as my eyes slipped past the husk into the black bottomlessness of the abyss. It was cool in the heat, yeah both the mouth in the earth and the material I held.

A gunshot ripped across the desert, its source behind me, its echo swallowed by the killing heat. Jagged had arrived, dude with the hair was dead, probably because he reminded her of me. Well, fuck you, Jag.

I jumped back in the jeep, took off in the direction of the near end of the crevice, looking back towards the barrier. The wooden frame was coming asunder as my eyes found the spot, a heat-captured, slow-motion event beneath the front end of her big truck. The fear like heights in the groin and alley darkness in the gut took hold of me. A fear familiar as the image of her face when she got the notion one sex-drenched day, in some bizarre, acid-paranoid moment, that I was banging her recently moved-in sister—like I needed *that* monkey too.

That monkey was dead now. Like at least three others—including Sunshine back there—that I knew about. Love is a many splintered thing.

Sliding around the end of the chasm, I pointed the jeep at an angle for the road again. In the distance, on the knife-edge horizon, the shapes of man-made structures materialized. A glance back showed Jagged coming fast. Maybe she'd be so intent on me spitting my little cloud of dust, that she'd run right into the hole. We can dream, even when we live a nightmare. Ahead, the group of buildings became a shabby town, a few old cars resting between the first of the buildings and my racing jeep. I looked back again before I reached the cars, noted she had made it around the crack, then *thump*, I hit something.

Reflexes slamming on the brakes for me, I clutched the wheel tightly as the jeep went sliding, screech-grazing the side of a station wagon before coming to rest facing back in the direction of the ravine, the barreling truck, and the thing I'd hit. The thing I'd hit writhed on the street. I fussed with the shifter, leg shaking crazily, grinding the gears to bone meal. As I finally got it in first, I spun forward, close enough to look down at the body, my heart hammering a ritual song. I felt the fist that resides inside come plunging up through my throat as I stared at the thing.

Long, gangling, with naked worm-like flesh and a sickly pearlish palor, it managed through all that to somehow possess humanoid characteristics. Its hips suggested it was bipedal, but the limbs were fantastically long, particularly the upper pair. Its features were grotesque to the degree of absurdity, with a flat, sort of winged upper face, while the lower part protruded in a snout large enough to contain the huge, ferocious, demonically keen teeth that gnashed wetly in the creature's jaws. Its eyes, lacking irises, were entirely pearly like its body, bulging from their sockets as they marked me. But maybe strangest of all were the tubes of moist, pulsing tissue that protruded from the top of its head, entering again behind the wings of its flounder face, and the whole bunch of coils twisting in a Gorgonian ecstasy.

Time was wasting. I laid hard on wheel and pedal, jerking her around back on track. Tearing through the center of town, I registered broken windows, debris strewn along the street, the absence of people, then I had to make a quick decision as a fork appeared in front of me. I chose right and was suddenly plummeting across the empty wastes again, reflections of the fucking apocalypse.

The fury of Jagged's pursuit grew in the mirror, and there was nowhere to go. I raised the Israeli handgun the bitch had been so proud of and prepared to go down firing. Two clips fell out of the glove box, one into my shaking hand, the other to the floor. I fished around for it, pushing it almost out of reach, finally managed to curl my fingers around it. When I came up, Jag's truck dominated the rearview and the sound of gunfire and exploding glass filled my ears.

I ducked down again, steering blindly with one hand, firing with the other. The first round glanced off the roll bar, ringing like a missionary at the door. As to the rest of them, sweet Jesus only knew how none of that flying lead, from my gun or hers, pierced the gas cans. Jagged began pounding on her horn, to add to the confusion. I might have been in the path of stampeding elephants, so noisy and imminent was the storm that descended. It all became one big drowning noise, the gunfire, the horn, the engines, my own yelling; I had to come up for air.

Through the dust and the bullet-riddled windshield my eyes fell on the yawning rupture in the ground ahead, that fucking black grin splitting the whole world apart. I swerved left, braking, skirting the awful wound in the desert. The world turned up, the sky sideways, and blackness came up out of the hole and devoured me.

I started from unconsciousness, a wet, spat-out Jonah, but it was my own sweat and blood that covered me. My skin was badly sunburned and the moisture was no comfort. I rose crookedly, but intact. The jeep was on its bars some eighty feet away, in the dust. A look to my left revealed a broken Ford truck wedged in the ground's gaping grin, even blacker now because evening had arrived.

In the twilight the desert was ashen; the stars appeared around a bright half moon. Blood fled down my neck from a wound reopened. Strange cries, wails, sounded in the distance. Vultures laughed off sleep in a rigid circle over the ravine. I began to walk that way. The idea that in another place I might have survived this thing, chase, wreck and all, teased me, amused me. Maybe I was somewhat delirious, but the fear was elsewhere. And the survival instinct seemed foolish.

Jagged hung from the driver's door of the truck, which appeared to have exploded open on impact. She hung in space, legs trapped inside the cab, head and arms reaching towards hell. Even so, an extended moan escaped her. I realized she could not have been hanging there with the blood filling her head all this time. She must have fallen out fairly recently, pulled by gravity, a wrong turn in her fever, a shift of the truck itself precariously spanning the gap.

I surprised myself with the thought of crawling out there for her. I surprised myself by pitying her. The memory of our arriving at this last crossroads in our lives flashed through my head. The horn. Her laying on the horn over and over again, almost as if she had been trying to warn me of the ravine. I halted at the edge of it, watching her body in space, swinging ever so slightly. A spasm passed from her shoulder to her hand, a feeble noise slipped from her mouth. With another look up at the vultures, I decided fuck her. Fuck you, Jagged.

A creaking shift in the hulk startled me. I looked down in time to see a second long-fingered hand reach up out of the blackness to join one that had already grasped part of the truck's frame. The creature's face turned my way as I leapt back, fear returning in one great wave. Its pearly eyes were luminous in the darkness, its teeth reflecting the light of the night sky as they parted in strings of viscous fluid. But it was in the other direction the creature went, causing the truck to tilt and moan as it found holds in the undercarriage, moving hand over hand as if on a rope in an obstacle course.

I moved slowly backwards, but I could not steal my eyes from the sight of it. When the creature reached the door, it swung up into the cab, found purchase with its legs, then dropped upside down so that its face was directly opposite hers. As two of the pulsing tubes separated from the sides of its head and plunged into her ears, its mouth closed over her scream and it began devouring her.

The choke that escaped me caused it to turn for a brief moment, and I saw the rapture written in the shocking orbs of its eyes, the blood and flesh in its teeth, the gaping hole in Jagged's face. Then the demon was on its meal again, head thrashing with the voraciousness and vigor that went into the feed.

As I finally got the right signals to my feet, I caught sight of another one of the creatures appearing over the lip of the chasm. My legs got tangled up, I hit a cactus and fell. My head instantly swiveled to see what plans this new arrival had. Halfway out of the pit, its body abruptly sank and another creature came riding over its back. Following that one came another, then another, and suddenly dozens and dozens of them, clawing and pulling at each other as they all strived to be the first over the brink, hands coming away with the tubes that coiled on the heads of those in the way.

My eyes went up to the still-circling vultures, the memory of the scavengers I had witnessed at work earlier coming back with force. Jesus God, how many of these devils had bled out of this rupture in the earth?

Lights appeared in the distance, out beyond the overturned jeep. Headlights. I leapt to my feet and ran. The creatures' heads lifted to watch the prey a moment before they gave chase, lanky legs producing strange spider-like strides, while their trunks had an ape-like, lumbering movement somewhat contradictory to their gangling frames. In flight my skin was on fire, and my working muscles and bones sore from the bruising and battering my body had taken. But worse by far was the pain in my head. Ripping fucking pain, no doubt from the injury that had left me unconscious for hours.

I shot by the jeep, wishing I had time to unbelt those gas cans, which had survived the crash thanks to the roll bars. An avid smoker of non-tobacco products, I'd a lighter in my pocket and the will to set the fucking universe aflame. The gun would be nice too, but God knew where that had landed.

A metallic noise which I knew in advance belonged to Jag's truck caused me to look back. Covered in the spidery fuckers, the hulk came unwedged at last, plunging into the abyss. But it was what was happening in the foreground that really piqued my interest. Pick your fucking poison. The creatures had multiplied, strike one, and closed way too much ground, strike two, in the seconds that had passed. So much that I could distinguish individual sets of eyes bobbing in the night, teeth snapping in anticipation of the frenzied feast to come.

The report of a rifle preceded the crashing of one of the creatures to the desert floor. Another, opening a gouge in the pulp of the night air. Now a whole torrent as the vehicle that bore the gunmen drew close enough to be recognizable as a pickup. Figures in the back leveled rifles, shouts rose over the riddle of bullets. But it was a brief hope as I felt the first of the long, reaching tendrils of their hands graze my back. Lead whizzed by my head. War zone was right on. Adrenaline pushed with an amphetamine insistence, but it wasn't going to be enough. Goodbye Jagged, goodbye me, please let my circle of hell be far from hers.

The weight behind me—I couldn't tell if it was one of them, two of them, or the whole goddamn army—drove me to the ground, desert searing my face as I slid across it. I turned to meet my death, to be introduced to it proper, to watch its robe swirl in the motionless wind and its sickle catch the light of the moon. Yeah like that, moon running like honey along the blade, falling in a long heavy drop.

The teeth and face before me exploded, bringing me instantly to life again.

"Get in the fucking truck, asshole!"

I turned against guns blasting like cannon fire around me. Arms reached out of the back of the spinning truck, dragging me up onto the open tailgate. My head struck the rim of the bed, bringing me even more awake, and I turned to see the fuckers falling like targets at a shooting range, only in fluid and meat, and teeth, fucking teeth, shattering in their misshapen skulls. "Hell yeah," I kept saying. "Hell yeah, you *fucks!*" As I watched them fold under the butts and barrels of rifles, the crash guard and the big tires of the truck.

"Anything in the jeep we might need?" one of them asked me.

"Gas?" I said.

We sped to the jeep. Men jumped out, cutting the belts, hauling the jugs aboard. A few last pops at the dispersed remainder of the devil mob and we moved away towards the sweep of sky ruled by the moon.

In the silence that settled, the temptation to ask questions flared and then died. The faces that stared back at me were worn to their frames. Eyes that had glinted as the gunfire rained were now dull and lifeless, routine. I became aware it wasn't the moon we were following but the wound in the earth that produced the vile. We were hunting.

There was only one more incident along the rupture, near the road I had driven in on, a few choicely placed shots in the heads of the scattered few we encountered, no passion really, no victory yells. Then we were beyond the rupture with only the moon in front of us. Again I felt the urge to ask, again it went away. There weren't any answers. Not in this game. If anything made sense anymore, I suspected it was the staying and battling it out, the protecting your own.

We rode for several miles before the silhouette of a town came into view. This one had lights, which meant life—totally unlike the one Jagged had chased me through. I began to see the slightest changes on the faces of the men as we got closer, as if here at least was something in a world gone mad.

"We got a doctor," the man nearest me said. "You look like you need one."

So goddamn routine.

A low rumbling sound began. I fantasized for a moment that maybe it was an escort coming out to meet us, then I watched the degenerating shades of the faces around me: curiosity to puzzlement to consternation to awe. The rumble grew into a tremor, rattling the tail gate, the cans, bone. The driver braked hard and the truck skidded sideways, throwing bodies against me as the rear passenger wheel suddenly dropped and the frame struck ground. Curses abounded but were swallowed by the noise of the earthquake, itself a curse, a curse upon the Earth. Though the truck had come to a dead halt, it did not stop moving because it was now being carried by the lip of the opening rupture. My eyes and mouth must have opened with it as I stared over the side of the truck at the unholy separation in the desert floor and the cords of tubular matter shot up like so many jellyfish tentacles searching for prey.

While these tentacles bore every resemblance to the things that protruded from the heads of the creatures, they came independently, feelers and ropes. One latched onto the side of the bed, followed by a second, then yet another. There appeared to be no threat of their tipping the truck as they burst easily beneath the butts of the rifles. I grabbed hold of one, steeling my nerves against its coolness as I wrapped it around my wrist, heaving upward. The problem with trying to detach it from its source was that the cord's slack was as incalculable as the depth of the fissure. Nonetheless, I felt resistance as the cord drew half-taut with a quivering spray of wet foulness. It was elastic as I kept winding and pulling, searching for the snapping point.

I felt its pulse in my palm and forearm, my own heartbeat threatening to join it. The line grew thinner and thinner as I was too committed now to unreel it and leap out of the truck like everyone else. The crack seemed to have opened as far as it was going to and still I concentrated on this lifeline from the pit of fucking Hades. "Hang tight!" came a voice from my right, outside the truck, then the blade of a hunting knife appeared. Another hand, fine-fingered and familiar, reached out of the darkness to grasp the wrist of the knife holder. The silvery arch of the blade caught the moonlight as the knife, followed by its wielder, fell into the chasm.

The rope shuddered as the hand reached up to seize my throat. Christ Jesus and the Cross as the hollowed-out face of its owner appeared, tubes dancing around a visage I recognized even in its ragged fleshlessness, only now more so because of the totally unobstructed view of her black soul. Though she'd no mouth, I could have sworn I heard her laughing as her tubes found my head and she swept up like the maw of oblivion to devour me.

A shot sounded in my ears. The tubes withdrew wetly. Jagged's face was the same pit it had always been as it hovered, knowing me. Then finally the cord snapped and down she went in a blaze of black nothingness, and maybe just maybe, as determined bodies managed to get the truck pushed up over the rim, I was going to get to see the other side of god-damn New Mexico.

Making Sense

Until he looked out the window that morning, Craig had almost decided to skip riding up to the spot where he had seen the thing. His ambivalence had calmed as he sat over coffee and nothingness, the wisdom of waiting a day or two filling the gulches left by last night's brutal dreams. But then he went to the kitchen and opened the roller blind to the bright March day. He found the faces out in full expression. Which was to say, possessing none at all.

Props.

Frau Schneider across the street looked back at him as she swept the already perfectly clean sidewalk in front of her house. She stood about four and a half feet tall, but her cast was no warmer for her diminutive stature. In fact it seemed the diametric opposite—if stoicism knows degrees. Craig waved, and she nodded in reply. The lines of her face never changed.

While Craig washed his mug and the coffee pot, Herr Friderich appeared, walking over from his house next door to visit with Frau Schneider. They spoke a few words, then in unison turned to look at Craig in his kitchen window. The stares cooled him more than they used to, even the dishwater losing heat around his hands. Someone went by on a scooter, older gentleman quintessential in his cap and patterned knee-high socks, looking for nowhere.

Props. Reminders.

Craig took his morning valium and put on his sweats and jacket and sunglasses. He stuffed two beers in a backpack otherwise empty, fetched his bike from the garage. The landlord and lady met him on the drive, their own aspects red with the exertion of being aspects. Their eyes and mouths told tales in spite of the *absence* that made their faces, like every-one else's, its home. How long will you stay now that she's gone, Craig?

The gears of his bike knew him better than his neighbors did, responding in quiet conformity as he began the ascent out of the village. The day a cloudless and mild precursor to spring, folk were buzzing about, finding excuses. Craig might have understood them better if they had whispered or made covert gestures. Instead they merely stared, as they had always done.

Even when he passed the place where it had happened, their expres-sions remained blankly inquisitive, forever uninspired.

Props. Reminders. Butchers.

He couldn't look there, by the curb, he couldn't bear to see the stain that had settled around the drain. Drain...cutting himself that morning when she surprised him from behind, causing his razor to slip off track. Making love on the vanity, the mirror steaming mysteriously, as if it knew what was coming.

At the right where the *Grillhütte* sign stood, Craig turned, passing the last of the houses and entering the forest. Through the *Wald* for two kilometers to the plateau and its pastures and interval crop fields. Wooden fences tilted from winter winds. Animal scents, piss, hay, faint taste of the shit fertilizer the farmers used to prepare the ground for the wheat and barley.

And at last, the bench overlooking the broad expanse of grass. This was the spot where Craig had been coming to make sense of things for three years. *Used* to come to make sense of things. For now it had become the spot where he had seen the alien thing. How Belinda would have marveled at it. She had sucked up her husband's tales of the dark and strange with a thirst that sustained him. For her, his fiction had been a parallel future, a thing beyond time, space, and her once-sexy international job.

Craig leaned his bike against the birch tree and sat on the bench. Around him songbirds heralded the rebirth season as he gazed out at that particular spot where he had watched the thing awaken on two occasions. Today was Friday of the week owned by this phenomenon, but it didn't matter what day it was anymore. The days were like the props' counte-nances, blurring into a canvas on which nothing would ever be painted.

Darren Speegle

A gentle disturbance out in the middle of the sun-drenched pasture marked the rousing of the thing. Dense red fog poured from the spot, filling an invisible, amorphous balloon which pulsed like the heart muscle in the breast. Craig found one of his beers, uncapped it, never taking his eyes off the trespasser in this place where he came to make sense of things. The mass pulsed and he drank his beer, letting the alcohol fall in drops from his eyes. He made sense of no thing.

Something was different today. The mass grew larger, deeper in color, and began to move *in his direction*. The fog took on a more gelatinous texture. The plateau, fields and forest alike, fell silent. The songbirds fell silent. Craig's heartbeat stretched out to join that of the body coming towards him, and the two fell into one, echoing in Craig's ears like Belinda united with him in passion. The drain in the road filled his eyes, the blood encircling it without dropping into the black abyss. And Belinda...reflected in skin, in faces made of skin and nothing more.

As the mass collected before him, he recognized features, fragments from his dreams, hints of a face gone reminiscently expressionless and inanimate as it stared blindly at Craig from the coffin. I can't see you, my husband. No one can see anyone. Everyone has been dead a long, long time. Kiss me where I lie and perhaps I will sleep.

Tendrils of vapor matter reached around Craig, gathering him in. He perceived her through his senses, essence there for an instant then lost among the odors of the farms and fields. But the gesture lived on, on his lips. A kiss containing the brightness and majesty of the steel blade he had brought with him lest the alien thing prove malevolent. Lest *he* prove so deserving. He had thought about it many times, doctor's valium fix or no.

His eyes opened. He was at the place where he came to make sense of it all, and he was beating like a drum. He studied his moment awhile as he put the second beer to use, tapping the cold hard metal against the glass, joining the rhythm, finding focus after long days and nights. Would they know him down in the village, so revived? He hoped so. He hoped for any spark of precognition.

At the first house no one answered, though a child watched from the yard behind the structure. The second house opened to Craig, singing with memory as the steely music formed dark pools in which to view past and future with equal nonchalance. At the third house, they inhaled

79

because they recognized his aspect as their own. On *Hauptstrasse* they came out by twos and threes to see what was taking place. Belinda might as well have still lain there, fresh from the skid on the ice, the bike sucked into the nearby chestnut tree, her body broken by the curb.

Craig found the exact spot in the road and, dripping blade tucked behind his wrist, beckoned them to come, knowing their fascination for oblivion, for watching blood leak away while no one lifted a hand to help. Recalling perfectly how they stood like stage set pieces as he crested the hill, minutes behind his wife, wholly unprepared for what he was about to discover.

Props.

Reminders.

Butchers.

Ghosts.

Triangle

So I was there and she was there and all three of us were there. So what.

So what? So it was my birthday and she had a gun pointed directly at Tiny's face, that's what.

Tiny, meantime, looked like he was about to shit his pants. There was no one else in the joint, thank God. Tiny being the bartender himself made matters a little less complicated. No witnesses, that way. Witnesses to *what*? That's what I was wonderin'. I mean, Christ, I lived with Debbie. Had she mentioned to me she was going to pull a gun on poor Tiny? Hell, I'd no idea she even had her piece with her.

So there's the gun in Tiny's face, and Tiny...well, he's looking at me like I know somethin' about somethin'. I can only shrug at him and wonder when Debbie's going to cool it so's I can have a damn beer. But Debbie, it seems, ain't gonna cool it.

"You are a mother prick, you know it, Tiny? And I'm a fucking dupe for lettin' it go on."

A *fuckin'* dupe, she says. Not just any dupe but a *fuckin'* one. I'm really troubled now because the only time Debbie ever uses that word is when she's especially steamed.

"I don't know what you're talking about, Deb."

"Don't call me Deb, Tiny," she says, sticking the nose of the revolver in his nostril.

"What do you want from me?" he squeals. Like he ain't no bigger than his title. Which he damned sure is—else his ass would have been kicked all over the joint fifty times and countin' by now.

81

"You know what I want."

"I don't, Debbie. I truly don't!"

"*You*, you big gorilla. It's you I want. Why do you think I moved in with this bum in the first place? Was to get to you, of course."

"Huh?" I'm not sure which one of us said it, Tiny or me. I knew this, though: absorbin' it was like absorbin' a punch in the ear, the 'verberations rollin' like a drum through me.

"Why, you ask, do I need a piece to make that point," she says to him matter-o'-factish, muzzle still in his nostril.

His big alarmed eyes are now fixed on yours truly. "Wh-why, Debbie?" he stammers.

"How else," she says kinda sexy-like, bending real close, "was I gonna get your attention?" The last word was a breath. Hot, I imagined.

Oh, but I don't know where I got the juice to do what I did next. I've been in some situations, some pretty damn hardcore situations, too, but I ain't never had a lady drop one on me like that. Not when I've been romancin' her and treatin' her right and, yeah, I ain't ashamed to admit it—thinkin' about marrying her. That's the fat and skinny of it right there. I loved the girl.

I pounced on her like a cat on a rat, five words tumblin' through my head. I'm gonna kill the bitch. I'm gonna kill the bitch! *I'm gonna kill you, bitch!* As I seized her throat in one hand, I grabbed at the gun with the other. It went off with a muffle more'n a bang, partly 'cause Tiny's head suppressed the noise, partly 'cause I was in another zone, the *killing* zone, and I wasn't hearin' much o' nothin' beyond those five words inside my skull. I think I must o' premonitioned the shot goin' off 'cause at that very instant my head jerked up, just in time to see Tiny's marbles go sprayin' across the bottles and the mirror behind the bar.

Suddenly people were rushin' into the room, from the back, from the bathrooms, from everywhere, it seemed, and all at once. A single word filled the air, but I was so consumed by the blood rage now, I couldn't have stopped myself if I'd wanted to. Clutching her head in both my hands, I bounced it off the cushioned edge of the bar. Dazed, she watched me lift the gun, level it, and fire.

She dropped like a weight. Behind the spot where she'd stood, balloons floated, mouths hung open, the word still lingered on the

blood-scented air...
Surprise!

The Smell of Sex

As India, she knew her body. She'd lived without anyone but Angela, the other woman inhabiting her body, for two decades now, and she had memorized its every blemish, its every suggestion. She knew how she appeared to men, how she affected their senses: she had the manner, the bearing and the speech of a woman skirting forty, but the softness of skin and absence of wrinkles of a girl of seventeen. She was naturally dark with hair that fell down her back in waves and eyes that spoke of exotic locales. She had taste, an elegance of dress and movement that both suited and was at odds with the manufactured ambiance of the piano bars where she spent her evenings. She possessed the sumptuousness of night, and no man, however unworldly, would ever have mistaken her for a day creature. She smelled of smoke—Angela hated it—and beneath the smoke, a hint of the perfume that Angela sold for a living.

And under the perfume, apparently, sex.

"Did you say...?" She stared at the man who had taken the stool beside hers, knowing she had heard him right, and that she was learning something new about herself—through the man, as always. Other than the barkeep, who read a newspaper by the impotent light intended to be synonymous with romance, and the pianist, whose icicle melody aspired to the same, they were alone. She had selected the stool at the far end of the bar, in relation to the hotel lobby, so she could be close to the mystery-lending darkness of the corner.

"Sex," he smiled, doing it again, taking in her aroma as if she were a wine. "You smell faintly of sex."

If she had been Angela, she would have tossed her drink in his face.

But then Angela wouldn't have been here, and Angela's drink of choice had ice cream in it, which didn't toss well.

"You have a lot of nerve."

"Don't pretend to be offended," he said. His voice was deep, with a soothing, intoning quality like a hypnotist's. His eyes were deeper yet, almost black, as he openly searched hers. The shadow of a beard accentuated a model's jaw line. His nose, rather beautiful itself, contributed to a predatory look. The flare of his nostrils told him hungry. Now.

She sipped her drink, unaroused, unimpressed. It was her game, India's game.

"Without lowering your eyes," he said, "tell me what I'm wearing."

"Black," she said. "You're always wearing black. Black suit, black leather jacket, black boots, black wingtips...what difference does it make?"

"I can tell you what you're wearing." He firmly held her gaze.

"Is that what you tell the girls you find in the phone book late at night?"

"Skin," he said, undeterred. "And the merest layer of sweat."

He knew. He knew what India had been doing before she emerged from her room tonight. It wasn't a line. He genuinely smelled it on her. She smelled his powers of perception, his acute senses, on him. He was starting to smell good.

It was still India's game, and she let him know it. "I carry a toy or two in my bags. It gets lonely on the road. That bitch I share a bed with is no good. I travel with Angela. She hasn't had sex since the day her husband walked out on her twenty years ago."

"Why did he walk out on her?" he said.

"She was screaming at me in the mirror. He dubbed her irremediably crazy. It was the last time she ever spoke to me. I don't think she knows I exist anymore."

"A woman you share a bed with?"

"Yes, well, I have night wings."

"Night wings," he echoed admiringly. "I've a pair of those myself. My name is Anton."

"I'm India," she said, extending her hand elegantly.

He did not stop at kissing her hand, but pulled her to him, brushing her cheek, her neck, with his lips. A slight exhalation escaped her mouth, and she knew he smelled that too: cognac, India's drink. She glanced up to find the bartender looking over his newspaper at her. She closed her eyes, sensually. When she opened them again, he had returned to his paper...out of boredom, embarrassment, desire, masculinity...

"India and Angela." His whisper was hot in her ear. "They don't even sound like they mix. India has a delicious flavor, like the odor of her body, but Angela..."

"Angela stinks of soap and hand lotion."

"The bartender, I noticed, stinks of soap and hand lotion. Maybe we should put the two together."

She thought how bizarre that would be, forcing Angela to let the bored, embarrassed, lustful bartender inside. How fitting for Angela, who was all of those things and didn't even know it.

She pushed him back, looking at him askew. "Do you know that Angela won't even wear the perfume she sells because she doesn't want to seem as if she's trying to be seductive?"

He looked at his watch. "The bar closes in twenty minutes."

She caught the barkeep looking at her again. Angela would be almost as attractive, almost India as she woke up to find him on top of her.

She raised her glass. He came lazily. She doubted that would be the case when they were in the room.

When no answer came after multiple knocks, India produced her card. She invited them to peruse the mini-bar while she went to see about Angela. She didn't elaborate except to offer a shrugging comment about "that mirror fetish of hers," after which she slipped into the bathroom, its door having been noticeably closed when they entered the room.

Inside the cubicle she stared at herself in the glass, hand absently going to the sample bottle, more like an ampule containing the elixir of her current need. She opened the bottle and touched the perfume to her slender neck, still conscious only of her face, delicate and exotic, daring in comparison to Angela's—though when the jets from the shower washed away the accessories, they were one and the same. For the briefest second

Angela's face breached the surface, scaring her with its sudden power and will to do so, then it sank back into the watery pool of the reflective glass, leaving her on the lip of anger, sexual and dark, like the mask.

When she watched her smirk twist into a grin, she knew she was still on her game. She began to talk, first in her own sexy voice, then in the reactive, weak, almost pathetic voice that she liked to put on Angela. Again the essence of Angela momentarily bled through the veil—uninvited, though not, upon reconsideration, unwelcome. Indeed she permitted herself the amusing notion that Angela might awaken to the night's reality prior to being summoned from her department store dreams. Relish our luscious fantasies.

Ending the dialogue with an expressive "You've got five minutes, Angela, then I'm sending our guest in after you," India emerged from the bathroom, closing the door behind her.

By *guest* she referred to the bartender of course. His name was Dave—she knew from the meaningless banter in the elevator—but she wasn't about to use it. At least Anton had the decency to don a handle for the night. Still, he had to be petted; he was, after all, the important and irresistible and superlative bartender. Accepting from Anton the cognac he had poured—her own addition to the mini-bar—she joined them at the table, sitting down on the bartender's lap without asking for his permission.

She placed his hand on her breast.

"Go ahead. Caress it. It is very much like hers. Consider it a taste."

He responded well. Both women wanted him—she could see the fantasy weaving itself in amongst the vanities dominating his features even before he clenched, rather than caressed, her breast. The pain stirred her in places already moist from the promises of the winged one who smelled sex on his victims. She thought to slap him, but figured he would pout, or worse yet, rough handle her. She suspected this would not be to Anton's liking, hence a black mark against the mixologist even before the sport began. Anton, meanwhile, was pitted against the fuckoverhaul of Angela's world in the game of India's desires. She thought to send Angela off, but no, Angela was always first choice.

The bartender's hand found its way beneath her form-fitting dress, groping, pinching the nipple. She felt him grow against her right cheek.

"I'm fascinated about Angela," Anton said, watching the movements of the bartender's hand. "Twenty years abstinent?"

"You wouldn't even smell the *desire* on her," India said.

"Really?" he said, amused. "There is always the desire."

"Yeah," grunted the barkeep, groping, pinching, rising.

India appreciated the idiotic quality of the bartender; the simpler they were, the more damage to Angela's big, glass, mannequin-dressed windows.

There was a sound, enough to turn heads towards the bathroom, which was only a wall's distance from the corridor, whence the noise had no doubt come. India played on it, rising to her feet, much to the discomfort of the bartender, unsure whether to seize her or seize himself. She went into the bathroom, closing the door behind her again.

"Angela!" she exclaimed, all shock. She quickly slipped out of her shoes, then her dress, then her stockings. She viewed herself naked in the mirror. The side of her right breast was red. "Angela," she said again, softly this time, touching the spot. She washed her face, put her hair in a pineapple, peed, then emerged from the cubicle unclothed.

Anton canted his head.

"We're twins," she said, blushing.

"Ah," he said. "It's a game."

"What do you mean?" India heard Angela in her voice, then retreating again, like radio interference.

"I mean there is the smell of sex on you too—Angela."

India did not know how to answer, so she didn't. She sat in the bartender's lap, whimpering, pining, widening her legs. Anton moved his chair nearer to her, leaning close as he asked, "So where is India now?"

She was a doe in the lights of an automobile, transfixed by him. The suspicion was odd on him, unworthy of his smooth, his cool.

The bartender, unable to contain himself any longer, suddenly grabbed her around the waist, surging to his feet. Anton got out of his way, but the table did not, India crying out in pain as her elbow caught its edge. The bartender threw her to the bed, pinning her down as he worked his pants undone. She resisted halfheartedly, watching with increasing interest as his zipper came down and the surprisingly impressive fullness of him sprang greedily from its containment. She heard Angela catch air, she heard Angela recalling a face in the mirror that was and was not her own, she heard Angela sniff at the mingled odors of smoke and perfume and sweat, every morning's fume as she woke from perverted dreams. She saw the aggressor through Angela's eyes, followed almost instantaneously by Angela's refusal to acknowledge him. She felt Angela withdraw, cursed her for the prude, coward, nun, and daughter of her mother that she was.

As she spread her legs to him, moistly seizing his organ with her own as she accepted him eagerly into her shared body, she saw the shape of the winged one rising up behind him, a distorted silhouette beyond the frame of her starting, nameless lover. Anton's mouth opened almost in unison with that of her driving adolescent, whose fit was bringing Angela back to the surface again, crucifix, soap, douche...all in hand. *Come on, Angie*, she thought. *Come up into the fuck with me.*

The bartender was perspiring already from the task of keeping up his jackhammer pace. India didn't care. She didn't need it slow from him; his simple, clumsy inability to control himself was aphrodisiac. It was the sort of thing Angela would call disgusting, brute and savage, animal. God, wasn't it so. His size was factoring in, massaging her most sensitive places without relent, denying her the simplest breath.

It was she who suffered the inability now, the inability to make a berth for Angela, the inability to delay her own orgasm until Angela had accepted that this was a gift to her, the inability to cry a warning about what came.

"*Ah, the aroma, delectable aroma of sex. How it strokes the appetite!*" issued Anton, one great claw raised, razors long and keen.

She wanted to demand of him an explanation. How had she been led to this frenzy of the body? This abandon? But she knew it was as much Angela's question as her own as she gave forth like a fountain, in harmony with her nameless lover, who spewed it all over the room, the hot red fluid of his body. Back and forth again, with a speed and ferocity that put the bartender's aggressions to shame, the winged one slashed him to tatters and ribbons.

With a last lurch of the upper torso, a richly dark rivulet spilled from the bartender's mouth and he fell sideways to the sheets, leaving Angela gaping up at the beast that had been Anton.

"You reek of it!" snarled the beast, saliva from its grinning mouth.

Her breathing was labored, fierce, as she stared up in wondrous terror. "Sex!" it spat.

She shook her head back and forth, a silent, terrified proclamation of innocence.

India broke the membrane, belching, "Not Angela! No! If it's the sex or the smell of sex that attracts you—"

"That *feeds* me!"

"Angela can't be what you're looking for. It isn't hers. She doesn't partake of the fruits I do." It came out of the shaft of a well, the shaft through which India was falling.

The beast glared down at the woman, nostrils twitching. With a long, keen talon it scraped moisture from her neck, sniffed it, now her belly, sniffed again, now between her legs.

"It has the scent..." it said. "And yet..." It glared again. "What is your name?!"

"Angela," she said feebly.

It frowned down at her, muttered something about abstinence, decades, then fretted off in the direction of the door. At the bathroom it paused, sniffing. It vanished for a moment, then reemerged with the vial of perfume.

Tossing the bottle at Angela, it said: "Hides the stink of abstinence."

A Dirge for the Temporal

When the ramshackle caravan rolled past, Yvette thought little of it. Faces stared out of the side windows of the campers, wild black hair surrounding various expressions. She had never encountered Gypsies, living as she did in the mountains, but she knew they wandered southern France. She found the experience mildly interesting, as she did the experience of people in general.

The last was a trailer, an ancient affair swaying past the narrow area where she had pulled off. As her gaze followed its sluggish progress up the grade, the curtains in the rear of its rounded silver body suddenly came open and a man's face appeared. His eyes found her, and as a result so did a momentary shudder, for they very closely resembled the round transfixing orbs of one of her instructors. Of course he could not be one of her instructors; they never appeared in human form.

His eyes remained on her until the trailer disappeared around a bend, then she was alone again, the face already forgotten. She returned to the edge of the shoulder, looking down into the gorge. It wasn't the same picture it had been when she'd gotten here. She stood for some minutes peering down at the strange tableau before returning to her car. She clicked on the radio, poised not for the music that was so hard to get in the Alpine pass, but for the whispered praises of her instructors.

Basking in them, she started back up the slope in the direction of home.

Another mild surprise awaited her when she arrived, a half-hour later, at her beloved village of St. Luc. The caravan had stopped at the campground across the road from her house, and several of its members stood around, drinking wine and waiting. As she pulled into her drive, one of the men crossed the road. She stepped out of her car to find herself looking at the set of eyes from the trailer.

The effect was different now, making him just another face. Darkly handsome, granted, but just another face. He seemed to think considerably more of hers, but that merely bored her. Once, it would have mattered. Once, a dark, exotic stranger would have made her blush.

"Yes?" she asked, knowing what was coming.

Eyes never leaving her, he gestured back at the campground. "The office is open, yet no one is there. We have knocked at the doors of nearby houses, but no one answers."

She shrugged. "They must be away."

"Everyone? And without locking the office? A bell chimes as you walk in. The sign says open."

Details, she thought. *Who knew you were coming, after all?*

She voiced, "I don't know how I can help you. If you will excuse me, please." She started to shut the door, but he caught her arm. She said coldly, "If you please, monsieur."

"There is a scent about you. Your clothes, your car," he said. He appeared to be taking it in as he spoke.

She removed his hand from her arm, slammed the car door, and strode to the entrance of her two-story stucco abode, not deigning to cast a glance back.

"What is your name?" he said after her.

At the door, key in her hand, she turned to look at him. His hair danced around his smile as he gave it his most dashing.

"My name is Yvette," she said. "What you smell is blood, because I buried my dog today. Is there anything more you would like to know?"

"Buried...over a cliff?"

"Yes."

"I am not fond of dogs," he said, eyes for an instant reclaiming that familiar quality.

"You don't even find them mildly interesting?" she asked.

He waved nonchalantly, dismissing the topic. "I have a very long name. I go by Jan."

"Good day, Jan." And she went in, shutting the door against dark, exotic strangers.

Evening called. Over the sink in the kitchen, she watched the Gypsies make fires without permission. She watched the smoke from those fires rove away in search of the June night, scattered already with stars. As she put away the soup pot, she noticed Jan's face over the nearest of the fires, watching.

Beyond, the twenty-some people who made up the caravan moved around in the night as if it belonged to them—an easy attitude to admire. Beyond their phantom shapes, the tops of the campground's cork trees were silhouetted against snow-capped peaks, which in turn radiantly contrasted the night. The snow whispered, even from such distances. It was in snow's whispering embrace that she had first come into contact with them. And to think, so much accomplished already, with spring only just departing, by one pupil about the work of catching eternity's sails as they swept by.

As the whispers of separation from the ephemeral seasons, from temporal existence, fluttered in her head, she realized the caravan was a sign—a sign of transience. The instructors hissed in the Gypsy fires, in Gypsy eyes.

A knock at the door. She looked to the fire again to find he wasn't there, prince of travelers, face hovering over the hissing flames.

She opened it to him, and he spoke her name. *Yvette, my fingers to caress your fading skin.* She could see it in him; she had seen it in every man in her village, followed by the strange jealousy in the eyes of their partners, the fascination in the children, who beheld the unfolding petals of the already rotten, already lost, already dead. It was as if the children knew that the transitory lives of men begot such desires, and such consequences.

"You want to see the dog," she said to the wildly dark figure standing there.

"I do. And more," Jan replied.

"How much more? Do you want to see the dirt slip from between the fingers of your clenched fist? The stars retreat?" She touched his vagabond hair with her fingers. "Do you want to forget what the mouth of oblivion looks like as it closes around you?"

His smile was worldly. "You would like to get to know me then?"

"Oh, I know you. I know you for the rascal that you are. I know you for the lustful, lascivious bastard that you are."

"Then you don't know me," he said. He offered his hand.

"We'll see," she smiled, accepting it.

They parked at the same spot where she had watched the caravan pass. He followed her to the shoulder's edge, and as they looked down into the gorge, he had never touched her. The canyon was so deep, no glove box torch would have penetrated. It didn't matter. The night was filled with stars. The tableau differed in its shadows, in the depths of those shadows, but it remained the same otherwise.

It was clearly a man sprawled on the rock, yet strangely Jan cared not for how he had gotten down there, only what his name was.

"His name?" she said. "Here is his name: the one who didn't make it over that last lip of rock and into the deeper ravine, where he would have been concealed from view, perhaps for years."

Jan stood at the very brink with her, hand now lightly touching her unflinching back as he asked, "Do you think you will be caught now?"

"Caught?" She turned to him. "I am beyond the reaches of mortal tendrils."

"Yes." His eyes grew round, transfixing, vessels out of her dreams. Beneath them his lips formed a part through which only whispers could escape. "*Yes Yvette you have done well, you have rid yourself of the most poisonous of transitory things, the infection that you have been surrounded by all your life. People.*"

Wonder bloomed. "It is you."

"In theory," he returned, winking. Then he turned and, drawing the sign he had described to her, the sign of the circle, lay back on the air, and dropped, never landing.

The caravan was gone when she arrived home. Unbothered, she walked across the road to study the vestiges of their human manifestation. The fires smoldered, necks of wine bottles protruding from the coals. In one of the trees was a twenty-centimeter gap where a knife had cut away a wedge of cork. A cigarette hung in the glum mouth.

She stepped into the office, lit up nicely in the night. It was she who smelled blood now, remembering it with no real interest as she glanced down at the floor, where the cleansing of St. Luc had begun. A reddish arc teased the eye, prompting her to drop to one knee, touching with delicate fingers the dried blood forming a circle around her. Ah yes, the handiwork of the moment. As if she'd really needed to remind herself.

Laying her head back, she began whispering from lips that had tasted the temporal and far preferred eternity.

The Call of Morzine

When the figure appeared in the mouth of the hillside cave, silhouetted darkly against the white sky, Philippe and his friends nearly jumped out of their skins. The visitor quickly issued a greeting, which eased their alarm somewhat, but there was more to answer for than his unexpected appearance. Crouching on his left shoulder was what appeared to be a monkey, though who could tell with only outlines visible.

In a man's voice to match his man-sized body, the visitor asked if he might enter. The boys, who were camping in the cave for the weekend, saw no harm in it. Secretly, their curiosity demanded it, particularly now that they observed some movement out of the man's companion. Philippe, oldest and pack leader, told the man he had their permission, and the man stepped inside, features emerging out of the dark mask of his face.

The face of the creature upon his shoulder remained in shadow as the man halted by the fire ring, but its naked body was visible now and it was definitely no monkey. Not only wasn't it covered in hair, it also wasn't built quite the same way, didn't crouch quite the same, didn't fidget or chatter. Its feet, while stained dirty, clearly bore human characteristics. The answer revealed itself as the man squatted, picking up a stick to poke at last night's embers.

The boys had seen many strange things in these hills—from wolves whose coats and eyes shone moonsilver in the night to hairy, unbathed wild folk who shunned villages and people—but they had never beheld the likes of this oddity. It resembled a man, and yet it was the size and shape of a monkey and had a long narrow tail curving up behind it. Its

96

face was squat, with large ears, and a mushed nose. Its mouth was big, but not enough to contain its teeth, which separated the thick lips to reveal a dull yellow gleam. The creature's eyes were a bright, gemstone green as they gazed steadily with more than a simian's intelligence.

"What *is* it?" said young Rémy, himself barely bigger than the anthropoid on its shoulder perch.

The features of the man whose shoulder it was on were rugged, carved liked the surrounding bluffs, this cave. His voice possessed a contrarily gentle quality:

"*Who* would be the more appropriate word, I think. His name is Morzine."

The creature blinked its bright eyes, as if to say, *That is I.*

"Have you heard of Morzine?" the man said.

The boys shook their heads.

"Morzine is a village that lies down along the Swiss border, in the Savoy. It was the site of strange and inexplicable events in the 1850s. People became possessed of some unknown malady that enabled them to climb buildings like squirrels, to speak in foreign tongues, Latin and German and even Arabic, and to reveal knowledge that they should not have known. They ran up and down the streets howling hysterically, shouting blasphemies, exhibiting every sign of insanity. My companion is named for that village."

The boys stared at Morzine, unsure what to say. Philippe spoke for them. "As I think about it, yes, I may have heard such tales. But what do they have to do with him?"

The man was about to reply when Morzine abandoned his shoulder, leaping onto a nearby stone then scurrying up the cave wall and perching inside a nook near the ceiling. While shadows concealed the creature's other features, twin green fires shone down.

"Don't settle in, Morzine," said the man. "We have business in the village below." He turned to Philippe. "The village in the valley, what is its name?"

"Merl," said Philippe.

"Can you show me the best route down to it?"

"Of course. Merl is our home."

The man smiled. Morzine leapt from his roost, following them to the entrance. As Philippe pointed out the trail winding down the hill, he felt the creature's cold hand on his knee.

In the pre-dawn hours, domain of the wolf and whisper, Philippe was awakened by eerie, distant sounds. At first he wasn't sure whether he was awake or in a dream, but the acrid smell of the fire's remnants and the slight hint of chill in the air counterbalanced the strange noises, breaking through membranes.

The others were asleep as he stumbled past in the dark, wrapped in his covers. Just as well, he thought as he stood in the mouth of the cave bending his ear towards the valley, because the disturbance would have scared them. These strains did not belong to wolves, who spoke in fluid and harmonious voices, in song. This discordant symphony belonged to the moon's other children...

Lunatics.

The Morzine story swelled to the surface, along with the face of the stranger, weathered lips speaking of business in the village. Beneath the light of the stars, Philippe made his way to the nearest outcrop, taking care not to let his bare feet lose the narrow path. As he stepped out onto the top of the bluff, he could see the lamps of Merl burning. They weren't stationary. Even from his lofty spot above the intricate patchwork of roofs, he could tell that the village had come under some fever.

He returned to the cave, calling to his brothers. "Adrien, Rémy, Pascal, up, *up!*"

Pascal moaned as he came awake first. "What is it, Philippe?"

"Something's happened in the village. We must go down."

"Tonight?"

"It is almost morning, Pascal. But that's just it. The village has risen before the sun. Can you not hear the commotion?"

The others sat up now as well, Philippe able to just make out their shapes. Little Rémy moved closer to Pascal, whose bedroll was beside his. In a voice as strange as the voices carrying up from Merl, Pascal said, "What's happened?"

"It's the monkey," whispered Rémy.

"Quiet with that," said Adrien.

"I don't know what's happening," Philippe said, "but we best go down. Rémy, get your boots—"

Rémy was otherwise engaged. His arm shook as he brought it up, pointing. For a moment Philippe thought the gesture was aimed at him, but then he turned to look over his shoulder, and there, in the niche near the ceiling, were twin gemstone fires staring down at them.

Philippe choked on his cry. In place of failed exclamations—for the others were deprived of their voices as well—came the sound of the dawn bell in Merl. The cave froze as the bell delivered the traditional three strokes of first light, but the tolling didn't end there. Not today.

"*Go away!*" Philippe screamed at the eyes. Their owner obeyed, leaping down and scampering out of the cave.

Philippe told the boys to put on their boots, and quickly. But as he minded his own words, jerking a knot in the laces, he realized that haste, like priests and remedies, wouldn't change a thing. He knew this with a certainty as cold as the impression left by Morzine's hand on his knee.

The gang forsook the cave for the trail that led down into the valley

Philippe looked back a last time as they broke out of the forest into pasture. He'd thought he saw movement once, farther up the hill, but it might have been his imagination. No matter now as the edge of the village lay up ahead. The closer they drew, the more definable the noises. The clanging of the bell, which had gone on an obscenely long time, had finally quit, making way for the darker clamor: the spontaneous howls of laughter, the outbursts of emotional or foul language, the baying of alarmed dogs. In the village of Merl the fever was in full sweat.

All four boys were focused on their homes. Pascal and Rémy split off before they reached the village. Their houses rested on the northern skirts of Merl, while Philippe and Adrien lived on the east side, which was across town as they approached. Adrien mused aloud about going around the whole village, but Philippe told him that he would being going alone if he did. As they reached the cul-de-sac that was Montpellier, they could already see the symptoms.

Observers were out in their yards, or safe behind their balconies and windows, pointing at a woman chasing a cat up and down the street. In the crook of a tree and rambling unintelligibly was what proved to be the baker, in full array, flour swirling like a halo around his wildly expressive face and hands. Philippe called up to him by name, but the words that returned were like burs in the ears.

The next disturbance was somewhat more unsettling.

Merl's priest was a wizened fellow, in his late seventies and generally imperturbable. That virtue wasn't in evidence this morning as he knelt in the street, pushing his bible towards the roof of one of the village's chateaus, of which Rue Montpellier was full. A girl whom Philippe knew from school perched on a high cornice, exposing her naked breasts to the priest and accusing him of lusting her, and of wanting to lick the Holy Sacrament off her body. While her brazenness was the priest's chagrin, the priest's chagrin was another party's amusement. That other party turned out to be the man upon whose shoulder the creature called Morzine had squatted.

The man's face expanded at the sight of the boys, reflecting their own expressions. The words that came out of him had a mocking flavor: "Aha! There you are!"

"What have you done?" Philippe demanded.

"What have *I* done?" the man said. "What have *you* done?"

The boys continued moving, keeping their distance from the man as he went to the priest, kneeling beside him and whispering in his ear.

"W-what can he be *doing?*" Adrien said, the pitch of his voice too high.

Looking up from his secret sharing, the man cast his head back and laughed through the morning and beyond.

Philippe's parents were safe, and full of relief at the sight of him. Locking the door behind him, his father stood there for several seconds, key in hand, as if assuring himself he had done as much as he could against the world beyond. A strange, uncomfortable silence surrounded the family as they sat around the dining table, Philippe's father with a brandy in his hand while the madness continued in the streets. Morning blazed like some kind of anticlimactic joke.

Some time passed, during which Philippe senior indulged his son in not one, but two strokes of the brandy. Philippe's mother sometimes rattled dishes in the kitchen, other times tried to sleep. At last Philippe brought forth the question.

"What do you know about Morzine in the Savoy?"

His parents met each other's eyes. They didn't ask what had prompted the question. Nor did they comment on any potential similarities between Morzine and Merl—perhaps out of superstition, as if to do so might bring the worst upon their village.

It had happened before Philippe was born. A single case of what appeared to be demonic possession had grown into several cases, and then an epidemic. As the contagion spread, so did the news of it, until it became an international incident. One writer had used the term "The Devils of Morzine," alluding to symptoms which included speaking in tongues, bodily contortions, levitation, and foretelling future events. When medicine, science, even troops proved unable to solve the problem, the archbishop of Paris had dispatched a team of exorcists. That too had failed. Eventually many of the two thousand or so afflicted were sent away to asylums. Soon after, the sickness died out.

The word sickness dissolved slowly. Silence returned, accentuated by cries from out in the streets. Philippe excused himself to his room, which, gratefully, overlooked fields rather than streets. Elbows on the windowsill, chin in his hands, he immersed himself in impressions, not least the cold one still lingering on his knee.

The sound of the front door extracted him from his reverie. Philippe senior called up, announcing the priest. Philippe junior thought he heard an undertone, even an underlying message in his father's voice, but he couldn't understand what it might mean. He stepped out of his room onto the interior balcony, looking down at the visitor.

The priest pointed at Philippe as he addressed Philippe's parents. "Your son was seen cavorting with a demon. It has been reported, by his own friends, that he has allowed a devil to sit upon his shoulder and whisper in his ear."

Philippe was appalled. "The stranger, he is the one!"

"Stranger?" said the priest. "What stranger?"

"Haven't you spoken to him, Father? Didn't you let *him* whisper in *your* ear?"

"I don't know what you're talking about, Philippe. But I do know that you have been seen with this monster in your company."

"So I am responsible for what is happening in the village?" His thigh became inflamed, with ice.

"Those who cavort with demons..."

Thank God Philippe's father saw the priest for his lunacy and threw him out into the street.

The next time the door sounded, a chaos of voices followed. But by the time they converged on Phillipe's room, he was out his window and down the side of the house.

Pasture spread before him, and the cold in his leg, though keen, wouldn't hinder him from getting there. The bluffs stood white against the hill, while the music of Merl fragmented to cries and murmurs; the voices of condemned sailors on the plank; wishes in the well of blood and madness. Philippe let it fall behind.

He recognized the man who had mocked him, standing exactly where Philippe himself had stood, on the outcrop, at the lip of dawn. He did an inventory of what he had to offer the man, what would make the man depart the village of Merl forever. It was a terribly short list. The icy mark on his knee emphasized that knowledge. As he made his way up the path, he had only his own flesh and blood, and sanity.

The man stood outside the cave. He gestured into the darkness in the hillside as he said, "When you fled, you left your scents behind. Particularly fear."

Muzzles and forequarters appeared. Coats diminished from luminous to merely silver as the wolves spotted Philippe and bolted into the trees. Philippe looked at the darkness from which they had emerged and imagined what might be perching among the lingering scents inside. He begged the man to take his creature and go. They'd done what they came to do, now leave Merl for the next village, plague that they were.

The man smiled at him then offered himself to the cave. The darkness seemed to reach out and pull him in, leaving Philippe alone on the hillside. Philippe waited, but the man didn't appear again. The sounds from Merl slithered up the hill like snakes. The sun fell behind the ridge, leaving a sea of blue shadow behind.

Philippe entered. He found the man lying on his back on the cave floor, eyes unseeing, chest unmoving, lips still. The other was there, in his dark niche, gemstone eyes gazing down on Philippe. The boy's instinct was to flee, but his feet would not move until Morzine dropped from his perch onto the stone, beckoning him with a cold finger. And then they moved in the wrong direction.

Michele and his friends were splashing in the waterfall's pool under the moonlight when a shape materialized out of the surrounding foliage. The visitor quickly issued a greeting, which eased their alarm somewhat, but there was more to answer for than his unexpected appearance. Crouching on his left shoulder was what appeared to be a monkey, though who could tell with only outlines visible.

Peering through the dark, Michele said, "What *is* that?"

"*Who* would be the better word," said Philippe. "And his name is Merl. Have you by chance heard of Merl?"

Eyes of Hazel, Kiss the Earth

It was supposed to have been a simple deal. I was there to get something from him. He was there to get something from me. It was the sort of transaction I had been involved in a dozen times before. The trouble was, he wanted more from me than was in our arrangement. He wanted not just the baby; he wanted me to deliver the seven-week-old package to a different spot, and on a different night. He had the money, which he gave to me, but he didn't have the means to see after the infant right now. Tomorrow night was better.

The means to see after it? What was that supposed to mean?

"Then why did I bring it along?" I asked, feeling uncomfortable beneath his discerning stare.

"It" was a boy. In this business you lose sight of such things...on purpose.

"I had to make sure it was healthy."

I didn't care how discerning he was, how the hell was he going to know that by looking at the infant? That particular episode of that particular prime time TV series which shall remain particularly nameless had shown us all that. Business dropped like a lead balloon for three months because of that show.

I didn't bother avoiding such issues anymore; I showed them the papers, I charged them half of what I once did, the rest was their concern. Now, don't get me wrong, mine was a legitimate business—any of my clients would have told you that—it's just that you can't ever be too sure, can you? I did all I could do at my end, even had my own pediatrician, to whom I gave a generous cut. No, the reason I got out of the business had nothing to do with baggage. It had to do with this gentleman standing here in front of me, although I'd no idea then I was headed for the unemployment line.

I voiced the thought. "How are you going to know if the baby's healthy by looking at it?"

"Oh, you know," he said, "...whether it's plump, colored, that sort of thing."

That should have been a dead giveaway. In fact I remember thinking—not for the first time in my dealings with this gentleman—that although he didn't have the *slick* of some of the lawyers with whom I'd crossed paths, there was still this hard-to-define, even askew something about him. Never mind that when he laid his judgmental eyes on me, he was accusing me less of unsavory practices than of being a lost soul. As far as I was concerned, righteousness itself had a funny smell to it. I asked myself a question I had asked myself more than once before. What did I know about the quality of the home into which the child was going? What about *their* health? Were they a plump couple? Were they colored? Were they *that sort of thing*? It's a beast, the living, no doubt about it. The questions abound, but the answers are scarce.

I eyed him, perhaps as openly as he eyed me. But in the end, one concern prevailed. What was I going to do with the baby for the next twenty-four hours?

I bade the gentleman goodnight and took my package home with me. I had nowhere else to take the little guy. The parents of the teenage girl, apparently of some status in the community, had told me quite plainly that they wanted to sever all contact now. I was to do as discussed with the money, and that was that. We did not know each other. We had never had any relations of any kind.

I phoned the doctor in my employ and asked him what I would need for the baby. I'm ashamed to say I was ignorant in that regard. I realize how unprofessional that must sound, considering the line of work I was in, but I was unmarried, an only child, and simply had never had to do the part before. The doctor told me not to be concerned; at that age the baby would be no trouble. He was kind enough to pick up the essentials and bring them to me, so I wouldn't have to drag the infant back out. I learned changing diapers, preparing formula, burping, a whole new discipline that evening.

My guest woke only once during the night. I held him for a while, singing what songs I could recall from my own weehood, telling him how I wished he had a name. His mother's parents had advised her against naming the baby. Which was understandable, I suppose, but it left me with this plump, pink baby with hazel eyes and no identity. I don't know, can a seven-week-old have an identity?

After spending the whole next day with him, I felt this little guy did. To the extent that when eight o'clock rolled around, I didn't want to take him to meet Mr. Doe. I had grown sort of used to him. He hardly ever cried, and spit up on me only a time or two. I was forced to remind myself that, although the service provided was a winner for all involved, the baby remained a product, and it was best not to lose sight of that fact.

We drove out to the designated spot, "Little Guy" nestled over there in his seat, quiet as you please. The church was in a more well-to-do neighborhood, where you might, in fact, expect to find a couple with means enough to purchase a baby boy. When I wheeled around behind the structure, I found that Mr. Doe hadn't arrived yet. Shutting off the engine, I said to my passenger, "Well, Little Guy, I guess we'll have to wait." But I was uneasy.

As I remember it, far worse than the nervousness of waiting in the darkness behind a church in that neighborhood was the discomforting silence that had settled over the interior of the car. It had the flavor of that thing that follows a spat with your date. Cry, I wished at the baby. *Goo. Gurgle. Babble. Do something.* I would have preferred he had been asleep, then I wouldn't have had to face those knowing hazel eyes.

Gratefully, less than five minutes after our arrival, a knock came at the rear passenger window. Mr. Doe's face looked in. With his thumb he motioned I unlock the door.

"What are you doing?" I said as he got in.

"Drive," he said. And pointed a handgun at my head.

Glancing over at the baby, I began, "I don't know what y—"

"Drive."

"Where?"

"I'll let you know."

I turned the key, put it in gear and drove. We pulled left out of the

106

church parking lot. A mile down we turned left again. In a few minutes he indicated a dirt road to the right. Though I took it slow, it was rough going, and Little Guy started crying.

"Yes, he does seem to be a healthy one," Mr. Doe said from the back seat.

I silently wished him a *rot in hell* as we bounced around a bend and the road came to an abrupt end at the edge of a field.

There must have been a hundred of them in the field, many with torches, all cloaked. They were material in the flash of the headlights, shadows as I shut the beams off at Mr. Doe's command. The night was young but deep. We were in that strange territory between the suburbs and the country, just beyond the fringes of the artificial light but not so far out that the land was cast in the unfiltered radiation of the starry sky. We were in that sightless territory where babies had no names and adults draped in dark garments bartered for them like packaged meats.

He had given me two commands. Shut off the lights. Shut off the engine. I obeyed only one. The little guy, you know. It was the little guy's party, no question about that, but no one had bothered to ask if he could make it. As his temporary guardian, I said uh-uh, he could not make it. Whatever these people were up to—ritual sacrifice, cannibalism, God only knew—they would have to go somewhere else for their plump, colored infant.

I threw the shifter in reverse, floored the pedal. The car surged but a huge weight resisted its going anywhere, as though the most functional emergency brake ever made were engaged. I pushed the pedal so hard, it's a wonder the thing didn't go through the floor. Then it was over. I'd had only as much time as it took for Mr. Doe to recover from the initial lurch of the vehicle, and that was mere seconds. He now had the nose of his gun against the top of the baby's wailing head, right there where I knew Little Guy's soft spot to be.

"Shut the fucking engine off!" he yelled.

I did.

"The keys," he ordered, gesturing with his free hand. As I handed him the ring, I saw faces staring in at me from all three of the back windows. The car fell. In my adrenaline storm, I hadn't even realized its rear wheels had been lifted off the ground. Needless to say, I have never owned another rear wheel drive vehicle.

"Out of the car!" Mr. Doe ordered.

I obeyed. They met me, torchlight flickering, distorted faces peering from deep within cowls. The déjà vu crawled over me like hairy spiders. I'd felt the first twinge when I saw their robes in the headlights, now was immersed in it. What in God's name were they going to do with the little fellow? I felt I should already know, that I had drifted through some amorphous foretelling of this nightmare...

The passenger door opened. Seconds passed as the straps were removed, then the bundle came up in the light for a moment before being gathered in to a chest. The crying weakened and died. As we moved across the field, I watched them pass the baby from one to another. I noticed how gingerly they handled it, how tenderly they touched those streaked cheeks—and not just the women but the men as well, as they passed their torches to their neighbors so they could experience the child personally.

I was pushed along in the tide of bodies, remaining unmolested otherwise. I wondered what would become of me but rather suspected I knew the answer. The how was the real question. As we approached the middle of the field, I felt the current slowing. We formed a circle around a spot where I presumed they had taken the baby. Gently, and by many hands, I was ushered through the bodies to the circle's center. Mr. Doe was there. So was the baby. He held the bundle up in his hands, up towards the heathen night sky. The baby was silent as he kissed it and brought it down to his chest again. He held out his hand to one of the figures nearby. I saw a glint of metal as the implement was placed in his hand. I rushed forward, unrestrained, unsure of what to do when I got there.

"But it's only a spade. See," he said, holding it up in the torchlight.

"W-what are you going to do with it?" I stammered.

"No, my friend," he laughed. "What are you going to do with it?"

I took a step back, shaking my head, the déjà vu bristling in my flesh, the sweat starting to twitch from my pores. "I won't. I won't."

"Have no fear," said Mr. Doe. "It's an *act*, that's all."

"An act?!"

"Only an act. Here, take the baby. I'll show you where."

Yes, the baby. Give me the baby. Let me touch it again before you do it.

He handed the bundle to me. I pulled back a bit of cloth, looked at its little—

"What have you done to it!" I cried.

Even as Little Guy gazed up at me, his eyes lost the last of their whites to the expanding, saturating pigment of their irises. The orbs were now entirely hazel.

"It's not *I* who have done it," said Mr. Doe. "The child's body knows it has found its way home."

"I don't want it!" I shrieked, holding the bundle out at arm's length. Towards him, the next person, anyone...

"Come. Come here to the spot." He put his boot on what looked like a random point in the grass. With a motion of his wrist, he flung the spade into the ground.

"Right there," he said. "That's where."

Although I saw the spot he had marked, although I had watched the blade pierce the earth, it was far from my focus. I continued to hold the baby out from my body, repulsed by it, terrified of it, and yet unable to drop it or to throw it at one of them for fear I would do it injury.

"I can help you," came a calm masculine voice. "Give me the baby."

It was the one who had supplied the spade.

I gave it willingly. He would not hurt the baby. I sensed he would not hurt him.

His hood got in the way as he bent to the baby. He removed it. The baby issued a sound, a cooing, affectionate sound. The young man issued a sound of his own. I could see the side of his head but little more as he gazed at the baby. I demanded he turn and look at me.

He did, and what I thought I had seen by the fragmented light was now confirmed. His face was only barely recognizable as the face of a man. It was gray in the torchlight, its texture rough, creased, even *knotted*. His hair—which I had at first thought to be a ritual wig, a prop of some kind—was not hair at all but a wild Gorgonian confusion of vine and earth and leaves.

I whirled, eyes darting around the circle, from figure to figure, hood to hood. Darkness stared back at me from within the cowls.

"Show yourselves," I demanded. "Drop the hoods. What in Christ's name *are you*?!"

One by one they began to remove their hoods. But the faces that were revealed were as normal as my own, each and every one of them, none even vaguely resembling the grotesque features of the young man or the baby.

I turned back to him. As terrified as I was, I found it within me to form words.

"What is the baby to you?"

"He is my son."

"But the girl...his mother?"

"When I am away from this hallowed place and walking among you, I am a handsome young man."

"What *are* you?" It was a whisper.

As he smiled, dry cracks formed at the corners of his mouth, threatening to spider web across his gray bark-like skin.

"I am not a god. I am a liaison."

"But...what do you want from me?"

He gestured. My eyes went there, but I didn't understand.

Mr. Doe retrieved the spade from the earth. "We want you," he said, "to dig."

I did not want to dig. Above all...*don't make me dig*. Sometimes, you see, on those rarest of occasions, you remember the déjà vu before the déjà vu remembers you. You recall the smell of the soil before you break it with the shovel. You glimpse, for the merest second, why you are here. And then it's gone, leaving only the knowledge that you are a baby merchant.

I accepted it from Mr. Doe in a hand that shook uncontrollably. I knelt down and began to dig.

"How deep?" As I threw the first scoop.

"Deep enough to plant a sapling," said Mr. Doe.

That at least I could fix on. It had substance to it. I dug until I thought the hole of adequate depth for the potted tree I pictured in my mind.

"Now?" I said.

"Keep digging."

I continued, rounding the hole out a certain way. A stroke here, a stroke there, another few inches in depth. That terrible knowledge I had glimpsed as he held the spade out to me still hovered, poised to descend on me. I paused, wiping my brow with the back of my hand. I was perspiring profusely, though it was only a spade. And a hole big enough to bury your cat in.

I glanced up at Mr. Doe. My lips quivered.

"A bit more," he said.

I went at it again. Scoop after scoop, but still rounding, still measuring, as if baby trading were only my day job.

At last he said, "That is sufficient."

I rose slowly, spitting dirt out of my mouth. As the circle moved closer, the torchlight dancing across the walls of the hole in the earth, I would look no place but there. They began to chant, the circle, and as their voice lifted, the knowledge descended, its talons like razors as they tore into my sweaty, dirty flesh.

Even when he offered it to me in his extended hands, my eyes remained on the pit I had made.

Mr. Doe put a hand on my shoulder, turned me around to face them. "Why me?" I implored. "Why *me*?"

"It didn't have to be you," Mr. Doe said. "In fact it was my full intention to take the child away last night and never see you again. Then I caught a glimpse of that empty place inside you and reconsidered. Since I was only going to take him home with me until the ceremony tonight, I decided I would let you experience him. As well as the ceremony itself."

My eyes, stinging with tears, drifted to the bundle that was being presented to me. The one presenting it peered at me through his hazel eyes and said, "No one could benefit more than you. Take him. Plant the sapling so that he may grow up to continue the cycle. Plant the sapling and let him take root in that desolate place in your soul. Go ahead. He is a liaison. Between man and the earth."

I heard the sound again. Despite the chanting around me, I heard the voice of Little Guy. Cooing, affectionate.

"Please," I choked. "I-I can't."

But I did. God help me, I did.

Though I've never managed to bring myself to return to that field to see what sort of boy he's growing up to be.

A Nasty Set of Circumstances

Katie had the nastiest set of circumstances Toby had ever come across. And as he'd told Blackie, whose girlfriend had hooked them up, there was definitely a double meaning in that evaluation. That was the problem; they were such an extraordinarily nasty set, men didn't want to give them up after they'd had a taste. No question Katie had a bad habit of flaunting her stuff, but shit, you'd think that would turn a guy away, not reel him in tighter.

Toby himself was reeled in about as tight as he could go. He was whipped, flogged, and lashed, and therefore had a sort of understanding with her stalker ex-husband, her stalker ex-boyfriend, and her other stalker ex-boyfriend. If she walked out tomorrow, he wasn't sure what he would do. He didn't love her; it was nothing like that. It wasn't even because she was a supreme lay, eye-popping, zipper-popping gorgeous, and superlative in every physical way. No, it was something crueler.

She was feeding off him. He had tried to explain what he meant by that to Blackie, but Blackie laughed at him and wanted to know if he was permanently stoned.

"Actually, that's kinda the way I feel. Like I'm constantly dazed. But it's more than that, too. It's like I'm being used up. Like the life force is being sucked out of me through a straw. And yet, the force is constantly being replenished by my lust for her. The whole thing is wearing me out, shriveling me up."

Blackie had shaken his head. "You're permanently stoned and you're getting too much snatch. Sounds like the curse of Paradise to me."

"Maybe you're right," Toby had mumbled, and then gone off to find her before she started sapping somebody else.

He was in bed now, mourning his bruised knuckles and occasionally glancing over at the toned contours of her back as she slept beside him. How she stayed in shape like that, he didn't know, unless it was pure, unbridled sex. Should have been her fighting off her ex this afternoon over at her place, but he guessed it didn't really matter, a man needed to keep sharp with his fists in this life. He only hoped he didn't turn them on her one day. She'd like that, he suspected. She would then have sucked all the self-composure and self-control and self-respect from yet another man.

From out of somewhere, or nowhere, came a very strange thought. A very morbid, even perverse thought. Would Katie retain her power over the opposite sex if she was dead? If she couldn't move those hips or shake that thang or breathe bourbon bubble gum through those sultry lips? He wondered.

As if catching his thoughts in her dreams, she stirred, murmuring the elongated version of his name. "Tobias, be good to me," he thought he heard. It really pissed him off when she called him that, Christian name or no.

"Go back to sleep," he said. But apparently she hadn't really been awake. For a moment he was flattered by the idea of being on her mind in her sleep, but then that pissed him off as well. He *should* be on her mind; they were a pair. Fuck, he thought. Fuck it.

He closed his eyes, tried to coax in the waves, but his hand was in pain. Maybe caplets would help. He rose and went to the bathroom, tried to piss while he fussed with the cotton, finally got out a pair of generic pain relievers—if nothing else. With the goods in hand, he moved on to the kitchen, where the clock registered a minute past dead midnight.

Dead, he thought. Dead. Then said it aloud: "Dead." Damn, what a flat word, for all its implications. As he reached for the cup, he caught the plastic handle of one of the cutlery pieces with his elbow. It was the big one, the one that always got in the way. The kitchen was so pathetically small. Cutlery set, toaster, microwave, paper towels, all these items shared the same slab of counter.

Slab. Like dead. Flat.

He unsheathed the big knife, not knowing why, just curious really. Just curious. Let one of those motherfuckers, Katie's formers, come round *his* pad. It'd be a trespass they'd not soon forget—or remember, rather, 'cause they'd be dead.

What was wrong with him anyway? He went to the sink, set the cup in the basin, drew enough water to douse down the caplets. Should be dousing his face. He wasn't himself at all. Why was he still holding the knife?

But really, how much power would she have in the permanent prone? Would she turn him into a necro? Would he wail and pull out his hair and throw himself at the mercy of the cops just for thinking of it? Of molesting the dead? There it was again. Dead. Just plain dead.

You must put this knife back in its place in that block. That's what you should and must be thinking. He took the caplets. Caplets. Fucking caplets. She had been grocery shopping with him just once and now he had fucking caplets. They went down so much easier, she had explained to him. Slut. Jesus, man, get a hold of yourself. I don't care. Slut.

Toby's mom had sung a song at his dad's funeral. It had struck him as exceedingly bold of her, considering how much she had hated the man. Maybe that's what this crisis he seemed to be having was all about. Pretending. Wasn't it a world easier just to come right out with the truth? *Katie, you ought to know real well how something goes down your throat, you fucking slut.*

"Tobe?" came her voice from behind him. He turned to find her standing there in her cotton pajama bottoms, her particular bedtime thing, squinting against the kitchen light. "Tobe, why do you have that knife in your hand?"

He was embarrassed one second, but then the next he found himself mulling it over. What *had* gotten into him, after all? Was this some kind of Jungian penis thing? Some kind of regaining his edge? I don't know, slut, why do I?

"Are you considering killing me?" she said in a voice that came out of sleep well, adopted its better points easily in the cold kitchen and its cold tile.

"Katie," he began. But there wasn't much to say to her. Her set of circumstances said it all. She dominated the room with her sexuality, she dominated him, she dominated the whole fucking world in the end. It would be like taking down Nero.

114

She smiled, squinty-eyed, as she stepped across the floor with her perfect feet. "Thanks," she said. "Thanks for taking care of me. With Jim and everything."

He let her put her arms around him, felt himself become liquid, oil. The knife clattered on the floor. Lay there, reflecting the light at one angle, dead at the next. Flat.

"Take me to bed, Katie," he whispered. "Fuck me."

The Ego Game

In the Nearspace I came upon a fella. He wore a pair of shorts, a hat, long hair bound in a ponytail, and he stood with his back to me, looking over the placid serene. Having never stumbled on male or female in the Nearspace, I was mildly surprised. I had naturally assumed the sphere existed solely for my treatment. As the Tone was fond of reminding me, the Nearspace was the relief at the heart of the egocentric mindview. The place where self-absorption beached one.

"Sir?" I inquired.

He turned and his face was as familiar to me as my own...because it was my own.

"A hesitant hello," he said, mirroring my own curious expression.

"What do you suppose they're up to now?" I wondered aloud.

"When the Tone last engaged me, the word *umbra* was used."

"Umbra?"

"Their expression for the Test's most recent introduction—your mechanical shadow."

"You are an android?"

"So it would seem."

"Memories?"

"Your very own...up to a point."

"What happens at that point?"

"A lesson in ontology. Who you thought you were all along is not who—nor even what—you actually are."

I considered. "So what do you suppose your purpose is?"

"The nature of the Test is to explore the true nature of man. I suppose

116

I further that by being a sort of alter-ego to man's representative—you."

"The Tone does not use the term, *man's representative.*"

"So?"

"So I would appreciate it if you wouldn't. It smacks of burdens and responsibilities. I was not approached for assets of that kind, remember?"

He laughed, which made me feel they had done a good job with him. He asked me if I would be willing to show him.

"Why? It's in your memory."

"Can I trust my memory? Can I trust *programs?*"

"I suppose not," I said, feeling for him. "But this is already a controlled environment. We might be in an airless vacuum even as we speak. I can't tell the difference, you know."

But of course he knew. If he had my memories, he knew all about how I came to be the subject in this Test. The Space Program had recruited me. In an environment simulator they had discovered for themselves the feature that made me an aberration among men, a first on the ladder of evolution.

The umbra shook his head. "My sensors say otherwise. Here in the Nearspace there is air."

I breathed of it, but my lungs did not taste.

We walked out across the placid serene, and I could see how eager my umbra was to witness this miracle of life. At the edge of the Outerspace, he gestured eloquently, inviting me to illustrate.

"What do your sensors say?" I asked him.

He dipped his head behind the invisible line, and immediately his eyes grew wide and he began to wheeze. "Air!" he gasped as he returned to our side of the membrane.

"Strange," I said. "I would have thought a robot…"

"…would need no air," he finished, reflecting my wonder, gulping oxygen like no robot ever had.

Like *I* never had.

Damn programs.

The Day it Rained Apricots

I was only a kid when Gretchen first hired me on at the bakery. I didn't know my pies from my cobblers, much less the array of finer delicacies her little shop offered. In spite of my ignorance of all things kitchen-related, she believed in me from the start, pointing out in her old-fashioned, grandmotherly way that I was after all a girl, and girls are made of no less than sugar and spice. We would compensate for those fourteen years of road life—"fancy a child being dragged all over the globe like that"—in no time at all. She was famous for this sort of frankness, as I suppose most Germans are. But I did love the lady, poor heart.

We settled in Bavaria, my parents' absolute favorite region in all the world, not long after my fourteenth birthday. It had taken that many years and more to build up the nest egg, and now I would have the simpler life they had always wanted for me. I don't know why they felt it necessary to carry around that air of apology. I had rather enjoyed the only life I had ever known. Just as I would enjoy this new life. I sometimes think they never completely understood that I was not just pretending to be a carefree, adaptable gal but that it was in my nature. Alas, what I am.

I fell into the job at the bakery. We had been living in the village of Meuerberg about two months at the time, and a Saturday morning ritual had developed of my picking up fresh *Brötchen* for breakfast. Gretchen and I had been on a first name basis almost since day one, when she had admired my straw hat in her thickly dialectal German, a gnarled forefinger helping to specify at least the object of her unintelligible compliment. Today I greeted her with the usual *Guten Morgen* as I stepped out of the cool November air into the warmth and delectable aromas of her shop.

118

When, rather than responding in kind, she gestured towards the back, where noises of clanging metals and swearing formed a discordant, even alarming symphony, I knew she was having a disagreement with her help again. The girl's name was Ina, and I went to school with her. She was a sassy one, to say the least, and I had wanted to punch her on her fat lip since the moment I first met her.

Gretchen served out the chosen pieces of bread silently—although I was a quick study, the language barrier would not be overcome for some time yet—while I considered, not seriously, stomping back to the kitchen to do some harmful thing to Ina. But she would not wait, even for a fantasy. As I passed the coins to Gretchen, Ina came storming out yelling something about *Arbeiten* (work) and *Hexe* (witch) tossing her apron at her employer and giving her the finger as she almost broke the front door with the force of her anger on her way out.

It was on that very day I was shown some of the finer points of making a brandied apricot-raison pie.

It was an alliance that would last well beyond the one year of our monopoly on the market. To this day I visit her, all the way from the States, and to this day she remembers most fondly that first year, when she had the corner, when she was the apricot queen and they would come from all the surrounding villages just to sink their teeth into her—into *our*—delicious pastries.

She was a wonderful teacher. There was an art, she said, not only to baking, not only to applying, but also to acquiring. "The apricots we use are only the best. Italian in the heart of the season, of the South of France on the season's fringes." She knew her apricots.

And that is how she almost put him out of business the moment he put up shop.

His name was Assen, he was only part German and he came from somewhere up north. He had always wanted to open a bakery, and our town was where he would do it. During the tourist season, what with all the skiers Meuerburg attracted, there was plenty of room for two bakeries. Out of season he would shut down, do his other thing (whatever that was), and no one would be hurt. Gretchen laughed at that, which meant she was already hurt, claiming that there was no way, even if he could compete with her at the most basic level of flour and yeast, that he could hope to succeed in the finer endeavors. Not with that schedule. Not when the crop schedule was so instrumental to a baker's success. With her knowledge and her connections, you see, she could stretch out the crop almost to the limits of any grown food.

To prove her point, on the day of his grand opening she had an outdoor tasting, which I myself managed, our apricot pastries lining three long tables. Herr Assen was forced to watch from across the street as his potential clients drifted towards the smell of Gretchen's unequalled baked goods.

It was not the sort of day for it, dark clouds gathering over the mountains to the south, the scent of precipitation on the air, the temperature unseasonably warm. But so we did, and I was not above doing a little taste-testing of my own, even offering some to Herr Assen himself when he rambled over to have a look.

"How can you bear to be in the employ of this woman?" he said. "Not that friendly competition bothers me, of course. But my own employee tells me stories of her..."

"Your own employee being the sweet-hearted Ina who once worked for Gretchen?"

He eyed me. "Perhaps *you* would consider..."

"I think you could not afford me, Herr Assen. Considering that you seem to be losing the friendly competition." I gestured around us.

As he acknowledged the flock of tourists and locals alike surrounding our tables, his face seemed to fall. "But you misunderstand me," he said. "I do not wish to steal her business, only to—"

"The devil, you say," came Gretchen's voice behind me. "That is precisely what you wish, and I stand here to tell you that you will wallow in your presumption before this day is through."

But thunder rumbled, and it looked as though we all might be wallowing before long.

"Truly, lady, you have me at a disadvantage."

"Oh? Because I know these people? Because they trust me? My goods?"

"Because I have misjudged the market, the taste of these people, the need for a fruit supplier—"

Something landed with a dull squish. We all lowered our faces to the pie to see what had disturbed its flaky surface. A yellowish fruit, some-what smaller than a peach, lay there, a dead weight in the pie's center. I was struck on the head, looked up to see what was about, was struck in the face. I turned to the others, saw that they too were staring up at the sky. Then all at once the clouds let loose and the sky began to fall in round downy missiles.

I reached out for Gretchen but she was not there. She had stumbled back beneath the eaves of the shop front, covering her ears as the mis-siles struck the aluminum, eyes wide with wonder as the apricots fell in a torrent over the street, her carefully laid tables, the stubborn head of Herr Assen as he held a specimen up for inspection.

Against the storefront across the way, leaned our notorious Ina, a look not of bewilderment on her face, as all the rest of the world seemed to share, but one of smug amusement. For it was her day in the rain.

Papa Bo's Big-Ass Barbeque

Everyone who worked for Papa Bo's Meats—which happened to be the whole town—came out for the annual barbecue. Three huge pigs turned on the spit, Angie McPherson's boy, Abel, working the crank this year. For two full days the fire had been burning in the big concrete pan that had been built for the purpose, and the embers now wriggled and writhed deliriously. Bright afternoon sunlight glanced off the buttered flesh of the pigs, stealing a prolonged kiss from the vibrant green grass of Papa Bo's barbecue yard.

Though it was only half past the hour normally set aside for cola and baseball practice, the ice-cold beer and wine coolers flowed liberally. Both work and school had let out at eleven a.m., as they did every year on the last Friday in June, and the good people of Downey had been splashing around in their merrymaking for some hours now. The kids played their games, the adults theirs, and the affair made every appearance of being the rich success it had nearly always been. Alas, it is what lies beneath appearances that counts.

As Papa Bo sat out on the veranda looking over his kingdom, he sensed he wasn't the only one feeling anxious. Here it was nearing five and Dogger, his master butcher, still hadn't arrived. Per tradition, Dogger had driven out of Downey bright and early yesterday morning, sporting the faded logo of Papa Bo's Meats. Not a word had been heard from him since. Usually he phoned on the morning of the event to say when to expect him; this morning, nothing. Papa Bo was generally a kind and patient man, yet this was an offense to rank up there with '92's notorious "storming of the roast pit," which unfortunate incident had inspired the transition to the current above-ground method of preparing the pork. If he'd told Dogger once, he'd told him a dozen times: yes, there are expectations, but don't feel obliged to satisfy them at all costs. If you run into a snag, then so be it. We'll get along.

But if Papa Bo knew one thing about Dogger, it was that he was dogged in his purpose, whatever the enterprise. He was a veritable motherfucker for getting the job done, and done right. Sadly, with regards to the present situation, that knowledge did not help put Papa Bo at ease. He extinguished his cigar and paced the porch. In the distance the abattoir stood majestic and beautiful on its patch of higher ground. Dogger was an artist within those walls, the worker's worker, an etcher of wonderfully un-thought-out manifestos. Something had to be wrong, didn't it? Dogger would never voluntarily cause discomfort to his fellow townsfolk.

Bo lit another cigar, puffed only a time or two before he put it out beneath his boot. He knew he should go down and mingle, but what news to give? He hated fielding questions. Dogger, unless you're dead or behind bars somewhere, you're in a world of trouble.

Dina rushed up to the old man as soon as she saw him, wanting to know when she would be moving up to the front office. Papa Bo, as usual, didn't have the heart to tell her that the smell of the slaughterhouse was so deep in her skin now, he could never bring her up to the fragrant offices and air conditioning and visitors.

"Where's Frank?" he asked her conversationally. Posing question for question might prove a worthwhile tactic.

"He's down there mixing. Got a cigar?" Ah yes, a little smoky flavor to the aroma already surrounding her thin frame. Before Frank she was Dogger's girl. Papa Bo had once caught them full-sweatin' it among the carcasses.

She smoked, inhaling, as he looked for help among the crowd. It soon came in the form of Josh and Vera Culpep. They proved thoroughly sloshed, spilling their beverages all over each other as they accompanied their slurred words with gestures.

"When's Dawg evuh gonna show?" Vera drawled, with more of the prison than the plantation in her deep southern voice.

"Yeah, what gives?" joined Josh. As if the whole cussed barbecue were about the two of them.

"He'll be along," said Papa Bo. "Don't you worry. Where's Bobby Boy?"

Josh looked around, craning strangely through his glaze. "Where is 'at boy, Vera?"

"He's such a good boy," she extolled. She might have been talking about a dog.

They went off in search of cheese moons, only to be scooped up by the Afftons, who doubtless wanted to know what the old man had had to say. Dina stared after them, blowing billows of smoke from her lungs. "They don't know where that boy is most of the time, Papa Bo. Wasn't it Bobby Boy who cut through the fence so he and his friends could get a look inside the slaughterhouse?"

"Sure," he said, reaching out to grab Den Helter's arm as the burly man passed.

"Keep walking," Papa Bo said in a low voice. "I'm trying to get away from Dina."

Den didn't seem his normal friendly self. It wasn't like him to over-look an excuse to make some inanely humorous remark. His hands remained stuffed in his overalls as the much smaller Papa Bo squeezed his shoulder affectionately. When they were out of range of Dina's radar ears, the old man asked Den if he was all right.

"People are gettin' uptight, Bo. You know what I mean. They're startin' to make jabs at me and Lou both. Just like last year, when it was so damn hot and me and my brother took off our shirts. People get uptight, what with the beer, the sun, the waitin' and all."

"Come on, Den," Papa Bo said encouragingly. "I think we need to get some suds in you, big fella. You'll be all right."

"Uh-uh, Papa Bo. Makes my belly poke out. I ain't drinkin' no more beer. Uh-uh."

"Okay," said Bo, "then why don't we go have a look at how the pigs are comin'? Whaddya say?"

Den was for that, though he sulked as they went. Bo rather suspected the sensuous assault of the hot, slathered hogs would take care of his blues—hell, Bo himself could do with a tease to his palate. Sure enough, as they bobbed through the midst of too many mixed expressions, Den's nose lifted, tasting the air. Very soon they found themselves encapsulated in the voluptuous coaxes of the pork and sauce bouquet. Ordinarily the designated applicator—in this case the normally imperturbable Ace Bolen—didn't start applying the sauce to the buttered meat till Dogger had arrived. The waiting, it seemed, had gotten to everyone.

Stepping out of Den's shadow, where he'd been hiding from potential inquisitors, Papa Bo asked after the sauce.

"Mona worked on it last night," Ace said. "I've been addin' beer here and there. You know."

"Well, it's looking delicious, Ace. Mouth-watering."

"Right. So where's Dog?"

Bo pursed his lips. "I was hoping you wouldn't ask me that, Ace. Because, unfortunately, I don't have an answer."

Ace nodded, adding more suds to the sauce. He stirred a moment then looked up, peering brightly into the old man's eyes. "I hate to think what might happen, boss. Already they're starting to gravitate towards certain folk." He glanced at Den.

Den didn't need the spelling. He said: "Just like I told you, Papa Bo."

Papa Bo nodded. "Why don't you and Lou go on home then, Den. I'll send somebody when Dogger gets here."

Den turned his hulking frame around to face the old man. "Huh?"

"I'll send somebody. Go home."

A dark expression came over Den's features. He'd lost the ax-throwing competition three years running because of losing focus to a very similar expression. "Are you tellin' me to go home before we've cut the meat, boss?"

Papa Bo regretted the suggestion. It wasn't Den's fault he was the big country boy he was—

A commotion caused both men to turn their heads. Den let out a yelp and began lumbering his way towards the crowd that had gathered around his brother. What next, thought Papa Bo, shaking his head at Ace Bolen and chasing after the big denim overalls. What damn next. Dogger, I'm going to kill you when you finally do get here.

The crowd brimmed with beer and uptightness. Fingers accused Lou of sins which weren't sins so much as lot and circumstance. What did he think he was going to get, shoveling it down like he did? Routinely devouring whole animals for snacks? Fattening himself up like a hog for slaughter? It was time his big-ass fessed up that he was nothing but a slab of meat.

Den loomed, two great hands poised to remove the first two heads within his reach. Papa Bo let out a warning, but just as it escaped his mouth, the cranky blare of a laid-on horn sounded in the waning afternoon. All eyes turned to see Dogger driving up the road in the old refrigerated truck he had last been seen in yesterday morning.

A spontaneous cheer rose, with the voices of Papa Bo and Den and Lou right in there with them. Dogger pulled up in an ecstasy of gravel and dust, jumping out with a "Sorry I'm late! Ran into some setbacks." In two long strides he was at the back of the truck, wrenching up the lever to release the bar. He cast both doors wide lest any eye miss the success he'd had on his mission for this year's barbecue.

The cloud of cool air parted like curtains to reveal what lay behind. An initial collective inhalation was followed by individual gasps of appreciation as news spread from person to person. Out of a hard-summoned respect, the folk in front backed up so those behind could see. Patches of skinned meat became torsos, then whole bodies drawn up on hooks, moist fleshy flanks teasing the shared appetite of the witnesses. Big meaty buttocks! And not just three, as was the usual, but *six*! Twice the number of the pigs on the spit. Goddamn, Dogger, do be late more often!

Tom Krants and Berry Louis stepped forward to help the veteran cut the prime portions. Shooing the lolling tongues back, they carried the cuts across the barbecue yard to where the swine turned lovingly on the spit. Angie McPherson's boy scampered out of the way, shaking his tired arm. Ace Bolen told the men to hang loose while he drew the skewer back out of the heat, then he helped them load the meat up under the ribs of the pigs. Now only to wait for the stuffing to warm up just right. The pigs had been cooked to a more than adequate depth to complement the choice flesh, and the choice flesh was best rare as possible.

Everybody was enraptured by the feast at last made whole, Papa Bo took Dogger aside. Before the old man could voice his mind, Dogger's hand came up as if he had been the one fielding the questions.

"I know what you're going to say, Bo. What can I tell you? There wasn't a single hitchhiker weighing over a hundred and a half. I had to visit the city."

"So you bring back *six?*"

"Yes, yes, but Papa Bo, the city has such a crop to choose from."

Papa Bo was about to ask his butcher if he'd ever heard of a telephone, then he reminded himself how despicable questions were—especially when the questioned had just saved the day.

Tousling Dogger's hair, Bo led him back into the revelry without another word on the matter. As they went, however, the old man couldn't resist sneaking a sidelong glance at his master butcher's spreading flanks.

Junkyard Fetish

Ooh, *had his sex,* unh, *had his body,*
Had him beggin' for my honey,
Had him chained and screamin' mercy,
Quench my hunger, suck my thirsty...

The *ooh* and the *unh* got him, as always. He didn't give a damn if he
was on the freeway, he was unzipping. Alice helped him get it out, but
when she bent down to do more, he pulled her away by the hair.

"What?"

He didn't answer. He had seized his nobility in his hands and was
stroking, hard.

Ooh, *shared his lust,* unh, *shared his naughty,*
We were bathin' in the honey...

He was swollen to bursting already, and the song was still in its
opening verse; the blood part hadn't even come yet.

"Save some for me, won't you?" Alice said.

"Shut up!" he panted.

Fucking Alice. She would never be the woman Amy was. *Never.*

"You're gonna get us killed, Ricky. Here, let me have the wheel."

He did, finding leverage with his free hand, giving it all he had with
the other.

When he went, he went with a bang. Just like Amy, who had left him

128

chained to the door of the Mercury.

Untwisting the wire that held the flaps of the torn fence together, they made their way among the wrecks to the same heap of mangled metal they always did. Alice was more eager than him today, maybe because of what she had witnessed on their way here. He remembered a time when he literally had to pin her down. An erstwhile stripper, having worked in one of the seediest spots in the city, she had encountered all sorts. But she had never played what he and Amy had always referred to as blood games until he introduced her. He didn't know where one went to find such sport; he and Amy had discovered it on their own, with a little unintended help from Amy's dad.

The rear door on the driver's side hung askew, open enough to slip a heavy chain around each side of the window frame, but little more. Bits of safety glass clung to rotting rubber, and in place of the vehicle's one shattered window was a thick piece of plywood, bolted in place, ragged from the claws of hounds, particularly around the holes the chains fed through. Dried blood still stained the area where the door had once molded with the car's body. The place where the damage had occurred, where the impact of the truck had been absorbed, was rusted almost through. Buck, Amy's dad, said the driver and two passengers were killed. Having been hired on at the junkyard long after the Mercury was dragged onto the lot, Ricky took the old man's word for it.

The appeal of the Merc went beyond its history, though. The car was back in the corner of the yard, about as far from the office as possible. It had a huge back seat, everything two starry-eyed bloodlovers could ask for in an afternoon escape. But most attractive was the element of danger, pungent like old oil, shrill like stripped metal on the tongue.

Each day at closing time, the old man took a ride around the lot in a forklift, satisfying himself that everyone was gone before he let loose the dogs. He couldn't see back in the niche where the Merc had been laid to rest, but they could hear him as he drove past. They knew they had minutes to attain the peak they had been teasing at for the last half hour or so, unlock the chains that bound whichever one was slab that day, and slip back through the rip in the fence. They had cut it close so many times, the old man thought nothing of his hounds racing off in that direction, howling their heads off. He assumed it was to do with the punks who lived on the next block, always pitching back tall boys and flipping people off.

The stupid old man probably never realized those were the very boys his daughter had formed her pop band with, went to fame and fortune with, leaving junkyard games to Daddy and Ricky and whomever else might want to experiment.

The visible links of chain worked at Ricky's nerves and appetites as he approached in the company of his inferior replacement partner. He hated Alice and supposed eventually the game would go too far and he would kill her, leave her body for the hounds. The old man didn't come back here any more, no need to worry about him finding what was left. And if he did, he wouldn't be able to tell her from the bones of the woman who started the whole cycle.

It was all cyclic. Ricky had watched the afternoon shows enough to know it was all fucking cyclic. TV was all he had to do before he found Alice at the strip bar; he had quit the junkyard when Amy left.

He looked at Alice and wondered why he hadn't told her everything—not through the casual remark, but in credible detail. In theory it would only enhance the experience. Maybe it was impatience. He'd virtually had to force her the first few times, before she finally admitted she had begun to crave their afternoons. He didn't have the wait power to let her come to terms with the fact that Amy, as a teen, had witnessed the old man in the Merc with his secretary. Amy had not just gotten her eyes' fill of their kinky backseat amusements—the plywood had no doubt been installed to keep out the gnashing, maniacal dogs, which the old man clearly liked to have about when he drilled the woman—she had watched the old man kill her.

From the lot's chain-link perimeter, Amy had looked on. It was night, no less than the fourth in a row that her father had made *her* let out the dogs. Terrified of them and their insanely possessive loyalty to their owner, she carried out his wishes from outside the fence, using a long rod to shove aside the beam that held the double doors of the ramshackle structure which contained the beasts. The fourth night she had dared to see what the hell was going on in the back of the lot.

The way the old man did it was an image that screwed itself in permanently; he had pushed his secretary's head into the crack of the askew door, where the dogs could get at it.

Ricky saw it in his mind's eye as he led Alice around to the passenger side rear, opening the door on screechy hinges and shoving her inside.

The tools were on the floor, scattered among the safety glass, screaming at him as always to be picked up and used in one fell, double-fisted stroke. He didn't. He wouldn't. Dead blood was no good to anybody. Besides, it was his turn slab. Alice got to work the instruments this afternoon.

"God, I loved watching you in the car," she breathed on his neck as she closed the locks.

Per routine, he tried the locks, remembering how he had tried them then, that last day with Amy. As always they were secure; he was bound; he was slab.

Alice removed her shirt, revealing the scarred mounds of her once beautiful breasts. She placed one nipple against the mutilated tissue at the top of his scalp, where the hair no longer grew. She thought the area a product of the game from the past, which indeed it was, only in a different way. That particular experience he would never share, in detail or otherwise. It wouldn't shrug off like Alice's electing not to believe him about his former blood partner being the same Amy who was known in the world of pop music as *Honeygirl*. Funny, if she only bothered to look outside the blood-tainted windows of her little dollhouse occasionally, she would eventually come across the former-junkyard-girl-rises-to-the-top-of-the-charts story. He'd seen it himself on a couple talk shows.

Yeah, he understood how an old man could grow sick of his dull, unimaginative partner. He could understand how one person might want to feed another to the dogs. This was why he did not hate Amy. He had forgiven her even before the unleashed beasts came howling and slinging their bloodthirst. He had loved her even as their snarling, salivating muzzles squeezed through the crack of the door, tearing at his head, which, thanks to her enviable, textbook expertise with the chain, she had rendered virtually immobile. He had delighted in her even as his fingers madly worked to get around the key, which she had left in the lock for him, like a last demented amusement. God did he love her.

Ooh. Unh.

"Come on," he said through his teeth. "Come on, Amy."

Alice was used to being Amy. She didn't care. She liked the song too. She wouldn't have cared if she had been presented proof that the Top Ten hit, *The Games We Played*, was silently dedicated to Ricky. Bloodlust just didn't fucking care.

Ricky had long since fixed it so the old cassette player could be turned on via a direct link to the battery. The recorded tape came on now, somewhere between *The Games We Played*, *The Games We Played* and *The Games We Played*, the constantly recycled song of songs stolen from her debut CD.

"What do you want from Amy, huh?" said Alice. "A little of the cut love?"

"Yeah, Honeygirl. Come on with the cut love. Bleed me, you twisted bitch."

She held a fillet knife with a flimsy blade. It had come from a tool or tackle box in the trunk of one of the wrecks. Ricky used to go around with Amy looking through the cars, hoping not to run into any customers lest the compulsion to contribute to the bones in the back of the lot come over them. Alice didn't know that, and didn't care. Her addiction had sucked all the superfluousness that plagues the unseasoned right out of her. Not that she wanted any blood but his. Ricky was the dealer. Ricky's was the best. No one detested her like Ricky.

> Ooh, *had his sex,* unh, *had his body,*
> *Had him beggin' for my honey...*

"Open your mouth, Ricky, stick out your tongue." She liked the tongue because it healed so well, so fast. He had always thought it weak of her, but admittedly enjoyed it himself.

> *Had him chained and screamin' mercy,*
> *Quench my hunger, "SUCK MY THIRSTY..."*

"What the hell?" It was Alice who spoke, reacting to Ricky's start as well as to the voice that had intruded on their game. He watched her eyes dart from window to window, back down at his amazed, inspired face.

> *"Yeah the taste buds, mmm the tickle*
> *Yeah the taste buds, mmm the trickle*
> *Of the blood*
> *Our married blood*
> Ooh, *the blood*
> *That is the honey..."*

"Hello, Amy!" he announced, rising against the chains.

"You've taken a whore," she said, still invisible to them.

"Tired of waiting for the old one," he said, laughing. "Get in here, you. Where are you?"

He was looking at Alice as he spoke, pasting her with it...this confused child, sorry excuse for a lover.

Still Amy did not show. She was a voice. That voice that had titillated the world...

> *Quench my hunger, suck my thirsty...*

"If I was the whore, I'd run," the voice said, "'cause my dad's coming and he's *mean*."

Sufficiently frightened, Alice grabbed her shirt, backing off him. "Save some for me," she spat. "For *me*, you fucker." Then she was shoving open the door, and dodging wreckage as she ran away.

"Get in here, you!" repeated Ricky. "I've missed—"

Then he heard the barking. Her face flashed in the window, made-up like MTV, and the *ooh* and the *unh* and a tire tool in her hand.

As it came crashing through the window, the noise of the dogs rose to a not altogether alien crescendo of bloodlust.

133

Clockwork

The clarity of the morning deteriorates to senselessness by noon, and then I cannot say it. Every word catches fire as it appears on the screen, chronicling a thrashing self-infliction and mutilating my eyes. Until, ritually, my head implodes. In sleep, that hour or two, they put my skull back together, delicately removing the fragments and shards from my brain. The rifts in the pulp will not heal, but the morning brings clarity again, slightly less than yesterday's and slightly more than tomorrow's.

It is twenty-nine minutes past ten now. Yesterday at this time it was twenty-eight minutes past ten.

The Glass Encrusted Nest

As the Colonel moved off the trail into the patch of young birches, the glint intensified, its source catching the sun in fragments and slivers. The trees were still skeletal after the stripping winter, and the object readily emerged from among the branches, revealing itself to be a large bird's nest. It rested a little above eye level, affording the Colonel an easy view of the pieces of glass that had lured him off the trail. Some clear, some colored, the bird had woven the shards in among the twigs. The creation might have been that of a touched basket weaver. Accident? Ornamentation? Defense? The Colonel had never seen its like.

It was a natural for the Colonel's collection of natural things, so he claimed it. Gently bending the branch down to assure himself that no eggs or nestlings occupied the strange basket, he pulled the nest free of the jointed woody fingers that clutched it. An edge cut him. A drop of blood rose, seeming to materialize on the glass that caused it. A sense of wonder bathed him. As part of his collection, this find would excel.

He had walked not ten steps when he heard a terrible caw-screech. He searched the sky over the naked birches, the tops of the surrounding firs, but he could not locate the voice. Offering a silent apology to avian mothers and their sylvan domain in general, he proceeded to the trail. The voice remained silent as he followed his tracks back to the cabin, but he imagined an eye watching him cradle the nest lovingly in his hands.

Inside his cabin, under the light, it was an amazing thing. The pieces of glass, having come mostly from broken bottles, were placed so that they curved into the circle, suggesting concentricity. Moreover, there seemed to be a pattern to their placement relative to each other. No two

135

fragments of similar size or color were neighbors. The variety simultaneously astounded and enchanted. Modern sculpture take note.

He walked over to the bookcase along the near wall. Before introducing the nest to its place of honor, he examined his collection of natural finds occupying the shelves. Seven years of living and hiking here in the Black Forest had produced a few interesting items. The fully intact marten skull, sharp fangs gleaming dryly, had been unearthed in a landslide. The sparkly *Edelstein* had been plucked from among the stones of a 2300-year-old Celtic ring-wall. The torn neon-blue wing of the mounted butterfly had actually been in a lizard's mouth when he happened upon it. The other shelves held similar oddities, all for his own enjoyment as few people ever came around.

Somehow these things meant more to him than the carvings he sold out of *Der Kuckuck Haus* in the village. The Black Forest relinquished such treasures less readily than the wood the Colonel sawed and whittled to form. This nest he held so delicately in his hand was certainly the rarest treasure *Der Schwarzwald* had yielded to date.

The nest worked well on the top shelf. The overhead bulb gave it added distinction, illuminating miracles in the shards, meaning and genius where none could logically apply. One thing lacked, however. A proper pedestal for this most unusual natural find. He went out to the woodshed to take care of the problem forthwith.

He liked the band saw because every corner could be observed as the sawdust flew and the figure took shape. He thought to save himself the trouble and grab a sufficiently sized piece of wood out of the trash receptacle, but the nest deserved more. He lay details to his eight-inch square pedestal that he never would have dreamed of adding to another piece—such that he was absorbed into the night, forgetting supper. It was sometime during those unknown hours, in that unknown zone, that the mother struck.

Three windows of his workshop faced three corners of the compass, while the door looked back towards the house. All of them were open, a ventilation system he could not have done without. The bird came through the north window, black and huge, shattering glass that was not there, shocking the Colonel out of his trance. It screamed as it landed on the pedestal in progress, tearing the chunk of wood free from the saw, causing the strip of flexible band to jump its pulley. Giant black wings slammed against everything the Colonel kept in his shed—tables, machines, him. He fought but it would not forgive.

By sheer instinct he grabbed the lighter fluid off the shelf, squirted it in the direction of the bird, which was everywhere. The bird screamed and stabbed at him as he groped for the emergency kit, where he knew a pack of matches to be. Shielding his efforts with his elbows, he managed to set the pack aflame, tossing it blindly into the shed as he forced the door to with his body.

He raced around the structure throwing the windows closed, but he'd no way of latching them from outside. No matter, the bird spent its furies upon the last window he held. Against its violence, he wedged a piece of rock, then ran.

The shed burned from within, its windows warping rather than dis-integrating. Outlets took the vapors away and in time the place was done. For two days the Colonel let the shed cool. He stayed inside the cabin mostly, admiring the nest, wondering over the fact that it was still in his possession. On the third day he had to see.

The bird was there, its mighty wings fused into the like material of the windows, its tail spread in plumes of sharp glass, its shiny claws still clutching the cinder.

Dance Therapeutic

Stepping into the doorway of the room was like coming home again. Events came surging out of the past, forcing him to grasp the doorjamb for support. Rarely a day went by that Domino didn't visit those images, but this brought it back all at once, with tremendous force. He had chosen his career field for personal therapy; this was beyond therapy. This was beyond bizarre. This was his most penetrating nightmare.

Hanging from the ceiling by what looked like fishing line were individual human organs: heart, liver, lung, kidney, spleen, stomach, etc. In each instance the line had been threaded through a hole, possibly made by an awl or large needle, and attached to the ceiling with industrial staples. The organs hung some twelve to fifteen inches from the ceiling, variously positioned over the queen-size bed. On the bed lay the naked dead body of a male in his mid-thirties, eye sockets empty and black, their contents among the internal parts suspended from the ceiling. Whatever mess had been made in the removal of the victim's eyes, it had been thoroughly cleaned up. Beneath the still fresh corpse the sheets were a pristine, virginal white. The body itself, at least the visible side, was marked in no other way. The eyes appeared to be the man's only contribution to the frozen dance of human parts.

Domino was here because of the nature of the scene, but it wasn't his trained professional eye which saw through the apparent lack of order in the locations of the separate organs. It was a little boy's eye—a little boy who had committed to unfading memory the unspeakable things he had seen.

A voice from the present saved him from falling into the pit opening before him. It came from behind, its owner looking over his shoulder into the room. "I don't fucking know with the crazies, Domino. Is this the weirdest thing you've seen to date?"

How to answer that in a grown-up's voice. "It's weird, Branton. It's weird."

He lingered there for five minutes, never venturing beyond where he stood framed in the doorway. When he turned away, he found Branton still standing behind him, viewing the tableau for his own reasons. Brushing past, Domino mumbled that the investigation team could have it now; he'd seen all he needed to see.

"There's something else," Branton said after him, causing him to stop in his tracks. "Something that was removed from the scene."

Domino turned. "Yes?"

"The body had candles in its eye sockets. They were burning. Instead of just pinching out the flames, Livac removed them. Both candles were black, if that says anything."

"Thanks, Bran," Domino said as he pushed his way through the uniforms, desperately seeking air.

An hour later he was home, standing in the kitchen with the phone in his hand, remembering the slow, fumbling rotary types of the past.

Daddy, Daddy, where are you? Answer the phone, Daddy.

Daddy had not answered the phone. Daddy wasn't at his office. Daddy had never gone to his office. Daddy wasn't Daddy anymore.

The now intruded on him again. "Dawn House," the cheerful voice spoke into his ear.

"Miss Fry? Excuse me, *Kay*, this is Michael Domino. I'm looking for my father."

"Hi Michael. Your father started his job today. Have you tried him there?"

"Kay, something's—no, actually, Kay, I had forgotten that was today. My apologies."

"Of course, Michael. We're so proud of him. He is doing so w—"

"Yes, thank you. Goodbye."

Oh Christ.

The phone rang the moment he put it back in its cradle.

"Yes?" said Domino.

"Heya, Domino. Nelson. What are you doing there? Branton said you disappeared from the scene."

"Yeah. Sorry." Daddy, Daddy, where are you?

"We need you at the station. Why the hell are you there?"

"How did you know to call here?" Domino said.

"Bran said you looked spooked. I figured I'd try your house. Seems it wasn't such a long shot. Are you? Spooked?"

"Never me, boss," he lied. "I'll be down in a bit."

Oh Christ.

His earliest memories of being his father's son were from age three, when whole words surrounded him in his bed. Yet he thought he remembered a three-year-old having memories of alphabet blocks in the playpen. He couldn't be sure though. Various psychologists had chased the use of these learning tools back to his crib, where the process of becoming the prodigy had begun in earnest.

He remembered being told by the magnificent IQ that was his father that he would accomplish great things. Make great discoveries. He remembered his mother's soft complement to the educator's voice. "Your father's right, Michael. You have so much potential, being your father's son. The universe is out there, waiting."

Daddy had despised the complement, Michael remembered as well. The various psychologists had traced that back to a young man of exceeding mental stature luring a young woman of exceptional good looks into his fascinating intellectual sphere, then becoming bored of her with age. They made it all seem so simple. Perhaps on some level Michael had become the psychologist to convince himself that it was cut and dry. Certainly he'd had identifiable reasons for going specifically into the criminal branch of the science.

He had been dissected so many times, by others and by himself, that there was little left to analyze. His father, on the other hand, was so densely layered as to be impossible to analyze completely. Which is why they should never have permitted the elder Domino to roam the earth a free man again. Michael himself had stated it most succinctly in one of his communications with his father through the Plexiglas barrier.

"Daddy, you need to realize that you are here for the duration. They haven't any real understanding, much less a panacea for the psychology of a man who kills his wife and leaves her body to bleed through the ceiling of their son's bedroom."

His father had looked back at him with eyes fogging in recollection, corners of his mouth tending dangerously towards a smile. And there was that reason, too: his father lacked any semblance of remorse or regret, though he seemed capable of revisiting the day on impulse.

But what haunted Michael the most was not the occasional crooked smile behind a synthetic barrier but rather the image of his room that afternoon when he returned from tutors. That is where the falseness of youth was unveiled; where magic and fantasy ended. The incomprehensible expressions of the lunatic in his sterile kingdom were after-tremors.

It had been a Friday, the best day of the week, the one evening he got to stay up late and watch TV. Exercises didn't start again till Sunday morning, a genius father's substitute for church. Of course he still had anatomy to study before dinner. The cardboard organs had only been up a week, having replaced the solar system, which had replaced the multiplication tables, which had replaced...Boy, being six sure tough.

"Hi Mom!" said the young Michael as he came through the front door. As on every Friday afternoon after returning home from "tutors" with Ms. Cocker, he was in a great mood. His tutor lived three doors down and had done something great for the world before arthritis set in.

When his mom didn't answer, Michael thought nothing of it; she was around somewhere. His dad would still be at the university. He poured a bowl of cereal, ate it while he read from *Robin Hood*, wincing a little as Robin caught the blade of the assassin's sword in his hand. When he was finished with his snack, he folded the corner of the page and ventured down the hallway to his bedroom. Opening the door, he was greeted by its familiar odor. He fell onto his bed, looking up at the lesson in human anatomy hanging from the ceiling. Body organs weren't nearly as fun as planets, but he knew it wasn't really about fun; it was about learning. Funtime was Friday evening with TV, and sometimes Saturday at the library.

The heart, he noticed, was moving slightly, as if there were a light draft. He wondered if it was his breath drifting around the room with nowhere else to go. As the angle of the cardboard cutout grew more obtuse, he noticed something behind it running along the ceiling back to the light fixture. Curious, he sat up, peering between the cutouts, finding a similar line—a dark red line, he observed—running between the fixture and the lung organ. He stood on the bed to better inspect this invader in his room. To his fascination, the line was fluid, and the fluid had run down the strings on which the organs hung and over the profiles themselves, beading at the bottom, poised to drop like tears.

He extended a hand, came away with one of the drops on his fingertip, smelled it.

"Mom!" he called, more out of an urge to introduce her to this oddity than anything else. He had concluded that the substance was blood, and that it had a source in the room above, but he did not associate it with human blood. People bled in smears mostly, as his knees and elbows had proven a time or two—not like this. A bucket had been tipped over, something his dad was working on, something like that. The room above was after all in the attic, where little boys were not allowed to go.

"Mah-uhhhm!" he called again on his way out into the hall.

Where was she? Once, when she didn't show for a half hour or so after he got back from his lessons, he had followed the footpath down to the neighborhood pond, where he found her sitting on a bench watching the ducks and weeping for all she had. It was her favorite place, she had told him once. The farthest extent of her world.

He headed that way now, thinking about blood wandering its own paths. When he reached the pond, he found only the boy from next door skipping stones. Brett, who was two years his better in age, looked at him as he always did, as if Michael were a freak because he didn't go to school like all the other kids. When Michael asked him if he had seen his mom, Brett's eyes grew sadistically bright and Michael knew the teases were coming.

"I thought you were s'posed to be so smart. Aren't you the boy genius? Can't even find your own mommy."

Michael retreated up the hill, tears stinging his eyes.

Inside, he called again, to no answer. He walked down the hall as though to his execution. He ascended the stairs as though to some after-life beyond the clouds of numbers and letters and planets and human organs that had drifted over his head all his days. The door didn't want to give beneath his little hands, but finally did, swinging to the left, open-ing up the attic and its mysteries to him. He had never been here alone. A few small steps showed him that he still wasn't. His mom waited with open arms, involuntarily pouring herself out to him.

He fell as he rushed down the stairs, struck his nose, producing further evidence that blood did run so profusely. The phone in his hand turned red. He managed to dial his dad's office. Daddy, Daddy, where are you? Answer the phone, Daddy. But Daddy wasn't there.

The hand on his head, as familiar a gesture as it was, made him scream. And scream.

Domino went to the station and sat with Nelson and the detectives assigned to the case in the lieutenant's closed office. Branton and Lundy occupied the chairs along the wall, while Domino and Nelson were separated by the big desk strewn with job litter.

Nelson regarded Domino for a moment, as if to satisfy himself that his psychologist hadn't lost his grip, then got right to it. "The body you saw belonged to one Brett Frier, CPA, unmarried, lived alone. Approximate time of death...Bran? Right, ten a.m. As for evidence, to this point they haven't found shit. All we can do for now is focus on the character of this creep. This is going to be a motherfucker if you ask me. To go to such detail to make your goddamn point—we got a real crazy on our hands."

That was Domino's cue. He only partially surprised himself when he skipped type, profile, and expert insight to offer this: "They let my dad out two weeks ago, Jack."

Nelson frowned, casting a glance at the detectives. "I heard," he said. "Have you been in touch?"

"Yeah. He wanted to see me, but I declined. He's been at a sort of halfway house. I wonder what the other residents think about having a psycho killer around."

"It's been, what, thirty years? That's a long time, Domino."

"Yeah."

"It's gotta be tough on you," Nelson said. "Look, best therapy is putting your mind on something else. Bury yourself in the current case. When I lost Vonda, that was how I got through. It shouldn't be too hard to do that on this one. Like I said, this creep's gonna be a challenge."

Domino thought about telling him to get his head out of his ass and listen, but instead merely nodded.

"Okay," Nelson said. "Let's start with the candles. What do you make of burning black candles? Satanist props?"

If only it were that simple, Domino thought.

Daddy wasn't Daddy anymore, that much was clear to the young Michael. The features behind the flickering light of the candles were familiar enough, but their expression was strange. And the voice...it might as well have been a stranger's voice speaking to Michael over the coffee table. He kept his eyes on the backs of his hands, which danced with reflections from the candles. His left hand was stained with blood from his nose.

"The flames are your mother's ghost in your eyes," said his father, delicately touching one of the columns of wax. "What truth those young eyes of yours have witnessed tonight. Do you understand about your mom?"

"I think so," Michael murmured.

"Where is she now, do you think?"

He didn't know. When his mom had spoken of heaven, his father had scoffed. He remembered hearing her once, through the bathroom wall, shouting at his father about that very topic. *What am I to teach him then?*

That he's going to the Great Equation when he dies?

"I don't know," he confessed to the face. "Where?"

"She's in your memories, Michael. Remember that. That's where they go when they have nothing else to offer us. Into our memories."

He thought about it, amid the candle flickers. But one question was not answered so easily.

"So where," he said to the stranger sitting across from him, "has my daddy gone?"

They were impatient to do the autopsy, so Domino was given the private viewing he requested right away. Standing over the body, looking into its empty eye sockets, he had a sense of the pit and the void and the nothingness of his upbringing. Yet what precisely had his father meant by that particular touch? The candles, the bodily organs—they clearly spoke to the past. What did the removal of the eyes say?

And what, for that matter, did Brett Frier have to do with anything? As Domino looked into the holes, he remembered the eyes they had once contained marking him as a freak. But how could his father have known about the way Brett and all the rest of them had looked at him?

"It was Daddy you should have been looking at, not me," he said over the dead face. "It was Daddy who made me the freak."

I thought you were s'posed to be so smart, it said back. *Can't even find your own mommy.*

He walked away, pressing at his headache, trying to work out how killers killed and moms went to flickers. He turned back suddenly, stabbing his finger at the face.

"It was Daddy, can you understand that?!"

I thought you were s'posed to be so smart. Aren't you the boy genius? it said.

He froze, staring. "What?"

Genius, it clarified mockingly.

The word was like a battering ram, smashing down doors inside him, revealing things that should have been left in the murk where they'd been buried.

"It was Daddy," he repeated, desperately. "Daddy, not me."

He stared into the sockets and saw flames, burning as they had only hours ago in Brett's room, shadows from the suspended organs dancing on the walls and ceiling, on his freshly stained hands.

"Where has my Daddy gone?" he whispered.

He's in your memories, Michael, came her voice. *Remember that. That's where they go when they have nothing else to offer us. Into our memories.*

Along the Footpath to Oblivion

Night fell like dark honey on the nothingland and one of the two men under the bridge wanted to know about something.

"Why do we do it, Mace?"

"Why do we do what, James?"

"Why do we kill?"

Mace didn't like the highwayman approach any more than his partner did. "What else is there to do, James?"

"I don't know—work?" He breathed on his glasses, wiped with his soiled teeshirt.

"We did that once. Remember? Let's talk about it over a beer, OK?"

"I want a motel. This time beer comes after. I need new glasses and I smell like blood."

"Fine." Mace knew it was a matter of waiting it out when James got like this.

"I mean it this time, Mace. Shower first."

"Glasses, too? Or can that at least wait till tomorrow?"

James had to admit that he really didn't want to *buy* a pair.

"Some'll come along," Mace said.

They watched a tanker out on the bay for a time. A ghostly moan-extending-into-a-screech sound came from over by the moorings, where one of the hulking captives tried its chains. Otherwise the night was in the grip of calm, the same calm that had settled over the two men. They always knew when they would score. It could be the most desolate, forbidden place, with the chances approaching nil, but that strange prescience was to be trusted.

Sometimes, however, the calm eluded them, and they roamed all night without success. James became hard to live with then, and Mace was not much better. Sometimes James would suggest they simply go to someone's home, do the ecstasy upon them right there, where they had all the comforts of the normals—shower, clean towels and sheets, a refrigerator with beer or yogurt. Mace patiently reminded him how he got, how enthusiastic, how loud, how *inspired* they both got in doing the thing. Oblivion became their only house, and for that reason they stayed out on the fringes, beyond ears more than eyes.

Voices stirred the calm. Two voices, heels on pavement, emerging from the unhardened pitch of night.

The one broke the surface with a confession. "I'm tired of this. Tired of this life, tired of this craving, tired of this disconnection."

"Arnold," said the other. "You need a fix, that's all."

"I hate it when you say that, Buzz. It ain't heroin, you know. It ain't crack. It ain't something you can just buy on the street corner."

"You forget if you think there's that much of a difference. Bottom line is, it's a hunger that screams to be satisfied."

"Don't you remember, Buzz, how it once was? How wide the margin separating this one thrill from all the others? It narrows with every trick."

Mace and James found themselves looking at each other by the thin light from the moorings. Above, the debaters drew nearer but weren't yet at the bridge.

"You hate it when I call it a fix, but you never hesitate to call it a trick."

Mace nodded his head.

"Yeah well, Buzz, it's become that cheap."

Now James nodded his.

There was a relatively long pause. Arnold, the raspier voice, broke it. "I wonder, man, you ever thought about performing the trick on me?"

They were on the bridge now. Even the tone of their steps had changed.

"I've thought about it. Especially when you get like this. But then who would I share the thing with? There aren't any others like us, you know. You ever really looked at the expression on Gramps when he gives us the key to our room? I'm sure we're not the only stained shirts to show up at the cheapest, seediest motel in the city, but he looks at us like he's looking at the face of God."

"Faces."

"What?"

"Faces, Buzz. We're two faces not one. I don't care how lost we are."

"It's God that has the one—did you say *lost*?"

Their approach stopped. Mace and James sensed it even before the footfalls were snatched away by night. The highwaymen raised their brows at one another, Mace mouthing the word *Now*?

But James shook his head.

The last spoken word, unlike the sound of the debaters' heels, still hung there, almost on top of the highwaymen. *Lost*.

The raspier voice: "What am I seeing in your face, Buzz?"

"*Lost*? As in *souls*? That's bringing religion into it. Never has religion been part of it."

"Is it fear I'm seeing in your face?"

"The blood vessel above my ear is throbbing. Fear is not the emotion."

"Ah." A pause separated this from his next words. "I've wondered what it would be like...at the receiving end."

Night bled with another wailing from the moorings.

"I've wondered if it would be different for one who has visited the act on others."

Silence from the occupant of space to whom he spoke. Silence from the trolls under the bridge, staring at each other, doing a bit of wondering themselves—wondering about the crazy mathematics of chance, about kindred souls on life's crazy roads. It was a more immediate prospect, though, that caused them to moisten their lips with their tongues.

There was a sound like that of air being knocked out of a set of lungs, a grunted exhalation followed by a moment's anticipatory lull. The next was a low, deep moan that gathered strength as it came, stretching into a rolling howl that in turn became something even fiercer, even stranger...

The notion of letting the song spread from victim to perpetrator and thereby to fullest blossom before acting was considered and discarded. Never had the two men under the bridge coveted the thing so. In spontaneous union they surged up the short bank, hoisted by the ripping, tearing, screaming stages they knew were on the razor's edge of taking command of the night.

The mouth formed an O as the eyes beheld the deed. The deed faltered only a second as it realized it was under scrutiny—how unimaginative its commencement wound must appear to these experts—then threw itself into its mutilations with all vigor.

He was alone, the perpetrator. Alone, the victim. They were one and the same man, and ribboning himself with the instrument jerking like a composer's wand in his hand.

Mace and James turned to look at each other, as synchronous a response as their aspiration towards oblivion. But neither found the other looking back as the music of the mutilator suddenly withered down a long tunnel to the single concentrated note of a great chain giving under stress.

Confounded, fragmented, but nothing so much as consumed by the lust, the two halves of the one man who had hidden under the bridge descended on the whirlwind to have a bath in its ecstasies themselves.

Hush Hush Little Kitty

Calendar year CC060, A-Dam on Uram. Central Port bustling with the comings and goings of tourists. Inside, the subtle fragrance of the air conditioning system; outside, the smell of crumbling fungus acrid on the mizzly air...staler for the weight of the moisture, which seemed to hold it in place against a useless breeze.

Unhappy faces as arrivals were forced to cross the distance between Landing and Receiving in the open air, thank you most graciously to a malfunction in the long tunnel which led to and from all gangways. The paneled glass façade that was the end to this particular inconvenience appeared to ripple like broken water as it accepted these unhappy faces into the giant main structure of Central Port.

Inside the hall, at Receiving, a sweeping arcing graffito scrawled over the entryway announced: *HUSH HUSH LITTLE KITTY AND YOU'LL HEAR IT WHISPERING BACK.* The words appeared to have been sprayed across the wall, shimmering delicately in the light of the over-heads, exhibiting a strange iridescence, harboring a strange meaning. Welcome to A-Dam on Uram. Check your psyches in at the main counter.

The river of bodies leading there, the various styles and cultures, the wide, eager eyes...and lost in it all, myself.

Myself...and the one who suddenly accosted me. An imparter of information, you know the type, inclined to brief me on the queer opalesque greeting that stared down at me.

"You know, man, if the power was shut down right now—you speak standard?—OK, if the whole port went black, you would find that message still glowing. You know why? Because it's biological, man. They keep the

151

shit in tanks, and spray it like paint. Only it's not paint. It's *alive*. It's alive in the tanks, it's alive on the wall. See the fuzzy edges—"

Cut off, as he was struck by a passing shoulder. Cursing as he turned back to me.

"Where was I?"

Where indeed. Stoned maybe, as I took him in. As I studied this moving photograph of him, gesture and garb. Certainly that look about him. That look of the free spirit, as my grandfather had referred to them. That same look, in fact, that the travel agent had worn.

I said, "The fuzzy edges."

"Yeah." A hesitant chuckle. "You get that too, do you? When you look at things?"

"Excuse me. I must be on my way."

"Yeah. Yeah, right. But hey, this your first visit to A-Dam?"

"Yes."

Regarding me wisely: "Do yourself a favor. Heed what it says. Take a moment and just listen. Listen beyond the surface clutter"—leaning in, as though to keep the secret between us—"and *you'll hear it whispering back*."

Then my imparter of information—yes, we all know the type— straightened up, satisfied with himself as he received a nod from me.

"I'll do that." And moved on my way.

Two hours later, and the bathroom mirror in Room 301, The Omni, etched with the little narcissisms we do ourselves before venturing out into new territory. The lobby door whispered to behind me, the charm and city lay before.

A-Dam on Uram was a beehive of activity, its tourism market in flowering array. I had been told it was a close replica of its mother city, and so it seemed to me, although I had never been to Terra's Amsterdam— which of course is off-limits now. What need, with the library of discs the travel agent had made available to me, with the memories of my grandfather, once stationed there, once in love with the place and its museums. Aesthetically anyway, Uram's copycat Mecca of tourism was exactly as I had imagined it—from the canals, the street lamps and the naughty window offerings right down to the expressions on the faces of the free-spirited mix of folk who thronged the place. All as advertised, all as remembered.

At least so far as my imagination could fit the pieces together.

I could not have known, for instance, precisely how a café would smell, with the smoky odors of its menu's herbal selections permeating the den's secret, moody confines. I could not have named the people glorified in its glass-protected antique posters, nor the artists whose eerie music bled from the boxes posted in no particular order about the hazy place.

No, I could only let my senses enhance the picture I had painted, and that to only a degree—then participation was required.

At my request, the recommendation. The recommendation, the substance *lustre*—as I had thought it might be.

Half of this corner of the galaxy recommended it. As such products went, this one had two distinct pluses. One, no harmful side effects; and two, the coming forth of who you really were. It was the second I was more interested in, although honestly I thought the whole thing a scam. I was more than a little suspicious of substance enhancers, especially when it came to their effect upon my identity. For if I wasn't who I thought I was, then why be me at all?

Who I thought I was, as it turned out, was still who I was—only without the static, the noise...the "clutter," as my hippie friend at Receiving had put it.

When I requested my check, I happened to drop my fist against the rubbery surface of the table, and a cloud of fine dust, very strong in smell, rose from the spot.

Stepping out of the café, I took in the fresh air, mizzly though it was. The acridness I had noticed before seemed so slight now, after the smoky interiors of the café, that it was hardly detectable. And yet it *was* detectable, to my heightened senses, and catching it in my nostrils made me remember the words that had welcomed me to this place. Amusing myself as much as anything else, I did as the graffito had instructed. I paused to listen. But just as the surface distractions were beginning to fade into the background, a woman stepped up to me.

She was lovely and soft, luminous hair, crystal eyes, and all the melodious substance of my mood.

"Who are you?" she asked.

I smiled at her. "That is a good question."

"Here..." she said, and placed in my hand a spongy object, a growth.

"What is this?" I asked.

"What isn't it," she said rhetorically. She looked into my eyes as she spoke—which wouldn't have been a thing, of itself, except that we were both participants.

"So..."

"So?" she echoed.

"So why are your eyes so bright on such a dreary day?"

"Hush," she said.

I did.

She watched me as I listened, and it seemed to me that she was listening, too, without trying, watching me.

As the noises of commercial A-Dam began to slip away, so did her command of me, that subtle, powerful effect of her as I stood before this woman, a victim of my senses.

"What is your name?" I reached, fearing I would lose her to the rising storm.

"Shhh. Listen."

I did, and I heard.

She touched my ear.

I heard it whispering back.

"Where is it coming from?" I asked her.

"There." She pointed at a sign. Its announcement spray-painted, so it appeared, and yet shivering in the awareness of itself.

"And there." Another.

"There!" She pointed at the thing in my hand. I looked at it, was certain it had begun to move. I resisted the urge to toss it away, to let the image of it writhing in my palm overtake me.

"Thank you," I said, handing it back to her, "but I have one of my own."

She smiled. "My name is Sha."

We walked along the crowded street, together, neither of us having invited the other, and the whole affair that was A-Dam on Uram stretching out before us like so much romance for the taking. We dodged bicycles, tossed coins to the colorful blankets of sidewalk musicians, amusedly declined the invitations of sprucely-dressed vendors and their often human wares. Together we visited another café, contributing to our certain *lustre* while enjoying the company of each other, without much talk, without much pressure, without the constraints of time or any of those other considerations that might stand out there in the way of pleasure and relaxation. We dined at a place called *Spores*, starting on sautéed mushrooms and moving on to a delicious something covered in mushroom sauce. We drank a bitter-tasting tea and desserted on a puffy "organic" bitter-tasting cake, and all the while loving it and complimenting the chef and laughing for the sheer joy of living the lustrous life.

When we were out among the busy sidewalks again, evening settling over the city, she pulled me to her with almost an urgency.

Whispering, "Where has the day gone?"

I couldn't tell her.

"Will we roam all night?"

"Wherever you wish."

And somehow we were away from there, and in her place, the sheets and the overhead fluorescence. Her elegance and my newly discovered freedom...

She sat atop me, naked. And mathematics were too severe, physics too limiting.

"So..."

"So."

"When my holiday is done..."

"We must return to our lives."

"It doesn't have to be so final."

After that first dialogue we had shared, strangers outside a café, I was never completely sure which one of us spoke, which one of us brought the thought to the surface.

"No, I suppose it doesn't."

"Then..."

She lowered herself to me, letting her breasts, the necklace she wore fall against my chest. We embraced tightly—lovingly, I thought, as I knew I was taking her back with me.

And then she was sitting again, the pressure of her thighs against my legs, the terrible beauty of her nearly overwhelming me.

I touched her necklace, pieces of gray pulpy matter strung along a chain.

"We only bloom for a day, you know."

"I know."

And that was enough. If it was all, it was enough.

There were no special arrangements to be made. Visas were a dime a dozen in this place. She might as well have been from here as anyplace else, and I suspected she had been here a long time. I noticed as we boarded the ship that she carried with her the scent of the place. She was smoking before we had set off. The stewardess said it was a nonrestrictive flight, she even brought us a pipe, and a package of the scented combustible crystals that aided in the burning of the stuff. I shared part of Sha's necklace with her as we were lifting off. We brought no more. On the other side of the galaxy it was forbidden.

We arrived on Abar Seven as the sun was completing its cycle. A pinkish glow possessed the northern skies, and the land was cast in a weird silvery-pink light. As we walked from the port toward the parking pad, I threw my arms wide, which was my way of welcoming my Sha to her new home. But she looked away to the north and the fading skies and said quietly, "Hush hush, little kitty..."

"We are not on Uram any longer," I reminded her.

"Shhh...listen."

I did as she bid, humoring her, thinking it would take some time to acclimatize her. At first I heard nothing, nothing unusual...then...

The whispering seemed to come from all around us, as though it had always been here, as though our arrival had nothing to do with it. I turned to Sha, who had fallen behind, and found her on the ground, on her knees, her arms failing her as she tried to reach out to me. Before my eyes she began to wilt, as from the strenuous task of living. The material of her, the flesh of her, becoming spongy, dry, brittle beneath the retreating eye of the day.

A Fixture on River Street

We had just come out of the Rumdog Café, feeling just about right, when Jamie drew our attention to the street musician on the next corner. The bright glint of his sax caught the eye first, then the man himself, black as the surrounding darkness, and every bit as ancient. The smell of the Mississippi was on the air, seeming to hover out here on the fringes, in accompaniment to the old man's soulful song. The din and bustle of thumping River Street to our backs, we might have been on the brink of a ghostland.

Jamie's first time to town, he was fascinated by the prospect of the lone jazz artist doing his thing in the soft light of an old-fashioned street lamp. They didn't have such fixtures where he came from. Tina and I were amused by his excitement, but followed him for the beacon of innocence that he was, not to be left out if any cosmic secrets were revealed.

Spotting us, the old man put more passion into it, bleeding through his instrument, summoning the longings of the night. As we crossed to the glow seeming to radiate from the musician himself, we saw that he was barefoot. Between his feet rested a tip bowl with scarcely a dime in it. Jamie immediately plunged his hand in his pocket, finding to his satisfaction a whole fistful of coins, which he tossed into the bowl when we reached the curb. The man played on, with renewed intensity, his eyes closed as he expressed his gratitude in the one way he knew how.

Tina, to my surprise, produced a bill of some denomination and let it waft down into the bowl. The old man pretended not to be aware of it, but I knew he could see through his lids. Men with bowls between their feet always can. I backed up into the street as the wailing reached a painful

157

pitch, but it proved to be the finale, taking what emotion had been called forth and warping it out of all context. Jazz. You wouldn't know I loved it by my wince.

"Man, you are the *shit!*" touted Jamie, shaking the old man's leathery hand.

"Where ya from?" the old man said in a gravelly voice.

"I'm from Knoxville. My friends here are from New Orleans. We're in town for a convention. Record industry thing."

"Good place for it."

"That's the truth." Jamie's fogged eyes seemed to catch another burst of revelation. "Man, do you *do.*"

The old man was used to the one-too-many sort, in fact seemed to appreciate Jamie's straightforward way of expressing his appreciation. Revealing an incongruous collection of nicotine-stained teeth, he said, "I been doin' it for a long time. Always comin' back here, where they love to groove the most."

"Good-looking instrument."

"Old as dirt. One day I'll be able to buy me a new one. It'll do til then, though. Hell, it's been doin' since Bobby Bones was cookin' up the blues on the corner. You'd be too young to remember him, I s'pose."

I thought I vaguely remembered the name, from down around the Quarter, but I told him I couldn't be sure.

"He was better known hereabouts," said the old man.

"Bobby Bones played that very sax?" asked Tina.

He nodded, eyes seeming to slip back in time.

She said, "The Rumdog Café'd probably give you a new one for it. They've got jazz paraphernalia hanging all over the walls."

"Nope. Gots to be on my terms," he said. "Hangin' it up like a museum piece is too damn final for my taste. I'd just as soon wait till I've collected enough pennies." He looked down at the bowl. "Which ain't gonna be too long with tips like that." He offered Tina a yellow grin.

"But..." Jamie's face had fallen under a shadow. He looked at the emptiness around us, down at the bowl. "Have you got nobody, Pops? Do you get by on tips?"

"No complaints, young man. I play my sax. I do my thang." He leaned forward, conspiratorially. "On top o' that, I got this other gig."

The way he said it made us all want to know what. Licking his lips, he said, "For a five-spot apiece—'ceptin' you, young lady—I can take ya to see Bobby's body."

"His bod—are you kiddin' me?" Jamie swayed on his feet, his body not up to its sudden reaction.

The old man waved his hand. "Never mind. It's for kids anyway."

"I'm a kid!" said Jamie. He turned to us. "How about you guys?"

Tina giggled. "A body? Sure, I'm a kid. What about you, Mark?"

Whatever Gramps was up to, I didn't see that any harm could be done. He was too old to mug, maul or molest. I was in.

Having stashed away his money, he led us, saxophone like a torch in his hand, down dark city blocks to a walled place near the river. Though I'm rather young to have to visit them often, cemeteries have never bothered me much. Tina, on the other hand, was thrilled to the point of latching on to me—for which I silently thanked our guide. Overhead, stars pierced the urban pall, bringing some light to the places lamps did not reach.

But it was into the deepest, darkest hearts of the cemetery that he led us, an interwoven canopy over our heads challenging any and all illumination, the markers and resting places of the dead darkening to shadows within shadows. He brought us to an impressive tomb amidst these, producing a key which clinked on its ring in the mute night.

"How did you get a key?" Tina whispered.

The façade of the tomb was columned, and before its massive door was a sill wide enough to accommodate the four of us as the key was inserted.

"Bobby had no one but me," said the old man. "His fans loved him enough that they paid for this beautiful tomb for him—he was truly a legend on River Street—but they were fans not family."

The door opened inward. The stony silence enveloped us as we entered. Along one wall was a ledge on which lay an open, rather scarred saxophone case. As the old man placed the instrument in the case, our eyes wandered to the opposite side of the vault, where an ornate iron handle provided access to the body's resting place.

"It's scary as hell," said Tina.

The old man held out his hand. Jamie and I produced the required fee.

Stuffing away the bills, he stepped over and grasped the handle. We stiffened for the worst as the drawer came open on its grinding runners.

It was empty.

All eyes fell on the saxophonist.

"One of these days I'm gonna have that brand-new sax," he said. "And when I do, I plan to set River Street on fire all over again." He tossed his key ring behind the instrument case.

Returning his attention to the void that had been revealed, he added, "I'd 'preciate it if you'd close it behind me. And the door, too, as ya leave. It will lock on its own."

And with that, he climbed with some clumsiness into his songless bed.

Mousse

Put a whole pile of mousse in my hair that evening. Best threads, packed wallet, Italian shoes. Gone hunting.

At the door, they took me at my style, waved me in ahead of the line. I felt the envy of the men like the spray of a flamethrower on my back. Fed on it. Took it for just what it was—inadequacy, weakness. I felt nothing from the women except the venomous greed slinging from their collagen-bloated lips onto their exposed, silicone-narrowed cleavage.

Stepped into the Spaceship, as I like to call it, with an air of supremacy. Whatever I said was the Word, whatever I did was the Example. Beneath the strobes, the globes, and the scent of perfume and smoke and sweat, all eyes were upon me. *Come to me*, they said. *Oh let it be me.*

I chose her for her delicateness, I chose her for her sass. I chose her for her fearlessness, I chose her for her ass. I chose her because she dripped superlatives. Because she was an exceptional wine. Because she was less impressed by me than the rest were. Because she thought herself my match.

"Are you a vampire?" she asked me.

"No."

"A psycho killer?" she asked me.

"Now, now."

"Do you find me alluring?"

"You appeal to my darker tastes."

Red tongue, clear green eyes, the viper. "I would not wish myself upon any man."

"Perhaps I am no man."

"What then?" Pressing herself closer.

Let us dance, I intimated. Dance we did. Killed each other, killed the house with our moves. Carnage strewn about the place. Seemed the lady and I did not honor the fair spirit of competition. Go home.

Suggested it to her. Tongue appeared, disappeared again.

"Of course."

"Are you a vampire?" I said.

"Are you the devil?" she returned.

"Perhaps that," I said. And out into the night, wings tucked in by our sides.

Her vehicle. Her suggestion. I had never played the game that way before. She drove a sports car, not dissimilar to my own. Will you drive, she offered.

With pleasure, lady. Did that. Fucked with the dial, brought up some jazz as we pulled out of the parking lot. My place?

She reached over, undid the three top buttons, ran her fingers across my chest.

"Anyplace dark," she said.

"My place is dark," I promised. And put the machine towards getting us there forthwith.

My place is beneath an overpass. My place isn't my home. My home is my home, my place is my place, two different sets of coordinates. She didn't mind.

Place is certainly dark, the murky river seeming to draw everything but the last glint in our eyes into its depths. I like to take her by the absence of light glancing off its opaque surfaces. Expression snatched in shadow, words lost in the black wind that does not blow. Fish lying dead and disoriented on the concrete bank. I do it with any one of my tools, sometimes my teeth, sometimes my knife, sometimes the wire. Would do it this night with my flask and a lighter. Because she dared so much. Because she would be my equal, venom bitch.

Took it out of my jacket pocket, like whiskey, like gin, drew a long mouthful, gasoline burns, yeah Jesus it does. She smelled it, I knew she smelled it, they always did, but it didn't make any sense, gasoline in a flask, gasoline killed. Yeah it did, come here, sweet temptation, matchbook

162

at the ready. I pretended to swallow.

But she wouldn't obey my gesture. She was cooler than that. You come, she said.

I could not verbalize. Mouth full of gasoline, pain. I would bathe her, baptize her, bring her to her belly, serpent, writhing and screaming in agony I love to inflict so. Only she was teasing me, backing away from me as I came, backing away, away, around the car and opening the door as if to jump inside the car—but then slamming it against me, watching with pleasure my facial contortions as the gasoline went down. When the fluid immediately lurched up again, she threw the door against me a second time. I dropped to my knees. She retrieved my matches, lit one, what is your wish, Word and Example?

I thought to welcome it. Deserved it, my inadequacy, my weakness...

"Too easy," she said, shaking it out. "Hurt a little." And climbed into her sports car and drove away.

Somewhere no doubt she's smiling, knowing I've been hunting her ever since.

Coeur de Vie

Passing a couple decked out in black, the scent of night and cologne about them, Cal Banes checked his watch. Almost midnight. He'd learned firsthand that the nightlife in Luxembourg City didn't get started until after twelve. Upon leaving the casino, which had made his pockets five hundred euros fatter, he'd taken the advice obtained from a hotel brochure and made Chez-nous Disco his next stop. The cabbie warned him, but Cal said he'd check it out for himself. Sure enough, the Friday night crowd was not only thin, but on average a generation younger than he was.

Not ready to call it a night, he wandered the streets. This was his first business trip to Europe in a while, and although the night around him wasn't quite as charged as he'd hoped, he wasn't about to let eccentric Luxembourger ways drive him to bed. The Grand Chateau, where he was staying, had its own various entertainments, but they were a little upscale for his tastes. As far as he was concerned, a man about town could do it on his own terms.

Ahead, a red neon sign—one of many adorned with either an *X* or a curvy female silhouette—flashed *Club Rouge*. While the higher-class amusements weren't Cal's style, neither necessarily were the lower. He strode past the bulging suit manning the sunken, nondescript door with a curt nod. Yet before he reached the end of the block he had replayed the subtle, mystery-infused head gesture of the doorman multiple times. What, after all, did go on in such places? Cal had seen similar establishments in other European cities and always assumed they were simply more brazen, less regulated cousins of the strip clubs found in the States.

164

He decided he would go in for one drink.

The suit smiled conspiratorially as he held the door open. Smoke and music welcomed the customer into the narrow confines of the club. Men sat around a bar drinking out of tall glasses, eyeballing a topless woman dancing sinuously on a small, hard-lit platform. Two other dancers, covered, were on hand as well. One of them drifted, while the second seemed locked in to the man she shared a drink with. Another bouncer type, maybe the clone of the suit manning the entrance, stood before a door of beads in the back. Otherwise—and this was what impressed Cal most keenly—the place was an excuse to play music of strange and bewildering origins.

"*Oui, Monsieur?*" said the bartender as Cal sat on the nearest stool.

"*Bonsoir,*" Cal said. "Do you by chance speak English?"

"Yes, of course. What can I get for you?"

"Recommendation?"

"Bloody Mary is our house drink, though perhaps it is too early?"

"Bloody Mary would be great."

Watching the bartender pour an almost equal amount of vodka and tomato juice over two ice cubes, dousing the blend liberally with tobasco and black pepper, Cal fished a cigarette out of his pocket. A slender hand produced a flame, which he used before turning to find the drifter standing there, her bare thigh lightly touching his knee. Her blue eyes had a lazy look to them as she sized him over. He hadn't bothered to notice at first glance, but she was an unexpectedly good-looking woman.

"You are new here, yes?" Her accent was heavily Slavic.

"The bar or Luxembourg in general?"

She shrugged, enhancing the gesture with a nuance of her nicely curved lips.

He said, "The answer is yes to both. But I might ask you the same thing."

"I am Sonja. I moved here recently from the Ukraine. Yana, the girl dancing on the stage, found this job for me."

"Five euros, please," the bartender said behind Cal.

"Can I run a tab?" he asked, turning that way.

The bartender and Sonja exchanged a pleased glance. Cal's remark suggested his intention to be around awhile.

"Sure," the barkeep said. "Just settle up here before you go upstairs."

Before he…

"Will I be going upstairs?"

The bartender struck him on the shoulder. "Surely you would not wish to hurt Sonja's feelings."

"No, of course not." He sucked on the cigarette before braving the concoction the man had prepared for him.

The mixture was surprisingly pleasing to the taste buds. Much like Sonja to the rest of the senses.

"So what does 'going upstairs' entail?" he asked her.

She mistook the question. "Four hundred euros."

"Four hundred—? Christ."

She pushed his thigh aside and slithered up against him. "And very much worth it."

He looked at her, her lips but an exhalation from his own. No way. No damn way.

She kissed him, convincingly, seeming to fully lose herself in the moment.

Against every instinct and ethic, he had to give consideration to the fact that his pockets were five hundred euros fatter from his casino winnings. "How long?" he said.

She touched his chin with her fingertip. "All night if you also buy my drinks."

"Are you…I mean, is it…"

"Safe? Yes, completely."

He measured her a moment longer, then turned to the bartender. "One for the lady, please. And I'll be settling up now."

The second floor was divided up not by partitions, but by long plush rugs forming paths between bunches of ornately covered mattresses and pillows. The smell of liquor, incense, smoke, and sweat filled the spaces. In the far wall was another door of beads, though this time no one manned it. Two of the sections were in use, their occupants giggling and fondling, but no one appeared to have gone any farther than that. With all night at their disposal, Cal thought, why indeed rush?

Sonja leaned back against the wall, the mattress beneath her emanating a perfumery—no doubt some spray to cloak deeper smells—that Cal might have found hard to swallow had his senses not been otherwise engaged. The euros had already been deposited in the hands of the man watching the beads downstairs, and the absoluteness of the thing hung there in direct opposition to the theory of romance. And yet, after only a little while in her company, Cal found himself liking her. What's more, she seemed to like him. He wasn't naïve enough to imagine this chemistry was anything more than business, but he did appreciate its relaxing effects.

"So what kind of music are we listening to, Sonja? It reminds me of a public radio program they used to run on Sunday mornings back when I was in college... *Tours through the Inner Cosmos*, they called it. Played all kinds of strange New Age music."

"New Age? They just call it *Vie* here. Life. My employers prefer this form for Club Rouge."

Form, she said. As though it was all about the music's artistic value. Sipping his vodka tomato, he concentrated a moment on the sometimes clear, sometimes hollow sounds, unable to determine what precise instruments they came from. While strings and keys and wind definitely contributed, most of the sounds were synthesized. The music was about mood more than melody, atmosphere more than beat. It was eerie, he thought. Whale songs with more sinister implications.

"Your employers have odd tastes," he said.

She smiled. "When you are rich, you can afford odd tastes."

"Isn't everyone in Luxembourg rich? That's what *my* employers told me, to prepare me for the mindset, I guess."

"Then you are here on business?"

"A conference."

"Your associates have left you to fend for yourself. Good for me."

"Ha. The moment these things end, I slip out the door. I don't need to be surrounded by work all night, which I've learned is exactly what you get when you go out with your associates." He smiled to himself, wondering what they would think of this place.

"So where do you come from in America?" she said, gliding a fingertip along his arm.

"Southwest," he said. "Boring."

She kissed his forehead. "Not boring. Do you have a family there?"

He frowned. "I don't know that I'd like to go there, Sonja. Why would you ask that?"

An unfamiliar face appeared with another Bloody Mary.

"I didn't order this," Cal said.

"And yet it is here," smiled the waiter, depositing it on the surface beside the bed. "This one is on the house."

"Would you bring the lady one too, then?"

He downed the rest of his first one, invited her to do the same with her mixture. As she complied, her eyes merged with the drink's similar color, supplying the clear blue depths for whalesong.

Though Cal knew he had downed at least three ounces of liquor in the house specialty, and on top of the four or five drinks he had already consumed tonight, he reached for the new glass. Maybe he needed a sampler of oblivion to help with the inhibitions. Family, she had asked. What nerve.

Before he returned the glass to its perch, Sonja abandoned her spot to him, coaxing him back against the wall. She began kissing him, her fingers unbuttoning his shirt, her lips roaming over his neck, chest, slightly neglected belly. A cold drop of liquid caused him to open his eyes abruptly; he realized she still held her drink aloft, while he had yet to return his to the ledge. He was feeling rather in limbo. What proof vodka had they used, anyway? When Sonja told him not to worry about such things, he didn't remember asking the question aloud.

"Hold on," he said, pushing her away. "Just cool it a sec, all right?"

"Yes?" she said, her sultry look defying his concerns.

"Yeah, thing is, I do have a family. My wife and I have been separated for more than a year. Two kids, boy and girl. Freedom don't taste much like freedom, y'know?"

"That depends on where one is from, yes?" she said. "Compared to my home, this"—she gestured around them—"is total liberation."

He looked at her for a minute then held up his drink. "To liberation."

"Liberation!" she said, meeting it with her own.

They might as well have been in Paris, at a revolutionists' convention.

"So what's through that door?" Cal asked, gesturing at the beads

168

stirring on the strange sounds that kept everything at a mesmerizing pitch.

"You are ready for the third floor already?"

He looked around the room. The other couples continued to play their soft games, contentedly. Maybe there would be some privacy after all.

"What is this, like the foreplay floor?"

"To foreplay," she said, holding up her drink.

He tapped it and drank yet again.

Her voice seemed to fade into the background, among the strains of the Inner Cosmos, as she asked, "Does anyone know where the bad boy has gone tonight?"

"Who's the bad boy?" he said, letting his eyelids droop deliriously.

"You are the bad boy, Cal. Does anyone know you are here?"

He laughed. "Yeah, I told everyone at the conference to meet me at the...what's the name of this joint, Natalie?"

"Club Rouge," came her underwater voice. "And my name is Sonja."

"Ohya, Natalie's that other harlot, the one I called a wife. Y'know, maybe I should put the drink down for awhile."

"Ah, so soon?" announced the voice of the waiter. "I've brought you another."

"I think Cal wants to take it upstairs," Sonja said.

Circumstances had changed. Environment. Things had become steadily clearer as Cal ascended the stairs. By the time he stepped foot on the third floor, everything was back into focus. The highly visual, almost dazzling sumptuousness of the furnishings only made things sharper to his receptors. Sonja, moving like liquid before him, was a goddess in her chamber.

Floor three was otherwise unoccupied. Its luxuries would be theirs alone once the waiter was on his way. Cal didn't notice the absence of the tall glass the guy had made a habit of bringing until the tray appeared before him. His pulse quickened as he saw what lay there.

"What is that?"

"Would you like to get high, Cal?" said Sonja.

169

"I don't know that I've ever thought about getting high like *that*." What he was looking at was a syringe, and beside it a small paper container of clear fluid.

"Look, there is nothing to be afraid of," Sonja said, motioning the waiter away. Picking up the syringe and drawing some of the fluid into it, she offered her arm for his examination. "See. No marks. Nothing like that. Only..."

She squeezed her fist, tapping the valley above her forearm, then pressed the fluid into a vein. "Liberation..." She lay her head back, and seemed to taste it on her lips.

"Christ, I'm just a businessman looking for a night on the town."

She lowered her head, eyes sleepily engaging him. "You can go searching the town for Natalie. Or you can forget her here."

He studied her. "Your English gets more impressive by the minute, Sonja. I wonder how long you've been out of the Ukraine—"

"Who cares?" she said, spitting fluid out of the needle.

He looked from the very obvious thing in her hand to the very obviousness of his surroundings. A deep red hue seemed to be the motif— cushions, art, carpet and all. Passion. Lust. Fierce emotion. The music, now that he stood back from it, had assumed the role of undertone. A poised, strangely majestic accompaniment. The difference in texture and quality from what he had been listening to downstairs was near impossible to pinpoint, yet it was different. As if the music moved with his own mood.

He gritted his teeth. "Yeah. Who cares."

Clenching his fist, he held out his arm, watched with determination. Blood rose into the cylinder. To his surprise she removed the needle from his arm, shot his blood into the depleted cup of clear fluid. She drew a few cc's of the blend back out, told him to be still, shot it into his arm.

Warmth chased the chill that ran through him, saturating him in wonder. "Drink your drink," she said. "I'll be back."

"But the waiter took my drink..."

"I'm here, sir," came the familiar masculine voice. "House drink, Bloody Mary."

Cal grasped the cool glass in his fist. "Is she really a Ukrainian?" he said.

"No, they're only make-believe, like us Luxembourgians."

Cal tried to chuckle. "I'd rather it was all real."

"Then quit trying to entomb yourself. Except for that flaw, you're a prime candidate."

"Prime candidate for what?"

"Vie, *mon ami.* Life! But let us wait and see how your blood tests before excitement takes us over." He bade *au revoir* and disappeared through the same door Sonja had disappeared through. Cal was sure he saw ascending stairs behind the settling beads; behind the mist that settled over his senses.

Eyes closed, he let the music have him. Tears from the aether fell around him in isolated drops, music from the moon levitated him. If only he'd had this to retreat to when Natalie became less a person and more a name. If only he'd been able to submerge in oblivious moonsong after Timmy and Lila had revealed that they were afraid of him because of a simple change in appearance—a haircut. The Club Rouge didn't know haircuts. Oblivion didn't know haircuts.

Tears from the aether, and here was his goddess again.

"Come, let's get our blood heated up," she said. "You've proved exactly what we're looking for. Lucky for all of us, yes?"

He sucked on his vodka tomato but it failed to illuminate. She pushed him back on cushions, licked his lips of excess, caressed his sensitive places, explored him as he became more fully aware of himself. Clothes strewn about in their wake, she led him on her words, promises of exaltation, to the fourth floor.

Beads, strong scent on the air, life itself. Sonja turned to him before what lay beyond was unveiled. "Remember," she said, "this is not about being lost. It's about being found." She stepped backwards into layers of beads, the smell growing increasingly stronger as the strings separated. The music grew less random, pulsing to the rhythms of multiple hearts.

"Come to me," she said. "She grasped his buttocks and pulled him against her body, meeting his fullness. "Yes, come to me," she breathed on his neck. The beads released their clutching bodies to the other side and the odor rose to a sharp, even shrill, crescendo.

"Jesus, I can feel it in my whole body," he said into her hair. *It* had no description.

"Me too," she said, pulling him with her as she moved backwards, up another stair, then another, into the mysterious embraces of the fourth floor. "Let go," she said. "Fall with me..."

Into warm deep thick liquid. He knew at once as his mouth tasted it, his skin recognized its texture and temperature, that he had plunged into a bath of blood. Losing track of Sonja, he surfaced, gasping for air, sucking in the copper oxygen his mind had failed to correctly associate. Sonja was in front of him, tongue swiping at her exhilarated lips, eyes for once fully awake and piercing like jewels.

Around them, arms resting along the circular rim of the spa, men and woman leisured like Roman senators. Watching him with senatorial amusement.

"Tash...Sonja, what...?" He hadn't the ability to finish it, too bound to his fascination even to retch.

"You've been invited to join in the *Coeur de Vie,* as we call it. Stand and you will be afforded a better view. Come." She urged with her hands, caressing his body as she did, reminding him in a soft voice that life was being celebrated here.

"*Vie,*" she said. "The Heart of Life surrounds us."

He stood, trailing fluid from his limbs, trapped in wonder terror as the whole scene opened before him. Whalesong blue tiles stretched from one end of the floor to the other, interrupted by oblong rectangular pools and the equipment that kept their sanguineous contents circulating. The pools were shallow, the fluid within stirring beneath frequent releases—from isolated individual drops to brief fan-like cascades—of the same unmistakable substance from the ceiling above. Suspended around the whole hideous operation were microphones, capturing the sounds produced.

Cal opened his mouth in soundless horror as he looked around him at these people pleasuring in all this bloody extravagance.

"Welcome," said one of the men. "Our house is your house."

"Oh God," was all he could manage. An emission of breath, with copper tints.

"God?" said another man. "Yes, life being divine, God is here. You might even call this a cathedral. For it is not just the material of life that we record and engineer into the symphony you hear. It is also its essence,

172

its spirit, its *âme*. When a drop of lifeblood is amplified into a perfectly clear note suspended in empty space, it is the soul we are hearing. Perhaps what is most difficult to capture about life is its grace, hence the delicate instrumental overtones we've added. But of course up here, where we immerse ourselves wholly in the miracle, nothing is lost."

Cal had no words for the face that spun such madness.

"Come, Cal," said Sonja. "I'll show you where it begins."

He did not want to know where it began, where it ended, or anything else to do with these people. But the voice to describe his aversion simply was not there. He stepped out of the spa, touched by the hand of the gray-haired woman nearest him, resisting the impulse to kick her face. Across reaches of Romanesque tile squares, Sonja led him, and as the tilt of reality readjusted, he reacted normally, by throwing up.

She ignored it. The music caught him again, chiding his insurrection. The *Coeur de Vie* pulsed uninterrupted, hungrily vibrant. His bodily movements merged with the tune of the rain forest and jungle, and Sonja led him into secret rooms, where those rhythms could be met at the source. "'Our house is your house,'" she quoted. "That welcome is a beginning. I envy you."

The face of the waiter grew before him. The blade felt cold as it opened the way for the heat to pour out of him and into their machinery.

Humpty Dumpty Had a Great Fall

I know I was never born; that I have existed forever. It is why I have brought her here.

She has come willingly because of my overwhelming innocence and...as she thinks of it, as they all think of it...naïvete. What they have never understood is that the wonder I express comes from holding reality up to the light and scrutinizing it for what it really is. What they have never understood is the light itself. Death is our preoccupation, we the deceivers of ourselves.

I told her she was a liar, the worst kind, deluding herself. I told her as I tied the belts around her wrists and, against her manufactured struggles, lashed her off at the fence posts, just wide enough to stretch the muscles, elegant contours along her taut sleek limbs. The stirrups are homemade, but sufficient for the task. She twists against her restraints, not disappointing me with the pretense; the symbolism is exquisite.

I invite her, not for the first time, to accuse me of contradiction, dichotomy, but she refuses. Because of my innocence, I am allowed my "fantasies."

Calming the motion of her bare belly with my hand, I proceed to tell her about the freshly laid eggs. When first I ate one whole and uncooked, the fragmenting shell cut my youthful lips. *Life unborn*, I tell her. How pure is that? Unspoiled. Undiluted. Or is that undeluded?

The first glimpse of doubt now as her innocent, naïve, trusted lover draws the blade from where it has lain superficially buried, more figuration, in the hay and loose earth. Still, we have played our games before; the death game comes to mind, where I pretend I am a corpse, so that I may show her how fiercely the light shines even when we are reduced to that physical state. She always indulges me, not knowing that my heartbeat has truly stopped, and forgets, at last, how peculiar she thinks the sport as I lift her to the crescendo and fountain that so represents the misguided thirst for animal consciousness. For these are the processes that ensure the whole race of men is a race of madmen, while its members know it not.

The fading shadow of concern, and the materializing smile, as I draw not the keen side of the blade, but the back of it, across her midsection, marking the spot. *Is this the way?* I ask her. *Or better here?* As I touch the moist crevice whose function it is to spill forth the graduate of the fetal waters. But I already know: the damage is greater from below; indeed the potential to extinguish the light, *very* real. Nevertheless, we must not abandon the ritual of birthing.

She squirms as I tease the spur, clever little garden of nerves that it is. Her legs relax as I pause to bask in a scented wind off a coming afternoon storm.

"Please," she breathes.

I touch there again. But my words carry into deeper realms. *"Push,"* I invite her. "I will give you that chance."

"Chance?" she manages in a slight gasp.

"Chance to bring it forth in the traditional way."

"It? Is this some new game? Are we pretending I am pregnant?"

"You are pregnant."

"Don't snap. I'll play."

Yes, you'll play. I caress her soft skin and imagine how smooth her offspring's will be. Like the unborn egg. It is fitting that we have come here, to my mother's home, where I was never really born on the kitchen floor, in a pool of fluids, the woman who carried me experiencing her last hour in agony, writhing in the delusion of our lunatic minds.

"Push," I command. And as the noise comes out of her nostrils flared in amusement and carnal curiosity, I remember that face.

My mother's sister, in whose house I was brought up, wore that face the first time she caught me fully exposed. I was on my bed, a bible before me, tearing out the pages of Genesis one by one, stuffing them in my mouth, ingesting them.

175

"Like the mother's milk you never had?" she suggested. And then she began to tell me, in greater detail than she ever had before, about my birth, shedding layers of clothing as she did, until she stood before me nude. My wonder made her laugh.

"You're still so amazed?" she said. "We've been doing this for a long time."

So we had. But the fluids had been ours and ours alone until that day.

At the funeral, which ritual I alone attended, I put a whole hen's egg in her mouth, a perfecting gleam to her still lascivious rictus.

"Push!" I demand of the woman before me. This time I will have it. This time I will not be tricked. This time my appetite will be satisfied.

I look up at her face. It is distorted by her desire to please me, yet I know I must enter her and find it myself. We can never trust them, these mothers; they are the doorways into this game of lunacy that is earthly existence. They defy the whole idea of perpetuity.

Her eyes are closed as I lift the knife. A strained high-pitched sound now as she puts her all into the exercise—*but what's this?*

A sudden light along the edge of the blade...

I look down to see it coming out of her, wrapped in brilliance.

Without hesitation, I cradle the egg in my hands, take it into my mouth, catch its mother's eyes as she cranes forward to observe more closely.

I recognize something there, in her face, in her eyes, as she watches me begin to chew.

She believes all of it a game.

I, on the other hand, *know* it's a game.

The Curse of Lianderin

Curious thing, I couldn't help but imagine it…

Fragments. Stained glass in deep Stygian shades…

Stygian? Had he really used that word? A word that I had never actually heard used in conversation.

…deep Stygian shades, alternately opaque and translucent, blacks and grays, seams shimmering in the effulgence of the rising moon…

There was a moon on this cold November night. A rising moon. Not quite full but bright.

…a silvery coin, imperfect, not circular but clipped, a Roman coin…

But that description had come before the elaborately articulated transformation of the sky, when the storyteller was still setting the stage.

Disconnected and nonsuccessive were the bits and pieces of his story coming to me now, almost twenty-four hours later, my eyes on the continuously unreeling center line, the deepening night and its antiquities meshing around me. As the road carelessly wound its way up the ridge, I couldn't help but imagine that when I arrived there, at the overlook, and the magnificent, multi-turreted castle that is Lianderin's offering to the world commanded my vision, the rich material of the sky would suddenly fragment, not a fabric at all but stained glass, seams shimmering.

…the answer to a warlord's arrogance and foolhardy ambition finally unfurling…

A great shadow, elegant and flickering, descend over the *Our* valley.

…a plague bestowed as by the thrust of a biblical staff, locusts showering down on the earth…

Funny, but I had never thought myself so suggestible.

A Dirge for the Temporal

They rushed the silent, undefended Schloss, the cry of victory on the air, and then all at once they detected a disturbance from high above and all four corners of the compass, a sound whose alienness alone, in the heavy quietude of the night, was cause for alarm...

How ostentatiously poetic he'd been in the telling of it, an innkeeper whose words of themselves were worth the francs. And Castle Larochette like a tomb outside the bar's slightly fogged window, a grim accent to his tale. His English had been as superb as his meticulous attention to detail, his language mitigating his accent such that I hadn't been able to tell whether he normally spoke French or German—I mean to his wife, his children, upstairs and asleep, oblivious to the terrors of the night. He'd said his town of birth was Bollendorf, but Bollendorf was even nearer the border than Larochette. Of course in the time of his tale there hadn't been a Luxembourg or a Germany. There had only been regions. And the lords of them.

High Lord Gilzern was a boar of a man, brawny, whiskered and smelling of sour beer. His one weakness was his fearlessness...

I had drunk entirely too much local while my host told his story. And perhaps that was the motive behind his lengthy elaborations. I was the inn's only guest, as I found out the next morning when I sat alone at the house's complimentary, and decidedly one-person, breakfast. A hard living, an inn and the off-season, tap never running dry. Please excuse, of course, the better-than-generous volume of beer to which my host treated himself.

"Witches," sneered Gilzern. "Humph! Neither witches nor bloodsuckers, devils nor ghouls shall alter my purpose. Lianderin is the prize and Lianderin I shall have, be the hordes of Darkness Itself there to defend her walls."

The crest was nearing now, and not far beyond it, I knew, stood the Schloss, grandly illuminated in the night. I had been here before, the naïve tourist arriving at a late hour. But not at this time of year. And not *this* year, this night. Strangely, there was no traffic on the road.

Tomorrow is the anniversary of that fateful night when Gilzern and his army crossed the Our River and rushed the castle...

I hadn't intended to be arriving so late—or after dark at all. Upon leaving the inn I had experienced car trouble. A certain hesitation (recently noticed and ignored) had evolved overnight, as my car sat idly

178

contemplating its own existence, into an outright sputtering. Resisting acceleration, the already languid hatchback had putted like the train that thought it could up a long gradual hill and then died without honor ten meters shy of the top.

I walked the three kilometers back to the *Gasthaus*, and the innkeeper put me in contact with a local garage. They pulled the car in (at an extravagant expense), and while it waited its turn, I explored Larochette's castle and the hiking trails surrounding it. Not until the third time I checked in did they actually have a man on my car. That was around two o'clock. It was four-thirty before he had chased the problem down, a clogged line, back near the fuel tank. The sun was setting as my keys were returned to me, my wallet significantly lighter for the inconvenience.

After a brief dinner at a nearby restaurant, I stopped by to thank the innkeeper before continuing on my journey. He looked at me disapprovingly when he learned my destination hadn't changed.

"You will go on to Lianderin anyway? At this hour?"

"I'm a man on holiday," I said. "Pleased to be without a schedule—"

"Then no harm will be done by your accepting my invitation to rest here another night."

"I will rest in Lianderin."

"The only rest you will find in Lianderin tonight is of the permanent variety."

There it was, right out in the open. And seeming somehow more than just an extension of his story. I studied him a protracted moment before letting the corners of my mouth lift in a grin. Although he smiled back, it didn't feel like a secret between us. Nay, 'twas I the fool.

And perhaps that was the job of the Third of the Three Angels on this mythological holiday of mine—to bring me, with a whisper in my ear, to that simple assessment. Her sisters had successfully performed their jobs: one to put a gremlin in my fuel system, the other to make it difficult to locate. All designed to keep me in Larochette, while Lianderin was only forty kilometers away.

And now, with all that in the rearview mirror, it seemed my guardians still had not abandoned me. The words of their mortal emissary kept me company every step of the way.

Fragments...

I pulled over before reaching the top of the ridge, wanting a clearer view of the sky than I would be afforded when first the rim of the village, and then the castle with all its floodlights, emerged out of my memory and into the sensory realm. Stepping out of the car, I gazed up at the sky. Glittering tapestry that it was, I could not imagine it quite as he had described it. Fragmented, perhaps. Stained glass, no. Alternately opaque and translucent, no. No light would show through when the vault was filled with their wings.

When High Lord Gilzern's scouts reported that both Schloss and surrounding village were empty and defenseless, Gilzern threw back his head and laughed. "You see!" he announced triumphantly. "They have fled like hares. I gave them a fortnight's notice and they have fled. Now what think you, you craven advisors of mine? 'Avoid Lianderin,' you said. 'Avoid Lianderin, for Lianderin is home to a great covey of witches.' So where are they now, these associates of Darkness?"

Gazing across the starry arch of night, I found myself wondering the same thing. I climbed back in the car, somewhat amused with myself.

"A shame," said Gilzern, "that my men, for their long march, will not be rewarded with a battle. But I say again, the real prize, when the horns have blown, is Lianderin." Yet even as he spoke these words, he was reminded by his instincts that not often were prizes of such rarity obtained without a cost...

A sign stated the proximity of the Schloss, and I wondered where my excitement had gone. The words of the innkeeper tarried, but without the haunting quality of before. My roadside study of the night sky seemed to have stolen the flutter.

I rounded a turn and the road leveled. Houses oddly modern, out of setting, slipped by. German symmetry, French nonchalance, American overtones. The trees among which they were built fell away, and, sooner perhaps than I had expected, I found myself looking out over the valley and upon the castle perched on its own hill above the surrounding village. The to-do I remembered was absent. The floodlights were off, the Schloss standing dark and silent at its enviable site amidst the hills, and yet all the more lovely for its solitude and lack of occasion.

As every eye turned to the firmament, Schloss Lianderin stood silently by. Solitudinous, majestic. A prize oh so easy, oh so effortlessly won, and yet, as they were about to find out, so profoundly, so utterly unobtainable.

Yes, it does seem to be that, I thought. Not in its design, for it lacked as a fortress. Not in its location, for wasn't it meant to impress more than to discourage? Its *presence* was what made it the prize it was, and no floodlight could adorn that perfect fact.

I sighed, moved.

Since then, upon every hundredth anniversary, as a reminder and a warning to any who would dare consider mounting an assault upon her, Lianderin has suffered no visitors. This is not to say that she has remained untouched by the great wars which have passed this way, for no thing has. But woe to those aggressors whose ambitions are within her power to thwart. Whatever form they may assume, it is to them she speaks. For even today the shadowy ones are among Lianderin's residents, and in spite of their swift and utter victory over the invaders that night, the insult remains.

The obligatory overlook before driving down into the village. Although a second-time visitor, I stopped here to absorb the vision, to enjoy it the way commercialism had not allowed the first time. But as I stepped out of the car, I detected a disturbance—

...from above and all four corners of the compass...

My eyes shot upward. The sky—yes, the gods above, it had become, in an instant, just as described—fragmented!

Not a whapping, leathery, batlike fury, as would seem to better fulfill the imagination, but a dance of glass, alternately opaque and translucent, the seam of every fragment shimmering in the light of the moon, and perhaps their own intrinsic energy as they gathered over this trespasser in their domain.

As I leapt into the car, they descended. As I swung the wheel and roared away in the direction from which I had come, they fell upon the car, faces flashing in the windshield, eyes telling the story in a way the innkeeper, eloquent as he was, never could have; mouths twisted in a savagery matched only by my desire and determination to be down the mountain and away from this place. How I managed to avoid wrapping the car around a tree during those first seconds of the ordeal I cannot accurately say. Perhaps it was that almost as soon as I began my flight, I brought the car to a screeching halt, failing to throw the creatures from the vehicle as it skidded sideways, coming to rest at odds with the direction of the road.

What inspired this reaction was not the vigor and madness of their assault, which I only wished to flee, but a sudden stench, an acrid, sickeningly pungent, almost palpable stench that entirely effused the interior of the car. I swung around, looking for the flames, the burning bodies, the whatever it was that fueled the foulness permeating the air, but found only a fresh perspective on the dark blizzard that consumed the car. I spun the wheel even before turning my shoulders square again, and laid hard on the accelerator. I was absolutely blind, my heartbeat racing to velocities incomprehensible as I called upon the intervention of a greater power—over and above any instinct I might have had at my disposal—to save me from the grab bag of fatal conclusions awaiting me.

Then all at once my attackers relented. They rose as one unit from the object of their assault, lifting up into the funnel of their own whirlwind, Elijah upon a chariot of black flames, from this earth and unto heaven.

The world whirred by with the kilometers I put between myself and unholy Lianderin. Within the hour I was brought, by destinies beyond my own to pilot, to the door of the inn in Larochette. Of the drive there I remember little, except how unbearably smothering the close confines of the car. Despite the cold November air, I drove the distance with my window down.

Presuming the bar would be empty, I went to the main door. I wondered what time it was. I had not thought to check the clock in the car. Apparently the house was yet to sleep, for soon after the bell rang, the door opened and the face of a pretty young girl greeted me.

"*Hallo*," she said—and even as the word issued from her mouth, that pretty face twisted into an ugly one, as though beset by something detestably foul.

The innkeeper's last, almost incidentally presented paragraph, a footnote of suddenly horrifying proportions, emerged from the revulsion I witnessed on his daughter's tender face. Words which could not begin to prepare me for the reactions that, starting here and tonight, would plague me for the rest of my days.

For those who are allowed to escape Lianderin on anniversary night, there is a fate infinitely worse than perishing at the hands of her shadowy residents. And that is, to be the bearers of the memory. A memory not as the mind provides but a physical one. A memory of that fateful night when the High Lord and as many of his soldiers as material would allow were mounted to poles around the castle, and piles of brush and branches were set to flame beneath their suspended feet. That same night when their often still conscious remnants were left to hang there on the scorched poles to be lusted over by scavengers until gracious death finally came. And after death had come and gone, still they hung there. Hung there to be ravaged by the carrion crows while decomposition took its lazy course. It is said that for weeks after, Lianderin stank of burnt and rotting flesh. But the memory of it never fades. In those who carry it with them from Lianderin, it survives in all its vivid, putrescent, reeking detail.

Dandelion Girl

Smiling, she held the tooth of the lion before her, between our faces, and dreamily blew its cottony wisp of a flower into a scatter of spinning weightless snowflakes. That is how I shall always remember her. With her light summer dress, green as the grass, anklets woven of silver and vine, and a dandelion in her hand. *The tooth of the lion*, she translated from the Latin. Because of its jagged leaves.

She brought a picnic basket along, and wore no shoes as she sat on the blanket, legs crossed, and braided the wild leaf of the forest into adornments. Of the food she had packed, she ate only an apple, and perhaps that was her way of speaking to the nature of evil without actually reviving the subject. It was one of many topics we had carelessly touched on at the party the night before. Last night when she announced, quite without preamble, that she was a witch.

"Are you a good witch or a bad witch?"

"Is there a difference?"

"Come now, Lyla..."

"Mm?"

I searched for the smartest words. "Next you'll be telling me you're a student of the philosophy that good and evil, truth and illusion, beauty and ugliness differ only in our interpretation of them."

"You have forgotten ecstasy and agony."

"Are you flirting with me, Lyla?" For she was already in the touching way by then. My arm, my knee, my beard.

She had been wearing a simple dress at the party, too. Only black, and of a more revealing cut. I picture her sitting there on the stool, tanned thighs exposed, reflections from the overheads captured in the elegant curve of her wineglass...I picture this, and the image, as always, fails. It dissolves, whether by preference or necessity, into the softer vision of the dandelion girl. Sleepy eyes, delicately rounded lips all the more alluring for the absence of makeup, that social apparatus behind which apparently even witches are inclined to disguise themselves. But it is the emotion involved that separates these images. For as the puff of flower was blown spinning on the air, I thought I might find it within me to love and treasure this creature, whomever, whatever she was.

"I want to take you to my special place," she told me after I kissed her goodnight. I thought for a fleeting, shallowly masculine moment that she had changed her mind, that she would invite me in after all, rewarding me at least with a nightcap. I would be instantly glad I misread her intentions, for we bachelors do not really enjoy floating from one party to the next, simultaneously camouflaged and exposed in our own brand of makeup, we just pretend we do. We are really just divorcés without former wives—divorcés of the stereotype, lonely and needing and loathing ourselves and each other.

"Your special place?" I said, recovering.

"My special place in the forest. It is there I have sought to explore the question we spoke of earlier."

"Which question?" For there had been a number of them. Spoken and unspoken.

"The nature of evil."

Perhaps I was being seduced at that. I hoped not. I hoped so. God, she was a beautiful creature.

But when I picked her up the next day, she was another sort of beautiful. A softer sort. The bloody shade of lipstick, the eye shadow blue, even the bun in which she had worn her hair, were gone. That soporific quality still, with her falling lids and the words coming lazily from her lips. But these traits, these features, were natural to her, at least long developed; not put on like coffee, the evening news, affectation. As I stood there at her door looking at her and her old-fashioned picnic basket, I decided I liked her very much.

"My Wiccan lady," I greeted her, our hands brushing as I took the basket. Even the touch of her was softer somehow.

She wore sandals which crisscrossed up over her sun-browned ankles. Her anklets shone silvery and delicate against the green leather, the windows of skin. She said something, I don't know what. I said something back. We touched again as I held the passenger door for her.

As we drove she offered these words which I haven't forgotten: "Daniel..." Which is my name actually, as lordly as it sounded from her. "Daniel, I enjoyed talking with you last night. I enjoyed our being together. Becoming acquainted is a necessity, I think."

A necessity? As applies to what...

"Before we can experiment further, I mean."

Experiment further? Was there a sexual connotation or was it my brute in-spite-of-myself acting up?

"Mind if I take off my sandals?"

I don't have a foot fetish, I won't be accused of having one, and I won't admit to it, needles under my fingernails. But damned if she hadn't worn the very sandal I so can't stand to look at. She saw me looking and simply smiled as if it were our secret.

She brought her feet up under her, cross-legged, hem rising carelessly, revealingly, with unabashed abandon. My eyes ached with the strain of keeping the road in front of them. We came to her special place none too soon for me.

A dirt road infrequently traveled, another perhaps never used anymore, and we were in the deep wood, and welcomed by the embrace of an easy summer breeze. Summer it was, and her bare feet and summer dress, and me in my shorts, less than bulbous muscles working to get us there. We followed a narrow deer path into the deeper domain, my eyes, her bottom and its melodious motion, and soon we came to her special place, how lovely it proved to be. We spread the blanket, brought forth the apples, the wine, the cheese, the ham. And all the while dandelions surrounding, swaying on the whispers of the wild clearing, island of weeds cut upon its rims and fringes by sheer, skyward rock progressions, bluffs and outcrops and still an hour of sunshine in which to explore.

With the flowers of her garden, she wove and braided, and her ankles were adorned, a wreath about her head. I kissed her, this the second time, and there was an alarming ease about it all, no, I absolutely *shan't* fall into the snare of matrimony, and my mom will die of shock and happiness

when she is informed. Lyla began to dance, to twirl among the wild
weeds, her hems catching upon her hips and her long legs, and the grace
of her amazing me, enchanting me. Wild Wiccan dreams and the tumult of
reality receding, and I had never been about town and its false pleasures
and the money in my suit, and my buying the lady a drink, and chatting
till the hour of bedtime and bedtime's false pleasures. I lurched to my
feet, and the gracelessness of me, spilling my wine as I came, and I swept
her up in my arms and the teasing suppleness, lightness of her in my
embrace. We spun and we spun, and the dandelions that blew, and the
whole universe exploding in cotton snowflakes and the whim and flurry
of the moment, cherished moment, smothering us in its ecstatic envelope.
We will die here, you in my arms, she laughed, pressing her breasts
against me, arching her head backwards, towards the waning day. You
will die in my arms and join the spirits that haunt this my special place,
the nature of things indeed.

I released her, wanting only to lay her in the weeds and thrust myself
inside her, hear the noise of her as we achieved fruition, shared souls that
we were. I wanted only to know her, to bathe myself in her, bleed with her
in our bliss and to die in her arms. But she fell, she crumpled, and she
was a dandelion herself, frail as the flower, and I had harmed her, I had
squeezed her too tightly, I heard the escape of a wounded and baleful
sound...

Song of liquid torturous pain and loss, grief and agony, rue and suffering and endless night flowing in waves as I realized it was not her
voice I heard but a collective one. Her estate was full of them, stretching
in endless torment and underscored by the rattle of bones, the chatter of
fleshless teeth, the suck, gargling suck of worms and insects upon the
deteriorating material of mortal vestiges and signs.

Her arms lifted as wings, and the magnificence of her was unimag-
inable as she stared down at me with those suddenly aware lucid vessels.

"What is it..." I uttered. Dumbly.

"What is the nature of evil?" she said back. "That has been the question since the beginning, when your eyes devoured me and the saliva
slung from your lips. You wanted me, *you want me now*, here I am Daniel
and you will die knowing what I am, for I am neither."

She bared her breasts to me, and the hunger was like a knife up through the abdominal regions, down through the bowels, through the groin. She seized the growing size of me and she laughed for my remembering her, for my acknowledgement of the Lyla of summer dresses.

"Come," she beckoned, and she flitted away towards the rock rising above, and in perpetual sighing accompaniment to, the acre of weeds and skeletal flowers amidst which we had spread a blanket and called it play.

A vertical cleft in the rock, its narrowing seam evident above the large stone that stood blocking the way. A gesture of her hand, black legerdemain, and the stone awoke, the sound like wrenching freedom and captivity as it moved out of the way and opened up the cave, lair of the dandelioness. The blast of stench and profundity momentarily swallowed me up, and then I let it be the progression of things, entering upon the offering of her hand and the phantom traces of her summer frock before.

"I," she said behind me. "I am that nature which is evil. I am that chasm which is night."

I whirled on the voice, confused as to our relative positions in space, and she was waiting for me, the lapels of her flesh and bony protection torn back and the heart that pulsed within the cavity exposed nakedly before me, muscular and black, shades of night and rapture eternal.

Holy sweet Christ and his disciples, I whispered without breath. How terrible and strange our nightmares, and what the fuck art thou, Lyla?

I moved backwards into the throat of her lair, pushed by her presence and anatomy and the truth and ghastly beauty of her. I stumbled over something, looked and beheld. Skull. And then another, and the scatter of bones, and the ragged bits of flesh that still clung. The clatter and innermost sanctum of her special place.

The song spread forth, echoing against the hidden walls of the cave, enshrouding us in its ecstatic, awful lament. Wisps of light and the texture of light as phantasmagoric, elongated shapes passed through the shadows, intertwining with one another and then escaping in reeling, spiraling moments of themselves, eternal moments, victims of Lyla and the nature, beautiful nature of evil. Evil...her substance and soul, what she was, the witch of dandelion fields and dreams, delights, sweet angel of truths simultaneously realized. I sought to pass but she stood in my way, heart hammering its black deathdrum, blood spewing from her mouth, spraying over me, seeking to drown me in the soaring bliss of becoming with her.

But I would not be hers. Though by all accounts Daniel had been in the lioness' den since the beginning, I would never be hers. I beckoned her, cravenly, as if it must be at her pleasure, my partaking of this meal she offered me. She came with a smile, a knowledge that was false, and yet utter like death itself. As she descended I brought my hands forward, two claws, seizing her black heart and its ventricles in the clamp formed of them. Her scream was one of purest ecstasy as the organ burst like a melon in my hands. The lantern-light dance of the phantasmagoria fluttered and died as it succumbed to a roiling, saturating pitch of shadow, perhaps the black soul of her as it filled the tomb. Darkness, stillness, Lyla and her shell clutching me as if I were the artery through which all blood flowed. Behind her, the entrance of the cave like the invite of her parted legs.

Clutching me, tongue searching for my mouth...

And then a terrible ferocity of motion and voice, an expression as chaotic and inexplicable as evil itself, as the victims of her seductions descended upon my Lyla, tearing her away from me and having her for their own.

In the twilight the blanket floated on a sea of dandelions. As I approached the spot I became momentarily confused, even touched by panic. Then I remembered they were in the car, on the floorboard where she had taken them off.

Dispossessed

It was a dry misery, tearless and bloodless, silent. Sometimes, with the passage of wind, the barn's boards sang, and the thrill of it vibrated through his thinly cocooned body, reminding him of music, long lost music. When would she come back, his *Ahraia* who had stolen all his tears, his blood, leaving him bound in this sheath?

He had been a farmer, a workhorse and widower starving for company, when she rapped on the door.

"Who...?"

"Has the Lord thy God abandoned thee?"

She wore a patterned dress, hair done up in conservative curls, and she carried a hefty tome which he mistook for the Good Book until he saw the runes in its animal skin cover.

"Are you a missionary of some kind?" he asked. "Are you here to save me?"

"I'm here," she said simply.

He was not an uneducated man, though perhaps he had regressed into naïvete through the decades of living out his chosen profession far from the mob. He let her in upon those two, forever elegant words.

"How did you get here?" he said as he gestured to a reupholstered chair in his handsome living room. He had noticed no car.

"I walked," she said.

Though it was autumn and cool, and the rural distances vast...

Sometimes an animal wandered in, unable to smell any residual vitality on him. Eyes luminous in the night, blinking on and off as they passed between the boards, reminded him of her. Not even the gopher rat that made residence beneath the barn knew of his existence. For a period of time an owl had enjoyed the loft. There were occasional bats. Once, a man; a vagabond.

Over a smoky fire of hay and rotting boards, what was left of the vagabond's drained soul drifted on the song that escaped his cracked, bloodless lips: *Yes the Lord my God has abandoned me, and Ahraia has left me to wither away...*

This had revived hope in the watcher behind the boards. He had been preserved in his cocoon for some purpose.

He would see her again, just as she had promised.

"I wonder why the milk hasn't arrived," he said one morning early in their courtship. He spoke as he removed his shorts, slipping back under the covers, where most of their strange, negligent hours were spent.

It wouldn't be the last question of its kind. There would be no mail, and no calls from widowed Willa Green, an interested party in her mid-sixties, some ten years his elder. The telephone never rang, airplanes never flew over, and cars never drove past.

Her way of soothing him was by telling him the world belonged to Ahraia now. At first he understood this as a personal proclamation, a sort of endearment. Then later, when the petals of isolation spread fully, he began to realize the larger scope of it. He did not lament the world's dispossession as long as she made love to him, stroked him and read to him from her book, which spoke so lovingly of the transcendence of humankind.

"Where do you come from, Ahraia?" he asked her in the third week.

"I cannot offer you heaven," was her reply. "No one can do that."

On clear nights when there was a moon, the light spilled through the cracks of the shambled roof of the barn, slashing his prison with white fire. As he watched the cobwebs in the corners capture the light in their threads, he wondered if the silken sheath in which he was wrapped glowed similarly, making him a radiant ghost.

On hazy nights he swore he saw her through the fog...cruelest of sirens who summons the petrified.

When it rained, the world was a mirror.

"What do you offer, Ahraia?"

"*Somewhere.* Can you believe in that? In somewhere?"

"I can."

"Will you let me restore your faith?"

"I will. Read to me, Ahraia."

She did.

It was a dry misery, even when the mirror roiled violently as it did tonight. Hymns and dirges wept from the boards as the feeble structure shook in the grip of the storm. He bathed in its memories, in the sweat of the farmer attacking the day before him, in the tears of the husband as he held his ruined wife in his hands, in the blood that fell from her split skull. Like a little girl in her excitement and carelessness, she had run out to give him the good news, had just caught his attention over the noise of the motor when she stumbled and fell into the blades behind the tractor.

"I love you! I love you! We're going to have a b—"

But they were memories only, for there was nothing left to weep, to bleed.

Ahraia had seeped it all out of him, for the restoration of his faith. If only she could be here now, to see how earnestly yet faithlessly he prayed for the destruction that a storm of this force might conceivably bring.

He closed his eyes and kept praying. He knew how forsaken he was.

Morning came with a mist. As his eyes focused on the distinct change in the pitch of reality, he knew that no mist inspired the manifestation of her, epiphany amidst the rubble of the devastated barn. No mist of the land, no mist of the imagination. She evolved of something more, and less.

"You have lost all faith then?" she said.

"Yes."

"You could not have waited till I came for you?"

"I waited. You never came."

"If I unbind you now, you will join the vagabonds who wander this wasteland, searching endlessly for what cannot be regained."

"I'm finished," he said.

Nodding, she stepped forward, holding the book aloft as she began to unturn the membrane.

Last Days of Solitude

With the snow came a hush. The gates of the city fell closed for the season. Lanterns on posts illuminated melancholy aspects in misted second-floor windows. Katrina's was one of these faces, caught between the permanence of winter and the ephemeral flames burning in the fireplace behind her.

In the dead of night she sat there by the window, sipping the cognac a neighbor had given her, unable to sleep because she knew she was in her last days of solitude. On the adjacent wall a wooden clock ticked off the seconds, collaborating with the diminishing stack of logs by the hearth to prove that time had not really come to a standstill. The big lazy snowflakes falling on the already blanketed roofs and roads made it seem like it had. The absence of wind tonight, the silence, the mystic hour...all these things made it seem so.

Raising her drink to her lips, seeing the flickers of the fire more clearly in the curve of the glass than in the sweating window, a sense told her there was movement beyond the reflections. She placed the glass on the flower table and wiped the window with the sleeve of her gown. Yes, there was something—a small girl, wrapped in fur and looking down the tunnel no longer recognizable as a street. No adult was to be seen, only this child of perhaps five or six standing shin-deep in the unshoveled snow. She appeared to be on the path leading to the door a short distance behind her, but Katrina didn't remember ever seeing a child at Miss Bettie's.

On an impulse she tapped the window. The child looked around, apparently uncertain as to where the noise came from. When she glanced up, expression revealed in the light of the lamp on its post,

194

Katrina recognized all the emotions the girl was experiencing. For once upon a time she had experienced them herself. Once upon a time she had wandered the night looking for answers. As she gazed down into the little girl's confused face, she felt herself hanging in emptiness, supported only by the ribbons of the moon. Then knife-sharp, icy water rushed over her, engulfing all the other emotions with shock.

Wrenching the window free of the night's cold grip, she hissed down at the child, "Go home, you! There's nothing out there but snow. Go *home!*"

The girl turned and started to run, but fell. She got up, wiped her face with her mittens, glanced back once at the window above, then resumed the effort.

In the morning the little girl's footprints were gone. Katrina tried not to think about her as she watched the milkman deliver his fresh goods to Miss Bettie's and the other doors along the street. Her own street was next, so she went downstairs to wait. She opened the curtains to a freshly white morning. The snow had ceased to fall, but she knew the city would have more about the time the snow covering the ground began to get dirty. It was the season's way. And next time, undoubtedly, the weather would come with wind.

She watched the milkman through the kitchen window as he walked up the path. They were so rare, the men. To watch them sometimes was nice. She suspected she was experiencing some maternal feelings as well. She touched her breast, cupped it in her palm, thinking about the milk it would produce. When she glanced up again, he was waving at her through the window. Had he seen her caressing herself? Had it moved him in any way? But no, of course not. Men took their nourishment in their work, their cognac, their rarity.

As she put the bottle of milk away, she realized the material of her gown over her breast was moist. She sighed, thinking how quickly the days passed, even as each one seemed to last an eternity. How many, three more now? As if she didn't know...

She went to the living room's cold fireplace, positioning some kindling under the grate. The fire crackled to life quickly on the seasoned fuel, reminding her she could do with spending more time down here where the spaces were more open, the mood brighter. Sitting on the hearth's edge, looking into the flames, her hand found its way beneath the neck of her gown again. She squeezed her breast and felt a drop emerge onto her finger. Carefully she brought it up to look at it. It was pale, not like pure milk but like a baby's teardrop laced with milk. She wondered if she would let her daughter suckle. Had she fed from her own mother's breast? She couldn't remember.

A commotion outside drew her attention. She went to the window and saw that the girls had surrounded Peter again, giggling and making fun, a common sight since school had let out for the break. Peter lived a few doors down and was the only boy in the neighborhood. At least ten girls surrounded him. He didn't stand a chance.

About noon of the next day the city bell rang seven times, signaling the opening of the seaward gates and making Katrina wonder if somehow she had her days wrong. The sky was almost clear and a salty scent off the sea hung pleasantly in the air. She had stayed up till ten or so the previous night, in bed with her cognac and book between infrequent trips to the window. There had been the occasional wanderer-by, but no sign of the girl. She had meant to check at a later hour, but fell asleep, and slept pleasantly until the morning.

The tolls of the bell, as it turned out, represented the return of the hunting party that had set out before the city, save for certain, prescribed business, had shut itself off from the outside for the cold months. All thirty-some men had returned intact, and with quite the fetch. Her street being near the city center, Katrina was able to look upon their haul as they rolled past her house in the four wagons of their caravan. As a boy was expected to do, Peter came out and examined the carcasses up close, then rode with the party for a short distance, feet dangling off the back of the last wagon. The hunters looked positive but exhausted, and ready to return home to whatever it was men returned home to. Katrina recalled having long ago asked her mother that very question, but whatever her mother's answer, it hadn't been worth remembering.

That evening Katrina didn't even bother to look outside. The cognac sat untouched by the bed while the book took her to places that even the rattling of the window didn't disturb. Sleep came easily, but the images weren't as benign as last night's, when the worst she'd had to endure was unburying herself from a strange soft substance that proved to be snow. White prevailed again tonight, but it was reinforced with the silver thread of clarity.

In front of her was the boat, a gray-eyed man in a seaman's coat urging the children aboard. As each of the girls stepped on deck, one of the crewmen lifted a sack onto his back. This went on, in the fashion of one sack for each passenger, until all fourteen girls—Katrina counted that many exactly—were on the boat. When the last one had stepped off the ramp, the man in his dingy coat searched the area with his gray eyes. Katrina felt a terrible, consuming dread as they passed over her once, twice, then returned to fix her in their snare.

She woke gasping for breath. The cognac by the bed was warm. The window was fogged. The night revealed no secrets.

The next morning Katrina answered a call at her door. She was surprised to find Peter standing there.

"My mom is ill," he told her. "She said maybe you would come."

Katrina did not know his mom, but she quickly got into her boots and coat and went with him. The snow had begun to fall again, lightly yet on an active wind. As she followed Peter around the building to the street where he lived, swirls formed in front of her, a map charting transitory, unknowable places. The sky over the city was ashen, the air trembled with the murmurs of the tomb, and a sense of fragility hung over all. Katrina removed her gloves to check Peter's cheeks. He glowed in the warmth of her hands for a moment but then made her keep going, the blush dissolving as quickly as it had come. His home was down the block from Miss Bettie's, smoke curling out of the stump of chimney protruding from the snow-laden roof.

The door opened inward across a dry mat. The interiors were unpleasantly cool, as if all the heat went out the chimney with the vapors.

There was a nondescriptness about Peter's home which made Katrina wonder about her own. The boy led her up a stairs, which made for better temperature, but the smell about the higher floor spoke of lingering. She had the sense of having been here before as she entered the room, knowing its weight if not exactly its fixtures. Peter's mom was on her bed, skin gray as the boatman's eyes.

"Thank you," said the woman. "I'm sorry to have asked for you, but I've seen you in your window."

Katrina did not ask what she meant. She knew the woman lived in reclusion, being the mother of the only boy for blocks.

"What afflicts you?" she said. Peter started to speak but his mother waved him silent.

"'Afflict' is a good word. For that is certainly what it feels like. But you must know that. In your own solitude, isolation."

"Yes, ma'am. But if you'll forgive me, mine is of my own choosing."

A strangled laugh came from the bed. "Your fate might have been negotiable, but your lot, I fear, is permanent."

"What can I do for you?" Katrina said.

"If my condition worsens, if I become irremediably invalid, or dead, see that my son arrives in the appropriate hands. He's young. He's never even been outside the neighborhood. He is alone."

"You have no one?"

"I have a son." The double meaning did not escape Katrina. She didn't know what to say to the woman. The task with which she was being charged was certainly no large one, but...

"I can agree only to deliver him," she said at last. "I can't have any more responsibility than that. My own time has come."

"Ah," said the woman, a faint smile touching at her gray lips.

"But I'll see that Peter is taken care of."

"Thank you. Pray with me, then."

The woman slept and Katrina told Peter she would see herself out. As she descended the stairs, she heard a noise, a rhythmic metallic tapping coming from a room off the hall below. She came to a door that stood

Darren Speegle

slightly ajar, pushed it open. The room appeared to be a playroom, with objects of various shapes and sizes lying about its wooden floor. In the rear stood a little girl dressed in tights and ruffles, whom she knew at once to be the same little girl who had looked up at her window from the street the other night. The girl let the spoons with which she had been tapping come to rest on the circular mouth of a heavy metal dairy container standing almost as tall as she.

"Hi," said the girl.

"Well, hi," said Katrina. "Do you remember me?"

The girl nodded.

"I'm sorry if I scared you," Katrina said. "It's just that, well, you scared me. What's your name?"

"Tasha."

"That's a pretty name, Tasha. I'm Katrina. Do you play over here a lot?"

"Are you going to tell my mommy? She doesn't know I'm here. I'm supposed to be at practice."

"What kind of practice?" Katrina said, rather guessing she knew. She stepped inside the room.

Tasha watched her with big green eyes. "I can show you. I have a special gift, Mommy says."

Katrina frowned. Her mother used to say the same thing. "Sure," she said. "I'd love to see."

The child set the spoons aside and took the handles of the big container on which she'd been making her music, carefully tilting it back against her body. Katrina hurried forward to help, but Tasha refused it adamantly. Crossing one hand over the other, she began to roll the vessel on its round base. Katrina hovered just by, in case her assistance prove necessary. When the vessel was free of the assorted objects among which it had stood, Tasha let it rest again. For a moment her breathing sounded like wind in dry snow, but she recovered swiftly, as if this were a daily exercise.

She fetched a small wooden box from the corner and placed it between herself and the big metal dairy container. "Watch," she said.

In one fluid and graceful motion, she stepped onto the box, grasped the handles of the vessel, and lifted her legs up over her head, standing to her fullest extent on her hands. Katrina held her breath as the display

199

did not end there. Tasha's arms trembled as she slowly arched her body backwards, letting her legs come all the way down so that her slippered feet hooked under the container's rim. She froze there, forming the most beautiful bow Katrina had ever seen. Katrina was afraid to clap, lest she somehow cause the child to fall from her magical pose.

Came the slightest noise, an exhalation from Tasha, then she unfurled, as gracefully as she had formed the bow, landing delicately on the box.

Katrina began to clap. At the door another set of hands joined her. Peter, come down to play with his friend.

That night the dream was so real that she was transformed into a girl again, escorted through the snow by her mother, whose cheeks glistened with ice crystals, perhaps frozen tears. She heard the bell, seven clear notes piercing the howling gale that had laid siege to the city. As they neared the seaward gates, the faces of other daughters appeared out of the blow, frightened, scrawled with uncertainty, like the mask of destiny itself. Mothers and daughters huddled inside the gates, words no comfort, therefore unspoken.

As the gates opened and the man with the seaman's coat and the gray eyes stood there, it seemed the weather receded from him, opening up to a night dominated by a huge ghostly moon, its silvery ribbons swinging across the sea. He walked amidst the huddled pairs, selecting from among the daughters with his gray eyes and the gesture of his finger. Those who were ignored shuffled away, murmuring prayers. In the end fifteen girls remained, kissing their mothers a last time before stepping through the raised gates. By the time they reached the dock, there were fourteen. For Katrina had drowned herself in shadow.

He beckoned them aboard, counting while he did. As each girl climbed on deck, one of the crewmen lifted a burlap sack, fat with its content, onto his back. This went on, in the fashion of one sack for each passenger, until all fourteen girls were on the boat. When the last one had stepped off the ramp, the man in his dingy coat searched the area with his gray eyes. Katrina felt a terrible, consuming dread as they passed over her once, twice, then returned to fix her in their snare.

His finger seemed drawn on one of the ribbons of moonlight as it marked her. Trembling, she emerged from her spot and feebly walked towards her beckoner. When she reached him, he invited her on board in silence. She wouldn't look at his eyes as she stepped across the ramp. No sooner had she planted her feet on the deck than the boat began to rock with the weight of bodies climbing out of the vessel. She turned to watch the men with the burlap sacks file towards the gates, which still had not closed over the shadowy figures who stood there hugging themselves and clutching their mouths as if to stifle cries. The crewmen deposited their bags at the entry and returned forthwith to the vessel.

The boat pushed out immediately, the moon-drenched, uneasy waters spreading out before it. Katrina averted her eyes from that eerie future in favor of the doings at the gates. Men showed up to hoist the burlap sacks onto their shoulders and tote them away into the city, while the stationary figures never took their eyes off the boat. She thought she knew which one was her mother, but she also knew it didn't matter, not anymore. A loud creaking noise made its way to her ears, prompting her to look above their heads, where the gates were just beginning to come down. She could tell by the body language of the silhouettes that their attention had been drawn by the descending teeth as well. In a surge of emotion too powerful to withstand, Katrina suddenly rushed forward, scrambled up on the stern's bulwark and leapt out over the silvery-dark water. She hung there for a moment in emptiness, supported only by the ribbons of the moon, then liquid ice shattered around her, inside her, through her head. Seconds to absorb the shock, to choose between the alluring embrace of darkness and the moonlight teasing the waves above her. Then she broke through the surface, taking in air and calling to her mother across the night.

She thought she heard her mother shout in return, but it might have been the ice in her ears as she swam towards the dock. She fought the knife of cold by concentrating on her mother's favorite words to her, words that had taught her to read, to solve, to swim, at so small an age. *You have a special gift and that gift is fortitude. They said you wouldn't survive when you were born, and we listened to them. But not you, Katrina. You wouldn't listen.* She concentrated on those words and they made every difference as she climbed up onto the pier, screaming at the jaws that were now halfway through their slow, deliberate journey towards mocking her with their cage-like grin.

Her mother's face grew before her, the fear, the confusion, the joy writing the beginning of a tale that would reveal much solitude and friendlessness as it unfolded.

For while the boat, once upon its course, could not come back for its lost passenger, there was a fifteenth burlap sack whose contents must simply melt away when dumped at the doorstep of their rightful recipient.

Katrina woke into a sweat. How had she fallen asleep? Was it *the* night? Perhaps she had missed it, perhaps there lay a puddle of ice at her doorstep. Dare she look? Dare she know?

But soon the rattling of the window and the odor of the coals, a merest splash of cognac and the ticking of the wooden clock on the wall...these things lulled her back to sleep. It was a fitful sleep, however, and once, when the hour was still small, she rose and went to the window and looked out from beneath half-closed lids. The wind was wild, the snow like needles disintegrating against the pane. The lamp on its post swung crazily. And yet, through it all, there was a kind of deep silence...perhaps she slept after all. Who could know?

The morning came with the same rattling silence. She went to the window and saw that a few people were out in the swirl, doing what it was people found necessary to do in such conditions. One was a girl, but she wasn't Tasha. No, Tasha's mother would have her inside today. Today there would be no practice, no wandering about outside, alone. Today she would be held and sung to, and told what a special gift she had. But Tasha, the daughter, would know.

Katrina went out to get the bottle of milk left at her doorstep, and her neighbor, the one who had given her the cognac, walked up tipping and nearly losing his hat. He was an older man, striking she thought, his hair like the snow, his skin like the weather, his eyes like the sea. Other than Peter, he was the only male within a certain radius of her home. She invited him in and neither of them spoke of today being the day, though they both knew. She suspected he knew everything. He asked if she had enjoyed the cognac and she said very much. Sleeping had been easier. He told her that if she ever needed another bottle, come to him. If she should need anything, come to him. She thought it both gracious and unusual of him. But then men seemed to be that way.

An hour before dinnertime Peter came by. His mom was feeling better, he said. Their prayers maybe had helped. Maybe, Katrina said. He asked if she wanted to come to his home for dinner. No, but thank you, she said. Maybe some other time. As he walked away, she noticed how the wind snatched at his hair, how the girls laughed and pointed, how he moved through their midst proudly, strangely, handsomely.

She dined on soup, not so hot that it burned her lips, for her lips mustn't be burnt, not tonight. Dark came slowly, the wind picked up again, the snow fell in a blinding white torrent until the clouds had spent themselves, then there was only the night. She went up to her bedroom to smooth out an impression on the blanket, burn a scented candle, retrieve a spot of lint from the corner, and eventually to stare at the words on a page that never turned as the wooden clock ticked. At that nameless hour, the city bell rang seven distinct times. Katrina rushed to the window. She thought she recognized Tasha, was sure of it for a moment as the child, who was led along by a woman in a cloak, looked up in her direction. But then it might as easily have been another little girl, distorted in the breath that rose in the wake of the snowfall. It might as easily have been Katrina, looking for reason.

Beyond the fading last note of the bell, she could do naught but tremble. Even after the last of the cognac was consumed in one great swallow, even when her hands hovered over the fire, drawing from its calm power...even then, she could do naught but tremble. When the knock finally came at her door, she thought she would simply seize up and die, as perhaps she should have done long ago.

The door opened to a freshly deposited pile of snow. The man and his burlap sack were gone, but the sack's contents remained. The snow hadn't melted away; it hadn't been spent on past transgressions; it stirred in lamplight, elegantly shapeless. As she sat before the mound, placing her hands gently over its surface, she happened to glance down the block at a woman on her porch doing the same. Katrina raised a hand to her, and the woman reciprocated. The night presented no disturbance otherwise; it was safely in the hands of the women, who were its sculptors.

Beneath Katrina's hands the mound of snow took shape. A body, at first lumpy and amorphous, began to reveal itself beneath her artistry. The thing itself assisted with the edges and the curves, the nuances and suggestions, the wholeness of the emerging being that would be partner to her. As it became a man, that rarest occasion, as it became beautiful, even rarer, she took his hand in hers and led him into her abode and up the stairs into the room where the fire seemed to have been burning forever. His eyes and his body were ethereal, yet physical to her every want and desire. And into the furthest morning did she satisfy herself upon him, exploring as she had never explored, experiencing such pleasures as she had never experienced. Into the furthest morning, and until the fragrances of her body filled the room and the light dimmed to an elongated wink.

When she woke the bed was saturated with water. Other than that, there was no sign of her lover. Snow fell ever so lightly outside her window and the seeds of the season had been planted. She sat by her fire, happier than she could remember, touching her belly, thinking of the voices of children, a music that made life livable. Inevitably, her thoughts drifted to Tasha, which caused her happiness to dissolve into the wan hues of the indecisive sky.

She did not want to go, yet she must know. Indeed, wouldn't sleep without knowing. Having no idea where Tasha lived, she went to Peter's house. Peter took her upstairs to visit with his mom for awhile. Obviously pleased to see Katrina, Peter's mom apologized for having neglected to introduce herself on their last visit. "Anna," she said, patting the bed beside her. As Katrina sat, Anna did not ask specifically how her night had gone, but she alluded, commenting on the glow, the freshness about her.

Katrina was not surprised to know that these signals seeped through her pensiveness. However, she could never let herself fully enjoy her situation without knowing about Tasha. She told Anna her fear, to which Peter's mom replied, "Hush now. Don't trouble yourself about things over which you have no control."

"Our lot is permanent," Katrina murmured.

"That is so."

"I'd like to know, nonetheless."

With a sidelong glance at Peter, Anna started to tell her directions, then scolded herself for her motherliness. "The boy's going to find out for himself soon enough. Peter, you take her there. And son...remember, we've talked about these things."

Kissing Anna's hand, Katrina whispered to her, "Have you? Really talked? My mother and I never did. Not about these things."

Anna returned the kiss and told her not to worry. Her days of solitude were over.

Peter led her downstairs, past the playroom and its objects, out into the gently falling snow. They walked along the street, ignoring the stares from windows, the occasional giggle. When Katrina asked Peter how he was doing, he shrugged. Feigned or real, his disinterest made her want to shake him. Tasha's was the last door on the block. Holding her breath, Katrina raised the knocker, let it fall. Once. She looked at Peter, and Peter looked away. Yes, his disinterest was certainly feigned, and poorly at that.

The door opened and a woman stood there, face revealing nothing, even when her eyes shifted to Peter. Katrina discovered that she hadn't taken the time to formulate the question in her mind. It had no shape, no sprout from which to grow. It was like the pile of snow that had appeared before her door.

"I'm...I'm wondering if..."

"Is Tasha here?" Peter said bluntly.

The woman let her eyes rest on him. A second passed, then another, and then her lips lifted slightly. "Yes," she said. "Yes, of course."

Katrina felt her breath, her heartbeat return. Beside her, Peter could pretend no more. He nearly leapt out of himself when Tasha's face appeared, smiling, alive, unselected.

In the coming weeks and months, Katrina stayed in touch with Peter, his mother, and Tasha, all of whom could be found on any given afternoon, after school and lessons, under the same roof. They all enjoyed watching Katrina grow towards motherhood, but particularly Tasha, who had a world of questions for her. Katrina answered them the best she could, but regularly reminded Tasha that she was new at this herself.

One day in the latter part of her term, Tasha surprised Katrina with an invitation from Tasha's mom.

Something about that afternoon, about the sun melting away in a golden splendor to rival the cognac which her neighbor hadn't let her beg off him since the day she came down with child, something about the reception she got from Tasha's mother, with whom she had never really discussed anything...it would stay with her long after.

Tasha's mom served hot buttered vegetables with a smile that struck Katrina as unlike her, though how could she know? They ate in relative silence, but when the meal was done, Tasha's mom glanced over at her daughter, letting out a sigh.

"I know," she said, fixing her gaze on Katrina, "that you know what I went through that night. I'm grateful that you have been able to show Tasha what the other end of it is like. I've had a difficult time. I was certain I had lost her."

Katrina left there thinking about her own mom, about the lack of communication, about the isolation imposed upon a mother because of her daughter's fortitude. She thought about such things and she thought about her own responsibility. As a daughter and as a mother.

That day came with gifts from those close to her—most importantly, their encouragement. The city had people available, but Katrina chose her own midwife. Peter's mom, now fully recovered, happened to be available, though it wasn't her first calling. Together they managed through it, through the toil of it, praying a little, cursing a little, finally opening their eyes and expressions in wonder as the baby came into the world.

At first Katrina didn't know how to react. The implications were such that she didn't even know where to begin. But gradually that evaporated. From next door and a tipped hat came help, how to deal with these rascals, what to feed them and what stories to tell. Rare as they were, there was an answer for them, and he'd help her along, whenever she needed it. Other neighbors, of course, shunned her. But Katrina was no stranger to that sort of thing. At least now she had her own child to keep her company.

rhyme or reason, Dear God

I sit here and wonder why I sit here and Satan howls outside.

> *I've nothing but my battered will*
> *An armrest at the windowsill*
> *Another day*
> *To waste away*
> *The headstone shapes on yonder hill*

Dear God, where are you? The day has grown cold, the sky wondrously dark. The wind has lifted to an infernal, incessant howling. I want to be away from this house *on the rocks by the sea, to swallow back the words that pour out of me.*

For it is only a pen, and a vision. Dear God.

Words.

About the Author

Darren Speegle's fiction has sold to such publications as *Chiaroscuro, Flesh and Blood, Fangoria Frightful Fiction,* and *Verte Brume: The Anthology of Absinthe. A Dirge for the Temporal* is his second short story collection. The first, *Gothic Wine,* was released in June 2004 by Aardwolf Press.

Darren lives in Germany with his wife, Julie, and their two daughters, who are in the German educational system and are called upon more than they like to act as translators for their parents. When he is not pounding his head on the keyboard, Darren enjoys biking and hiking and experiencing Europe by its less beaten paths.

LaVergne, TN USA
26 August 2010
194737LV00003B/136/A